I0690147

The

Christmas Village

LINDA ANDREWS

ZUMAYA EMBRACES   AUSTIN TX

2011

This book is a work of fiction. Names, characters, places and incidents are products of the author's imagination or are used fictitiously. Any resemblance to actual locales events or persons living or dead is entirely coincidental.

THE CHRISTMAS VILLAGE
© 2003, 2011 by Linda Andrews
ISBN 978-1-936144-44-0
Cover Art and Design © Charles Bernard

"Zumaya Embraces" and the dove colophon are trademarks of Zumaya Publications LLC, Austin TX.

Look for us online at
http://www.zumayapublications.com/embraces.php

Library of Congress Cataloging-in-Publication Data

Andrews, Linda, 1967-
  The Christmas village / Linda Andrews.
      p. cm.
   ISBN 978-1-936144-44-0 (trade pbk. : alk. paper) -- ISBN 978-1-936144-45-7 (electronic/multiple format) -- ISBN 978-1-936144-39-6 (electronic/epub)
1. Christmas stories. I. Title.
 PS3601.N55267C47 2011
 813'.6--dc23
                              2011043900

🔔 Dedication 🔔

To everyone who believes Christmas should be celebrated all year long

Chapter I

"Did you hear me, dear?" Margaret Starr's exasperation filled the line like static.

"Yes, Mom." Egypt tucked the cordless phone between her ear and shoulder then closed the lid on the suitcase. The teeth of the zipper remained four inches apart. Maybe she should have used a bigger suitcase.

A splash of red caught her eye. The American Tourister was larger. It also had a broken clasp. She smacked open the suitcase lid. Wads of sweaters and pants rose above the soft-sided confines. Maybe she should have packed less stuff.

"I don't think you know how hard this is on your sister."

"Weddings are hard on everyone." Egypt buffered her mother's irritation with a well-rehearsed line. Thirteen weddings had taught her something—a patient, well-modulated tone calmed fretful brides, harried mothers and a bevy of bridesmaids. Too bad it couldn't shrink the contents of her suitcase. She had packed only the essentials, hadn't she? Air stirred the papers on her coffee table as she swatted the lid closed and took a seat on top. Fabric oozed out the sides.

"Yes, well, this kind of thing just does not happen to me." Irritation chased the anxiety from her mother's voice. "Paris has had her wedding planned since the fourth grade. The dress design was in pink crayon with purple butterflies and blue

1

hearts floating around it. Oh, why did Minnie Houser have to move to Phoenix six weeks before the wedding?"

Egypt's gaze traveled around the small studio apartment. Had she forgotten anything? Undoubtedly. She combed her hands through her short hair then shook the strand from her fingers. Perhaps she should get into the habit of making lists. Heaven knew her mother and sister were constantly giving her pads of paper with cutesy logos and patterns. She picked up a note with hearts stamped across the top. Her sister's handwriting accused her: *Leave on December 22nd at seven a.m. Arrive Dragoon's Springs Country Club at 1:30 p.m. for bridal shower.* It was 8:17 a.m. on the twenty-third.

"Guess Paris can't plan everything."

"Egypt!" Disapproval whipped down the line. "That is not a very nice thing to say. You know your sister is under a lot of strain. Weddings are stressful on everyone."

She blinked as a recap of her own words echoed back to her. Merciless monkeys, she had turned into her mother. Egypt shook the unpleasant thought from her head.

"I only meant that the quadruple bypass kind of snuck up on Max and Minnie Houser."

She crossed her fingers behind her back. What her mother didn't know wouldn't cause high long distance charges to invade her parent's phone bill.

"Yes, well..." Suspicion dragged the words.

Egypt's stomach flipped in her belly. She had better change the subject quickly. Her gaze flicked to the white confection draped over the back of the Bentwood rocker.

"Paris's dress turned out beautifully. Mrs. Houser even sewed iridescent seed beads on the bodice. Lavender butterflies, just like Paris drew when she was ten."

Air hissed through the miles of phone line. "Paris *had* wanted, dear. Our budget—"

"She sewed them on for free." The words gushed past Egypt's lips. Her mother hated being interrupted almost as

2

much as she hated glitches in her plans. "She said she owed you something for driving to Phoenix for the fittings. Sewing gave her something to do and stopped her from worrying so much while she sat in the hospital waiting room."

"Well..." The scales tipped in her favor. "That was very nice of Minnie. I'll make certain Paris sends her an extra-special thank you note, maybe even a few pictures."

"I'm certain she'd appreciate that. She misses Dragoon's Springs." Egypt made one last sweep of the room. She seemed to have everything. "According to Minnie, she hasn't had a nice chat or a decent cup of coffee since she came to the big city." She paused. Her words surfed the gasp of breath in the receiver. "Except for my visits, of course."

"That sounds like Minnie. With all that worry, I should have known there would be a mix-up in the dresses." Plastic swished and satin rustled. "I suppose no real harm has occurred. You have Paris's dress and I have yours. It turned out very lovely, by the way. The color will flatter your skin tone and the style is timeless."

Egypt stuffed the blobs of fabric inside her suitcase. Plastic teeth scraped her flesh. Cold metal bit into the pads of her thumb and index finger. The zipper grumbled along its track then stopped halfway around the corner. The metal tab buttoned the suitcase at a single point, the remaining teeth curled back in a ferocious snarl. A growl rumbled up her throat. She jerked the zipper backwards. Pink silk bubbled around the tab.

"Unbelievable." Egypt rocketed from her seat and glared at the tapestry luggage. "Stupid, idiotic, overgrown handbag."

"I beg your pardon."

"Not you, Mom." Egypt unclenched one fist and strangled the phone. She stormed across the room, bones rattling with every step. Why did this happen every time she was late? Why couldn't everything go right just once? Would the universe come to a crashing halt? Would the cure for cancer be postponed? How important could thwarting her every plan be to world peace? Metal jingled as she yanked open her junk drawer. She scooped up the pliers and stomped back to the mocking baggage. "It's this stupid luggage. The zipper broke."

"Is that the Marshalls' American Tourister or the Andersons' Fancy French one?"

"The Andersons'." Egypt shoved the carry-on into a better position and clamped the phone between her ear and shoulder. Maybe if she backed the zipper up it would catch and hold. The pliers clamped onto the pull-tab. Such a method had worked before. Her knee dug into the soft top; fabric extruded out the side. She released the zipper and prodded her clothes back inside the suitcase.

"Well, that did get a bit of wear on their honeymoon. Everyone knows those airport people toss bags around like footballs." Her mother's monologue gathered steam. Was her mouth pleased to be released from its prison of wedding talk? Or was it simply a reminder that wedding related misery included more people than just the Starr family? "And then they were stopped not once but three times while they toured Europe for all those weeks. You would think since it was made over there it would have been able to survive the rough handling they put it through. Of course, if Sheila hadn't been so determined to visit so many countries on their six-week honeymoon..."

Honeymoon. Blood slogged through Egypt's heart. It was only natural to be a little depressed. All of her friends were pairing up like animals before the Flood. Her plight was no different than any other thirty-year-old spinster, no matter the circumstance of the bride and groom's meeting.

Sheesh, after thirteen weddings, she should have constructed a better pep talk than that. Silence buzzed in her ear. Had she missed an opportunity to grunt in support?

"Are you all right, dear?"

Egypt's sigh fluttered her bangs. No missed cue, just the end of her mother's soliloquy.

"Yeah, I mean, yes, Mom. I'm fine." She clamped the pliers onto the metal tab and tugged. "I was just thinking if I'd need a jacket."

"Are you sure that's what's bothering you? I mean, you can talk to me about anything. You know that, don't you, dear?"

"I know, Mom." The zipper refused to budge. Egypt yanked. Fabric ripped. The zipper closed as the tab retreated. She tugged it in the other direction, and the zipper held.

"Mrs. Houser did remind me this was the sixteenth time."

Irritation flayed Egypt's skin. For a seamstress, Mrs. Houser needed help with her math.

"Fourteenth time, Mom. This will be the fourteenth time I've been a bridesmaid."

A rainbow of satin dresses was the consolation prize. Along with her sofa, the rocker, the broken luggage—even her cat and hamster—all were the relics of her friends' abandoned single life, willed to their good friend Egypt.

"Well, you're bound to be the bride next time." False cheer rang hollowly in her mother's voice. "I mean, you don't have any more single friends left. Do you, Egypt?"

Did she? There always seemed to be a few hovering close by, vultures waiting for a fresh kill. There were bound to be some disappointed ladies at Paris's wedding when Egypt appeared solo. However, that was in Dragoon's Springs, not Phoenix. In Phoenix, she knew only one single woman.

"Well, we did hire a new girl for the holiday season."

"Surely, that's not long enough to become good friends." Margaret Starr squeaked. "All the girls whose...whose weddings you were in, you'd been friends since childhood."

"I know, Mom. Besides, she has a boyfriend."

Nutz jumped onto the suitcase. The marmalade cat rolled onto his back and swatted at a patch of pink fluttering on the back of the sofa's blue slipcover. Egypt tugged a piece of gum out of her pocket. Cinnamon exploded across her tongue. Light sparked off the silver foil as it sailed onto the coffee table. She should probably remove the damaged camisole. Should but wouldn't. Gum popped in her mouth. She already had one side zipped. She only had two to go.

"Well, that's a relief. Not that I believe you're cursed or anything, dear."

"No one believes I'm cursed." Egypt yanked the zipper around the corner, tucking clothes inside as she went. "Everyone just comes to me for their husbands."

Nutz jumped onto the sofa back as she slid the baggage off the cushion. She jerked the plastic extension handle up as the carry-on wheels thudded onto the carpet.

Dead air filled the phone connection. "The dress really is lovely. Your sister picked out the turquoise especially to flatter your complexion."

Phase one of bridal pity: a modification of wedding colors to flatter the poor slob whose ex-boyfriend you just happen to be marrying. Phase two: the pairing of said poor slob with an eligible party specifically imported for the occasion. Egypt shuddered as the memories resurrected her dread.

She snapped the bungee cord around her suitcase. If it had been anyone else but her sister she would have bowed out of the wedding. As it was, she must endure the warm-up torture and the coup de grace, phase three. Her favorite. Should phases one or two fail, subject poor slob to endless introductions to single males, including passing waiters and, if necessary, the valet. How long could someone wear a phony smile before the expression became permanent? Hopefully, longer than her sister's wedding and reception.

"Egypt?"

"It's a pretty color."

"And you'll be able to use the dress again." Strain sharpened her mother's voice. "Maybe for that New Year's party you told me about. Not that we wouldn't want you to spend the holiday with us. I understand all about young single girls, liv-

6

ing in the big city and all. We do get *Sex and the City* up here, you know."

"Mom."

"I do hope you are protecting yourself." Hinges creaked. A door closed. "Sexually, I mean." Her mother's voice dropped to a whisper.

"Mom!" Egypt raised her shoulder, pressing the phone closer to her ear. Was her mother's voice muffled?

"Minnie says they have entire stores devoted to experimentation of a certain sort." Definitely muffled. Her mother had retreated to the closet, that sanctuary where only the most sacred of subjects were discussed on the phone—divorce, unexpected pregnancies and hurried marriages. "Not that there's anything wrong with it. You're young, and you always were the curious one. There is absolutely no cause for embarrassment. In my day, well, really we—"

"Mo-ther!" Emphasis on both syllables. The tone perfected by teenagers everywhere. Egypt cringed. Why did she always revert to a child whenever she talked with her mother?

"Yes, dear?"

Egypt's chest expanded as she filled her lungs with air. She had flirted with the line in the sand long enough. It was time to commit herself to battle. Utterly. Completely.

"I'm spending New Year's in Dragoon's Springs."

"Really?" Disappointment trimmed the happiness in her mother's voice.

"Really." Cowardice beat against her skull. It wasn't too late. She could still back out. Egypt shored up her courage. No surrender, no prisoners. She would spend a week at home, visiting with friends, catching up with family, being the object of pity and speculation and answering impertinent questions. Small-town America. Is it any wonder she left?

"You're not still in love with Darrell, are you? He really isn't right for you."

Egypt nodded, rubbed at the ache spreading across her chest. None of them had been. But knowing the truth didn't lessen the sting.

"I know, Mom. There were signs. Darrell is obnoxious and controlling, hates pets of any kind, can't dance, despises big band music and would rather buy one front-row ticket to the hockey game than two in the nosebleed seats."

"He's also marrying your sister, dear."

"Yes," Stitches jumped as she lifted his cage. The teddy-bear hamster blinked up at her then scurried up the pink plastic tube to the room above. Metal rattled as she secured it to the carry-on with another bungee cord. "He's perfect for Paris."

"And you are definitely over him?" *Will you make trouble at the wedding?*

The unspoken question hovered like an eavesdropper on the line.

"Yes, Mom. I feel the same about Darrell as I feel for Diego." Exasperated, irritated and not a little perturbed by his existence. "Brotherly feelings, nothing more." Except for the disappointment, not that she'd mention that to her mother.

"Good. Did I tell you we've rounded up four eligible men for the wedding?"

Egypt sighed. Phase two, and she hadn't even left her apartment. New Year's Day seemed very far away.

"Of course, three are divorced, but, well, I suppose that's to be expected. After all, they are in their thirties. Except for Doug—he's forty-one."

Egypt's knees buckled. She bounced twice on the sofa before collapsing into a boneless mass. How had her life come to this? What atrocity had she committed in another life?

"Don't worry, dear. We capped the age at fifty. That would be much too close to your father's age. Minnie says we should take their previously married state as a blessing. I mean, they took the plunge once so they're not liable to be as gun-shy as men in the Big City."

Big City. Egypt struggled against the waves of despondency. She could do this. She had done this before. She liked her single life, preferred living with her hamster and her cat. Men were smelly. They hogged the remote. Her New Year's resolution involved remaining as far away from them as possible. Her reasoning was sound. Her mother's logic was another story.

"Darrell is from a big city, Mom. So were Adam and Brad and Zachary and—"

"I know that, dear."

One-by-one, the men in her past faced her. Wanted posters hovering above tasteful wedding invitations. Other women's husbands. She had never been wanted by any of them. Bitterness welled up inside her.

"Only Todd wasn't. I think the mayor should give me a medal or something. Egypt Starr, the woman personally responsible for introducing new blood to Dragoon's Springs, population twenty-four hundred thirteen. No, make that population twenty-four hundred twenty-seven."

She choked on a ragged breath. This should be easy. Why wasn't this easier? She hugged herself close, half-afraid she'd shatter, half-afraid hers would be the only arms to hold her in the future.

"That's not funny, Egypt." Her mother cleared her throat. "You'll find the right man. He'll come riding to your rescue and knock you right off your feet."

"I don't believe in fairy tales anymore, Mom." Nutz padded across the sofa, rasped his rough tongue over her white knuckles. Despair's grip eased. She would be all right. Her hand slicked down the cat's body. Everything would be all right.

"That's precisely why Fate will send Prince Charming to your rescue."

"I definitely do not need rescuing."

"We'll see."

9

The omniscient tone grated on Egypt's nerves. She shoved to her feet. At least, the anger could be channeled. She grabbed her sweater and shoved her arm into the sleeve.

"Mother."

"I'm glad you're staying for New Year's, dear. That will give your father time to look at your car."

"My car?" Gum lodged in her throat. She coughed it up and pulverized the tasteless mass. That rat fink Darrell had snitched. He was the one who'd told her to wrap the hoses in duct tape. He was the one who hadn't wanted to waste time while she made the appropriate repairs.

"Darrell mentioned you were having engine troubles, and you know your father."

"My car is fine." Plastic crinkled as she tossed the roll of duct tape and a handful of garbage ties into the grocery bag. It clunked against the cans of cat food and crunched into the hamster seed. Of course, she had continued down the path of madness by wrapping the next hose in the tape, then the next. She had meant to replace them properly. There just never seemed to be any time.

"I'm sure it is, dear. No daughter of mine would make the long drive home without having a properly serviced and maintained car."

"Of course not." Egypt crossed her fingers. If their conversation took any more turns, her fingers might become permanently twisted around each other.

"It was never in question," her mother agreed. "But Darrell mentioned something the other day. And your father just won't let it go until he's satisfied himself. And, really, dear, where's the harm in allowing him a little peek under the hood?"

Out-flanked and out-maneuvered. Surrender loomed. Egypt had one more tactic and that was more whine than winning.

"But if we all agree..."

"We know you're an adult, but you're still our child. We like to feel useful. Growing old isn't very pleasant, dear." Her mother's sigh undoubtedly bowed telephone lines all across Arizona. "Nowadays, we old folks just get stuck in a retirement village somewhere while you young ones get on with your busy lives. Forgotten. Ignored."

Guilt. The weapon specifically designed to find the chinks in a child's armor. Egypt mentally surrendered. One day, she might actually find her backbone.

"You are not old, Mother. And no one is talking about sticking you or Dad in a retirement home. You're not even retired." She spat her gum into the trash and knotted the grocery sack.

"Will you let your father do this for you? You know Doc Matheson has forbidden him from undertaking any construction projects until his wrist heals."

Her dad and construction projects. It was a standing joke in the community that the walls of the Starr house moved more quickly than an ancient Egyptian booby trap.

"Dad can look at my car, Mom."

"Oh, my goodness. Is that the time? You should have left fifteen minutes ago. Do try to hurry, dear. Paris won't listen to a word of reason until she has that dress in her hands."

Fifteen minutes. The revised schedule that had been faxed twenty-two minutes after she called to let them know she would have to work an extra day. Egypt shuffled toward the phone recharger.

"Bye, Mom. I'll see you at lunch."

"At Granetti's. You do remember where it is, don't you, dear?"

"Yes, Mom. And even if I'd forgotten in the six years I've been living in Phoenix, I'd be able to find it from one of the seven maps you faxed me."

"Leave the attitude in Phoenix, dear. It's not really becoming in a woman your age."

"Bye, Mom." Egypt hung up the phone as the first giggles tickled her tongue. After three decades on this Earth, she had yet to reach the age where her attitude was becoming. Maybe she was only six hours away from reaching that point.

Then again, maybe not.

"Well, this should be an interesting trip." The cat sauntered beside her as she dragged the squeaking suitcase into the parking lot. She opened the Volkswagen door and the cat leapt inside. "Make yourself at home. It's going to be a long drive."

Nutz blinked his yellow eyes, batted at the silver bell adorning one of her gifts for the happy couple then curled up on the backseat. His tail twitched as she wedged the hamster cage between the passenger's seat and the dashboard.

Egypt merged onto the freeway just as her brain registered the missing wedding dress. She smacked on the blinker and veered towards the closest exit. Backtracking to her apartment would cost her fifteen minutes tops; forgetting her sister's wedding dress could prove fatal.

"Please, God, let this is the last thing that goes wrong."

Chapter II

"The lights are out?" Cade Dugan squinted at the silhouette moving through the brightness of the afternoon sun.

"Just a few bulbs." Metal rattled. The shadow shifted. Paul Browning, the Mayor of Holly, climbed down the ladder. Colored-glass bulbs dribbled from his fingertips into the garbage can. "Were you expecting something different?"

"Not at all," Cade answered, rocking back on his heels. He hadn't paid the lights of Holly much attention lately. Other things had occupied his thoughts.

Blue flashed in the corner of his eye. Pine needles scratched his leather jacket and glass tinkled as he pressed further between the decorated trees lining the town square.

"Season's almost over." A horse-drawn omnibus swayed down Main Street. Happy tourists laughed and chattered into the steam rising from the mugs gripped in their mittens. "I'll be glad not to have to worry about the lights going out."

Cade peered around the edge of his sanctuary. That obnoxious shade of blue was nowhere in sight. Snow crunched as he stepped forward, tension draining off his shoulders.

"No need to worry about that now."

"Is that why you cringe every time you see the color blue?"

"The cold has affected your brain."

"You should have stopped using the townsfolk as inspiration for your figurines when the city council asked."

Cade snorted. "Two councilmen volunteered to model for me if I agreed to create a companion piece according to their specifications."

"Life does imitate art."

"That's a cliché, not the moral of the story."

"Even the outsiders have commented on the resemblance between the locals and the featured artwork." The mayor moved the ladder down the red brick walk and fished fresh bulbs out of the paper bag by his feet. "They don't realize half the people in the sets didn't meet until after you created them."

"The Blue Coats know," Cade spat.

"Babbette, Sherry and Emma are more than happy to keep the legend alive. Heck, they even leave the pieces up all year round and point them out to everyone."

"They're stupid figurines."

"That you created." Paul glanced at the string of lights above his head then at Cade. Humor lifted his lips. "If you didn't want the legend to continue why did you produce another couple? Face it, you want to meet your own soul mate."

Unease disturbed Cade's equilibrium. The set had been crafted to destroy the rumors of his artistic matchmaking. If he really were a twisted incarnation of Cupid, a woman would appear wearing a purple scarf and a blue coat. None had; they'd all aped the figurines available to the public—blue scarf and blue coat.

"Wearing a blue coat doesn't mean a woman is destined to be my lifelong companion."

"Then, why are you hiding?"

Irritation flayed Cade. His shoulders squared.

"I am not hiding." He had paused between the trees to catch his breath, not to hide. He scanned the town square. Hiding from the Blue Coats required more finesse than simply stepping between a few scrawny trees.

"I suppose your work has kept you locked in your house."

"I *work* in my house. It's where my studio is." Cade shoved his fists into his pockets. A man understood a harmless bet; being transformed into a walking human punchline was too much. "You do remember my studio—it's that big addition you labored all summer to build."

"I thought artists like light. You cower behind drawn curtains and locked doors."

"I'm not cowering."

"Cade Dugan, Holly High football captain and debate champ." Paul carved a marquee in the air. "Afraid of a teeny, tiny woman."

"Women, not woman. There's more than one of them." Cade scanned the square. Length and width. Width and length. Superman had it easy. Every man should have x-ray vision. "They pop up everywhere, like toadstools after the rain."

"Careful where you step, Cade. You might crush that egg under your tail feathers."

Cade fisted his hands in his pockets. His gaze landed on the mayor. "I might crush something but it won't be an egg."

"Ohhh, I'm so scared."

Cade stepped forward. A tiny fist thudded against his chest, laughter gurgled in his ears. Irritation dissolved in his growing confusion. He glanced down.

Brown eyes peered at him from under a mop of curly brown hair. A smile forced the concern from Emma Browning's elfin features. The scent of rosewater mingled with that of baby powder drifting wafting from the infant wiggling in her arms.

"Don't mind him, Cade." The mayor's wife hitched her son higher on her hip, winced as a hank of hair was captured in a chubby fist. "He checks the lights every time someone new arrives in town." She kissed her son's hair while extricating her own. "It's the price we pay for living in a magical town."

"Enchanted town, dear." Mayor Browning lifted his son from her arms. "Like the sign says." Husband and wife glanced towards the crowd huddled in the town square's gazebo.

Outsiders. The town was flooded with them. They visited Holly from Thanksgiving till New Year's, wallowed in the charm and quaintness of an old-fashioned Christmas. Applause filled the square, as much for the trio of Victorian carolers as to beat the feeling back into their frozen hands. Hums of appreciation greeted the town's baker, Babbette, when she arrived with her tray of roasted chestnuts and tiny mince pies.

Pride swelled Cade's chest. He loved his hometown. He just wished there were a few less people in it today. Not the harried outsiders. They could stay. But the Blue Coats...

Fleece brushed his ears. The Blue Coats had to go. Especially since their numbers continued to swell.

"Someone new arrived in town?"

Paul Browning grinned. "I thought you weren't concerned about the lights."

Cade winced. He should never have stopped to talk with the mayor. The slimy politician was bound to mention his interest in the lights. And if he snitched about Cade's question regarding the newest Blue Coat...

A shudder rippled up his spine. Damn. It's a good thing he was headed home. This little conversation was going to require major damage control.

"Don't tease Cade," Emma chided, picking up the bag of lights from the path and setting it next to the strings of lights on the green park bench. "You were just as nervous when I arrived in town."

Browning took his son's fist out of his mouth and glared at his wife.

"I was stunned by your beauty, not scared that the love of my life had arrived."

"You hid in your house for two days." Emma winked at Cade and maneuvered the ladder under the next dark bulb. "Straight."

Cade held the ladder as she climbed up the rungs. Finally, he had an ally. One person sympathetic to his plight. Things were looking up.

"I had the flu. Geez, a guy does his civic duty by staying home when he's sick and you turn it into a conspiracy." Browning pinned Cade with a glare. "And we're not talking about my behavior. We're talking about the poultry essence wafting off Cade."

"Poultry essence?" Color left his knuckles as he tightened his grip on the ladder. Browning danced beyond Cade's reach. Damn manners. He couldn't allow Emma to fall, even if he intended to make her a widow. Browning's son grinned up at him. He re-evaluated his plan. Okay, not a widow, just a hospital visitor for the next several weeks.

"If it runs like a chicken..." Browning shrugged.

"Boys, boys." Emma hopped off the last step of the ladder and stepped between her husband and Cade. "This isn't helping. Obviously, the newest Blue Coat isn't Cade's match. The lights haven't gone out." She shoved the ladder a few feet down the path then rummaged through the bag for a red bulb.

Coward, Cade mouthed as the mayor kept his wife and son between them.

Jealous, Browning mouthed back before turning his attention to his wife.

"It doesn't work that way, love."

Emma Browning spun on her heel. "You said that when the lights in Holly fall dark someone has met their match. Did you lie to me?" she asked, poking her husband with the bulb.

"No. No, I would never lie to you."

Cade grinned. Misery was better shared. Especially when someone else got the bigger share. Especially when that someone had been enjoying Cade's suffering for the last two months.

Yes, sir. This almost made up for those insufferable city council meetings. Almost, but not quite. There was still the matter of the bet.

"You know that, don't you?" Wheedling infused the Mayor's question.

Cade cleared his throat. Now, if he could get the rest of the gambling populace in trouble with their spouses...

"I thought I did. I thought that's why we were checking the lights every day." Emma cocked an eyebrow at Cade. He blinked then held the ladder steady. "I thought we were checking to see if Cade's match has arrived. It has to be soon, or they'll be forced to accept dates in January."

Another month of betting. Another month of Blue Coats. Bile soured Cade's tongue. Better to endure another month of Blue Coats than to marry one. A thought popped inside his skull. He glared at Emma's back.

"Are you part of the betting pool out of Babbette's?"

"You asked for it." Browning smirked.

"Don't mind him." Emma chucked the burnt-out bulb into the trashcan then snapped her fingers. "Give me a green one. This one is flickering."

Cade reached in the bag. Glass slid over his fingers. He plucked out two bulbs. Both blue. He was beginning to hate that color. Another dip in the bag; he caught a yellow and a green. He offered Emma her choice.

"I never pay your husband any mind."

"Paul's just cranky because he picked the eighteenth."

"The eighteenth." Five days ago. Five more losers. Cade smiled. Maybe he'd mention the town's wagering epidemic to Father Bridges. Surely, the priest would come up with a suitable sermon. After all, gambling was one of the seven deadly sins, wasn't it?

"Hey, I figured you'd have wised up after a month and a half." Browning dangled his son above his head. Drool dripped from the giggling infant. "Didn't figure you for a runner."

"I'm not a runner," Cade snapped. He was a survivor. A survivor knew when to retreat.

"You're avoiding them." Browning tucked his son next to his chest and swiped at the moisture on his cheek.

"What does it matter?" Emma jumped off the last step and glared at her husband. "The lights haven't gone out."

"The lights go out when someone meets their match. Cade hasn't met half of them. He's been holed up in his house."

Cade folded his arms over his chest. Holed up. He wasn't hiding. He was biding his time. Waiting. "I fixed Babbette's oven yesterday." And was grilled while doing it. He hadn't enjoyed his cinnamon roll, thanks to those Blue Coats. "There were four of them in the bakery." Four blue-coated women touring Babbette's small kitchen. How convenient for her oven to malfunction on the very day she selected.

"Four out of what?" Paul shuffled down the path next to his wife. "How many did Charity say are staying at the hotel?"

"Fifteen."

"Sixteen." Metal complained as Cade folded the ladder. That made eighteen altogether. Two had given up and gone home. "I took one over this morning." He resisted the urge to stick out his tongue. It was enough to win and foolish to gloat. Fate always smote those who gloated, and Charity's Bed and Breakfast only had one unoccupied room.

Emma twirled a lock of hair around her finger. "I hadn't realized Babbette was so clever. Imagine needing a repair..." Her brown eyes fixed on Cade. "Are you attending the city council meeting tonight?"

"No." Cade shuddered as rows of Blue Coats filled his mind's town hall. One-by-one, they would take the microphone and ask him questions. One kid or two? Long honeymoon or short? Boxers or briefs? He'd be dissected in front of his family and friends. Except, he wouldn't. "The meeting was cancelled on account of the holidays."

"Did you pick today, wife?" Browning peered at her over their son's head.

"I most certainly did not." Emma tugged her jacket over her belly. "I ran into Charity while picking up groceries. She said they're guzzling cocoa faster than Santa in a blizzard and needed to know if she could bring tea to tonight's meeting instead of hot chocolate."

"So, what day did you pick?"

Cade swallowed his groan. The whole town was against him. He wouldn't be surprised if the damn newspaper started printing the odds.

"I wasn't going to. But then Marlene added a free highlighting kit to the pot and Janelle added three hours of babysitting."

"Ha! I knew it." Browning tossed the baby in the air. "Mommy bet. You know what that means, don't you? No more preaching and lots of crow eating." He set the laughing baby on his hip and regarded his wife. "So, if you didn't pick today, what day did you chose?"

"Tomorrow."

"Tomorrow?" Browning smacked his forehead. "Tomorrow's Christmas Eve. Who's going to be traveling on Christmas Eve? You should have picked the day after Christmas when people are returning home."

"There weren't that many choices left," Emma sniffed.

Cade's jaw clicked shut. The sound echoed in his skull. The world had gone mad. And these two were leading the loonies. "I can't believe you two."

"Why not?" Browning placed his arm around his wife's shoulders. "You helped bring us together."

Cade raked his hand through his hair. What did it take to get through to people?

"*Fate* brought you together. *God* brought you together." The same lines, a touch more anger. He should have the message recorded for posterity. Hell, he should have it broadcasted 24/7 on the radio. "If you two had just kept your mouths shut..."

"Babbette talks, and so does Sherry. Between them, they've talked to everyone in Holly at least once. And almost everyone in Holly has friends and family in other towns." Emma crossed her arms and glared at him. "There are three couples as living proof of fate and destiny."

"Face it, you were doomed when the die was cast." Browning elbowed his wife. "Get it? Dye cast?"

"Doomed?" Emma shrugged off her husband's embrace. She snatched her son from his arms. A muscle twitched in her jaw. "He is destined to meet the future Mrs. Dugan, and you say he's doomed." Her voice climbed an octave on the last syllable.

"Now, honey, you know I didn't mean it that way." Browning flashed his palms at his wife.

"Really?" She raised her chin and marched down the path. "Cade's suit has certainly put our courtship in a whole new perspective."

"Thanks a lot, Cade." Browning tossed a glare over his shoulder as he loped after his wife. "You better meet Miss Right tomorrow, or my wife will never talk to me."

"Hey, you cast your own dye."

Browning made an obscene gesture than skidded to a halt. He turned left, cupped his hands around his mouth and shouted, "Oh, ladies! If you're looking for the artist formerly known as Cade Dugan, he's over here!"

"Son of a— " Cade pivoted about. Bones shuddered under flesh as he aborted his flight.

"Wouldn't waste your time swearing, boy." The town's oldest resident planted himself on the path, as insubstantial as a blade of grass and as firmly rooted as a centuries-old oak. His cane thumped Cade's boot.

Pain rattled up his shin. Great! Now he'd have a limp. "Mr. Henderson, I didn't see you there." Cade glanced through the tufts of hair on the old man's pink pate. He could still make it to the corner, but he'd have to hurry.

"Wasn't here a moment ago. Just came to see who won."

"Won?" Cade stepped left. The wizened man shadowed his movements.

"Your mama's family is known for their wit, boy. Guess you take after your pa's side."

This time the older man thumped his cane on Cade's chest. Excited chatter disturbed the air behind him. Damn, the Blue Coats were gaining, and Old Man Henderson was settling in for a chat. "I—I— "

"You resemble a fish with your jaw flapping like that." The old man rubbed his hands together. "I'm talking about the bet, boy. The bet. Today's my day, came to see if I could give the odds a little nudge in my favor."

Cade smoothed his furrowed brow. He should have stayed home. He was safe at home. He placed his hands on the human blockade's shoulders. Either the man stayed put, or he'd find himself on the bottom of a game of leapfrog. "I have to go now."

"I understand." Mischief twinkled in Mr. Henderson's rheumy blue eyes. A gnarled hand rested on Cade's forearm. "Just want ya ta know one thing."

"What." The jabber increased in volume. They were closer now. Cade's muscles locked. He refused to look. The hunted always tripped if they looked over their shoulder.

"I'm real sorry."

"Sorry?" Cade snapped his attention back to Mr. Henderson. Was someone actually apologizing for trying to profit from his misery?

"Yep." Gnarled hands gripped the cane.

"For what?"

"This."

The cane moved with the fluid grace of a striking cobra. Its brass knob plunged into Cade's gut, prodded the air out of his lungs. Muscles contracted, folding him over at the waist. Blue filled in his peripheral vision. The lead Blue Coat tackled him, knocking him to the ground, rattling the teeth in his head. Arms and legs tangled around his. Something hard banged into his ankle, added to the cacophony jangling along his nerves. The cool pavement leached his body heat, numbed some of the pain.

A fluffy white cloud scuttled across the blue sky. White. Surrender. Cade shook his head. He might not be able to escape at the moment, but he would never surrender.

He sipped air into his lungs. The pain receded to distant thunder. When he got out of this mess he would need a peek at that betting book. It was the only thing that could tell him who to avoid on what day.

A shadow blocked out the sky. Gradually, his eyes adjusted and a face appeared. A female face.

"Oh." Hands pressed into his chest, pinning him to the ground. "Oh, it's you."

Cade spit the blue scarf out of his mouth then gazed at the string of lights twinkling overhead. She wasn't his mate. Not that he'd actually believed differently. The pairings of local townsfolk had been a coincidence, nothing more.

"Darn." A cane tapped the ground beside Cade's head. "I thought she'd be the one."

Cade shoved the Blue Coat off his lap and sat up. Pain stitched up his side. Great, now he'd have to deal with one of them plus some bruised ribs. He glared at Mr. Henderson. Meddlesome old coot. It was past time someone locked up the old fart. He gingerly rose to his feet.

"This is so perfect." A well-manicured hand latched on his forearm. "Look, I'm even wearing pink skates like the figurine.

I bet none of the others wore skates. That just proves I'm your true love."

Cade plucked at the fingers. They wouldn't budge. Damn, now he knew why trapped animals gnawed off their legs to escape. Too bad he needed both of his hands in his line of work.

"I see, Miss— "

"Petrie. Deborah Petrie. I hope you don't mind, but I plan to keep my name after we're married."

"Damn Blue Coats."

"Blue Coat? Is that what you call them?" She flashed her straight teeth at him. "No wonder they're cooped up in the hotel drowning their sorrows with Christmas cookies and hot chocolate. Blue." She shook her head woefully. "The coat is distinctly turquoise, not blue. I took the figurine to the milliners. We matched it perfectly."

"You did?" Colored glass winked at Cade from the bench. Someone had forgotten to put away the extra strings of lights.

"Of course. It will make lovely bridesmaids' dresses, too. We are planning to marry in the spring, aren't we?"

An idea grew in his skull. It might work. He wouldn't know until he tried. He smiled at her. "I think you should sit down."

He gestured to the bench and gallantly scooped the string of lights out of her way. To his surprise, she released her grip and complied. Laughter buoyed his spirits. This was almost too easy.

"Oh, yes. Yes, of course." She hand-pressed her wool coat. "I knew it would be like this."

"You did?" The bulbs clunked together as he looped one end.

"Everyone knows the man proposes on bended knee. It's very romantic."

Cade's thoughts skipped two steps ahead. He'd loop the strand of lights around the back of the bench and tie it off around the opposite end. A small delay that would allow him to escape. But how to draw them across her without giving away his plan?

"You will propose on bended knee?"

He returned to the moment. "Uh, I hadn't— "

"Don't be silly." She jerked on his coat. "Just bend down. Everyone is expecting it." A storm brewed in her eyes. She didn't like being thwarted.

Good thing he wasn't planning on being caught.

"I'll get on my knees if you close your eyes, Deborah."

"Close my eyes?"

"Just for a moment." Just long enough for him to lash her to the bench. "I want to compose my thoughts. It wouldn't do to mess this up. It's too important." His freedom hung in the balance.

"All right." Her eyes flickered closed.

Cade waited a few seconds then looped one end of the string of lights around the bench. He winced as the bulbs clacked together. His soon-to-be-captive audience didn't seem to notice. Guilt nudged his determination. He wasn't her soul mate. The lights proved it. The scarf proved it. She would be better with someone else. This would simply help her see that.

He threaded the string around the bench seat and tied the ends together. Besides, it wasn't as if she would be stuck here all night. Someone would rescue her in a few minutes.

"You don't have to think of anything fancy, Cade. Just ask."

Cade straightened and backed away. Not one word. His tone could give away his intentions. Another step. Five more and he should be able to break into a run.

"Cade?" Irritation honed her notes. She shifted on the bench.

Two more steps. He pivoted on his heel. Old Man Henderson shook his head then stepped aside.

"I'll see she gets to Charity's."

"Really, Cade, I—" The shrill notes cut through the air as he rounded the corner. "Where did he go?"

"Home would be my guess." Mr. Henderson answered.

"Home?" Confusion and doubt rippled through the trees.

Cade stopped at the corner as a horse and carriage jingled past. His leg jumped. Two Blue Coats stood on the opposite side of the street. Damn. He couldn't tie those two up. A sleigh and another omnibus clattered by, and judging by the sound of voices, the latest Blue Coat was free and on the move. He'd have to cut across the park, take the alley behind the courthouse and slip through the Arts and Crafts neighborhood.

"But he can't. I'm the one he's waiting for."

"The lights told him otherwise."

"Lights?"

"They always go dark when someone's match arrives."

"Oh, drat. I should have known Holly would have something like that. So, now what am I supposed to do?"

Blue flashed. He plunged through the trees where the pine needles scratched his cheek. Snow crunched under his feet. He would make it home and not come out until after New Year's Day.

"Don't worry. I believe Charity has just made a fresh batch of sugar cookies."

Chapter III

"Egypt, thank God I didn't miss you." Helen Weaver, nee O'Connell, stood on Egypt's apartment stoop. Her very swollen belly pointed directly at Egypt, blocking the route to the almost-forgotten wedding dress.

"Hello, Helen." Egypt's sneakers squealed to a halt. Jingling keys dangled from her fingertips. Her heart slowed to a normal beat. "What brings you here?"

"This. It's a wedding scrapbook." She giggled and shoved the gaily wrapped box off her belly and towards Egypt. "I've made thirteen of them so far. Well, fourteen, if you count my own. Your sister admired mine so much I made her one."

Blue ribbon crawled over the silver wrapping paper. A bell tinkled. Egypt balanced the gift on her fingertips.

"I'm certain she'll love it."

"You are planning on attending the wedding, aren't you?" Helen waddled closer; her gaze swept up Egypt's blue jeans and stopped on the embroidered sweater.

She resisted the urge to squirm. Helen had always been the fashion plate. Even now, every hair lay neatly against her head and her clothes emphasized her trim legs while hugging her ripe belly. Egypt swallowed her inadequacies, tucked the gift under her arm and rammed her key into her lock.

"Of course, I'm going to the wedding. Paris is my sister."

"And Darrell is your ex-boyfriend, just like Adam."

Disappointment gripped Egypt's lungs. She forced air in and out despite the constriction. Today's reminders were the humidity before the thunderstorm. Once she was in Dragoon's Springs, they would come faster than water in a cloudburst. "I attended your wedding to Adam and then Brad's to Marie and Zach's to—"

"My, you've certainly introduced many of us girls to our husbands." Helen giggled, backing up a step. Her gaze fell on the steps before she looked back at Egypt.

Fourteen girls, to be exact. And her heart had broken every time.

"Maybe you should start your own matchmaking service." Helen's laugh was forced, the notes dropping like stones on asphalt.

Egypt strode across her apartment, shoved up the sleeves of her sweater. A studio. One room. Large enough for one person. A hovel compared to Helen's four-bedroom Arts and Crafts home in Dragoon's Springs.

Plastic crinkled as she tossed the wedding dress over her shoulder.

"I really need to get on the road."

"Oh, is someone waiting for you?" Hope flashed on Helen's round face before fear drew the shutters on her expression. "My sister Karen asked if you were bringing a boyfriend. She just graduated from high school, you know."

Egypt shooed her old friend outside and faced the door. Karen had been a skinny, scraped-kneed teenager when Egypt left Dragoon's Springs for college. Now the brat was a young woman prowling for a husband.

"No, I didn't know." She hadn't wanted to put names and relationships to those females awaiting her return. No, not her return home but the arrival of an escort, ripe for the picking. "And no, no one's waiting for me. I'm fresh out of broken-in boyfriends who make perfect husbands for someone else."

She turned around in time to see the tears well up in Helen's eyes. A dainty handkerchief dabbed at her pink nose. Guilt lashed Egypt. Great, now she'd made a pregnant woman cry. Where were the puppies she was supposed to kick?

"Helen, I'm sorry. I—"

"Don't worry about it." She sniffed, waving the white cloth. "Stupid hormones. Adam comes home and finds me bawling over Hallmark commercials."

"Still, even an idiot like me could see you two belong together."

She nodded. "Adam would not have made you a good husband, Egypt. He's so practical and you're..." She cleared her throat and tucked her sodden handkerchief in her purse. "You're so..."

"Flighty."

"Whimsical." Helen's perfectly manicured hand slipped around Egypt's and squeezed gently. "You always used to create the most elaborate fairy tales for our Barbies. I guess you were pairing up people even then."

Egypt fidgeted in her skin. Fairy tales. Those words had crept up once too often today.

"I'll give Paris your present."

"I know you will but that's not really why I'm here."

"It's not?"

Helen took a deep breath and caressed her belly.

"We were going to name the baby after you, but then Adam noticed there are already five girls in Dragoon's Springs with your name and so we were hoping you'd be her godmother instead." She released her belly to grab Egypt's hand. "Will you? I mean, she wouldn't even be here if you hadn't brought Adam home that Fourth of July."

That Fourth of July. Egypt's first summer after college. She couldn't wait to show off her cosmopolitan air, not to mention her handsome new boyfriend. She literally ran into Helen at the grocery store, and Adam had ignored his stum-

29

bling girlfriend in favor of his future wife. It had taken Egypt twenty minutes to realize *she* was the third wheel at the fireworks display and not her grade-school friend. Loneliness threatened to drown her. She missed her friend.

"I'd be honored to be her godmother."

"Thanks. Egypt. You're such a sweet person. Be sure to stop by my mom's house before you leave Dragoon's Springs—I have something for you."

"You don't have to give me anything."

"It's just Auntie Jane's old mirror. We converted the guest bedroom into a nursery and were going to get rid of it when I remembered that summer when we were five and you pretended to be Alice and that mirror was our entrance into Wonderland. Do you remember?"

"Yes. You always wanted to be the Cheshire Cat instead of the White Rabbit."

"I like cats." Helen frowned at Egypt. "You're not taking that jacket, are you? Really, Egypt, you've lived in the desert too long. The mountains get cold, even in Arizona."

She shrugged. The weatherman had predicted clear skies and above-normal temperatures for the next week. If it got too cold she would borrow something from her mother or sister. "It's the only one I have."

"What about the blue one from our senior trip? You loved that jacket. The whole class was taking bets whether or not you'd sleep in it."

Egypt strolled to her car and balanced the gift on the pile in the backseat.

"That's about how long it's been since I last wore it."

"You should find it. Honestly, Egypt, you're going to need something warmer."

"I'll be fine. Really."

Helen squeezed between Egypt and the door and tapped her foot against the pavement.

"Look, the jacket's probably still at my mother's."

"Nope. I checked. She said she gave it to you when you were up there last Christmas."

Last Christmas. The day she'd introduced Paris to Darrell. A pinpoint of clarity amidst the haze of memory. Egypt shook off the thoughts.

"You checked?"

"I needed an excuse to see you, all right? I know you haven't quite forgiven me for stealing Adam. I haven't forgiven myself for hurting you and..."

"That's why you haven't talked to me?" Egypt's spirits lifted. "I thought you weren't speaking to me because of what we did to your car?"

"My car? What did you do to my car?" Helen searched the parking lot before her gaze rested on a tan Volvo.

"Uh, I think my jacket is still in the trunk." Egypt quickly shut the door and walked to the front of the Volkswagen. Either Helen had forgotten about the flat tires on the car or she never found out Egypt had been responsible. Who was she to enlighten her?

With a twist of her wrist, the trunk sprang open. The turquoise jacket lay folded across two smashed boxes. Her mother would kill her if she found out Egypt had been carting around boxes for a whole year.

"It even has the lift ticket." Helen tugged out a purple scarf from the inside and looped it around Egypt's shoulders. "Now you're ready for cold weather."

Egypt ripped off the ticket and shoved it in the pocket.

"I better be off. I've deviated thirty-three minutes from The Plan."

"Oh, no! The dreaded Plan. I swear that was the first four-letter word I learned. Plan." Helen shuddered.

Egypt felt herself smile. "You have no idea how many times they've had to revise it." She tossed her jacket onto the passenger seat. Her cat rose from his perch and sauntered over.

"Hey, is that Nutz?"

"Yep." Nutz sniffed the air before strolling closer.

"Hey, Nutz. Do you remember me? I can't believe you're taking him. He absolutely hates the snow." Helen stroked the cat once before he walked away to lie on the coat. "Wouldn't go outside for anything. And he couldn't stay inside because of Adam's allergies. He looks good."

Nutz preened under the attention.

"I'm taking good care of him."

"That's why I agreed to give him to you. Take care, Egypt." After a brief, awkward hug Helen walked toward her Volvo. "I'll see you at your parents' New Year's Eve party if this baby ever decides to come."

"Take care, Helen."

The VW rocked as Egypt shut the door. That hadn't been too bad. Perhaps her luck had finally changed.

Cade slammed the deadbolt home and rested his head against the door. Safe. At last. His heart slowed to a normal rhythm. Two of the Blue Coats had almost caught him behind the King house. Almost but not quite. Only longtime residents knew about the break in the hedges. The break that opened onto the alley that cut behind his house.

He shifted his weight to his right leg. Cold metal stung his finger as he separated a few slats of the blinds. They were still there, circling his house like buzzards over a lost desert wanderer. A third joined the set. Damn women. He'd have to run the gauntlet to get his dog. He ripped off his baseball cap and raked his fingers through his hair. He would have to call his mother, make sure Pete could stay the night.

The hair on the back of his neck stood up. Awareness pricked along his skin just as perfume teased his nose.

Someone was in his house.

"Alone at last."

He spun on his heel and stepped back. His head collided with the door; stars exploded inside his skull. Good God. They were invading his house.

"You are a hard man to get alone, Cade Dugan."

"I—I am."

She stalked towards him. Her hips undulated suggestively. Cade blinked. There was something wrong with her clothes.

"Yes, indeed." Long crimson nails raked the back of his sofa as her green-eyed gaze traveled up and down his body. "But definitely worth waiting for."

"I feel at a disadvantage." The doorknob ground into his back. He never should have left Pete at his parents'. No one would have broken into his house with a wolf-dog on duty.

"I'm Maybelle—Maybelle Collins." She extended her hand. Blue and purple paint stained her palm.

Cade's heart raced. She wouldn't. He scrutinized her clothes. Good Lord, the woman had painted on her clothes. If anyone ever found out he had entertained a naked woman in his house...

A shudder scrambled his thoughts.

"What brings you here, Maybelle?" *More important, how can I get you to leave?*

"I thought playing hard-to-get was a woman's prerogative."

"That's okay. I thought choosing whom to court was a man's." Cade sidled away from her. Ridding himself of Blue Coats was becoming trickier. He couldn't toss her naked butt out his front door. This would require more finesse.

"I was tired of waiting at the hotel." She pouted. "And I missed you at the bakery."

"I doubt many men missed you looking like that." Cade reached the kitchen, turned and faced her. She was still there, following him in a stable orbit. Maybe he could shove her out the back door. First, he'd have to find her clothes.

"Do you like it?" Her hands slipped over her blue hips.

33

A groan slipped past his lips. He had a pulse, didn't he? Cade shook the insanity from his skull. He couldn't encourage her. She wasn't who she wanted to be, even if her curves got him hotter than a NASCAR driver the second before the flag dropped.

"It shows a definite artistic bent." The uniqueness of the canvas was definitely bent. God save him. Where were her clothes? His gaze swept the living room. Nothing. "Did you use my paint?"

She nodded, trailing her hand along the countertop. "I thought this might help me stand out, make you notice who I am."

Great, the nuts grew nuttier just to be noticed. And they were touching his stuff. Even his mother knew better than to touch his stuff. Everything was where it was supposed to be, and she had to go and touch it. No one went into his studio unless he was with them, and she had just sashayed into his house. He tramped down the rising anger.

She had to go.

"It worked," he stated, although not in the way she had wanted.

"You don't think I'm her, do you?" Her gaze flew around the room, alighted briefly on each breakable item before coming to rest on the glass near her hand.

Great. She was a smasher. His house wouldn't be able to withstand her wrath. He had to get her out before she inflicted too much damage.

"I'd say you were the closest one yet."

"Do you mean it?"

"I—" Blue flashed in the foliage outside his dining room window. God save him. More were arriving. Arriving. An idea sparked in his head. He had to try, although it might not be effective on a woman who strolled around a complete stranger's house in nothing but paint and skin. Still, he hadn't come up with anything else. "Good grief, my parents."

"Your parents?" she squeaked. Her hands and arms shifted to cover strategic parts of her anatomy.

"Yes." Relief. He should have known such a crazy idea would work. "They're here. You have to get dressed." He inched towards her. No touching, absolutely no touching. He swept the air in front of him, shooing her backwards.

"Dressed?" Her eyes widened in her chalky face.

"You certainly don't want to meet my folks dressed like that, do you?"

"No. No, I don't." She snatched a towel off the counter and held it in front of her.

"Quickly. Where are your clothes?"

"I...I...They're in there." She pointed to the bathroom then glanced at her blue-and-purple palms. "Perhaps I should take a shower."

"Shower." Cade exaggerated his grimace and added a shudder for good measure. "No. Definitely not. My parents are very old-fashioned. They once thought my high school sweetheart was fast because we kissed after a month of dating."

"A month?" She streaked across the room, slipped into the bathroom. Fabric rustled. Grunting drifted out.

Cade fixed his gaze on the landscape above the fireplace.

"Thirty-six days, to be exact."

"Yes, but we're meant to be together. I'm sure— "

"To this day they cross the street when they see her walking towards them."

"Oh, dear. I can't find my shoes." Flesh slapped tile.

Cade shook his head. No excuses. Shoes or no, she had to go. He wouldn't mind cleaning up after her. With a smile, he pressed his point.

"I could probably explain why you are here without a chaperone. I mean, I know first impressions are so important. I even think Mom'll forgive you in a couple years."

The activity picked up. Her panic was palpable. Now all he had to do is spur her to dress more quickly, or she'd grow suspicious when his parents failed to materialize. "Of course, that might make those first years of living with them a bit awkward."

She poked her head out the door. The rest of her followed.

"We're going to live with your parents?"

"Oh, yes. We can't leave Mom to push Dad's wheelchair about in the snow. You're young and healthy. I don't want you to worry, I'm certain you can learn how to place the leeches just so. I mean, no one wants Dad's leg to putrefy again. The bathrooms still smells..."

"You know, maybe I should wait on the porch." She stuffed her feet into her shoes and scooted across the carpet.

"Really?"

"Yes, yes." Her laces slapped the wood floor. Her hands jammed into her jacket. "I wouldn't want to get off on the wrong foot."

"No need to worry about that—Dad only has the one." Her jaw hung open. Cade smacked his forehead. "Oh, you mean figuratively." He moved toward her. She held up her hand.

"Yes."

"Perhaps you're right. Mom always said women know best. And Mom is never wrong. I'm sure she'll like you," He frowned at her. "Given time."

"I—I'll be outside." Metal rattled as she tried to open the door with the deadbolt in place. "Just give me a few minutes then I'll knock."

"You'll knock?"

"Yes, I'll knock." She sobbed, twisted the knob and retracted the bolt. "Don't come looking for me, okay? That way, your mother won't suspect I've been here."

"Oh, you're smart. Mom said I should marry a smart one. She'll be so glad when we walk down the aisle. She has the wedding all planned—she even decorated our new room. I don't get to live there until after the wedding. Mom insisted."

"Okay." She wrenched open the door

"You like blue, don't you?" Cade stepped after her. She was so frantic to leave she might leave the door open for other Blue Coats. "Of course, you do, you painted yourself with that very color."

"I'm going to leave now."

"Leave?"

"Yes, like we planned. I'll go and..." She stepped onto the porch, pivoted about and faced him. "And this is very important. You stay here until I come back."

"Right. I forgot." Cade leaned against the doorjamb. His hand rested on the knob, in case anyone else thought to enter his house. "I'll be sure to act surprised when you come back."

"Bye, Cade."

"Bye, Maybelle." He waited until she had cleared his driveway before he shut the door. Laughter bounced off the rafters, buoyed his spirit. Who knew revenge could be this satisfying?

Chapter IV

"Obviously, whatever's wrong is beyond the powers of duct tape and garbage ties." Egypt slammed the hood, cleaned her greasy hands on her jeans and climbed into the car. Red lights glared back at her from the dash. On the passenger seat Nutz's tail swished. One yellow eye stared at her.

Cold air pressed against the window. A frigid blast coughed out of the vents before the engine died. She slapped off the heater and pounded her fist against the steering wheel. Tingles raced up her arm.

"Mom is going to kill me." The sound of grinding teeth filled the air. Egypt forced her jaw to relax. Yellow caution lights cast a jaundice pall over the pristine snow.

Walk or wait, the choice of every stranded traveler. Egypt stared down the two-lane road. Snow on the left, snow on the right, snow dripping from the trees crowding the empty road. Neither a construction crew nor another car was in sight. Leather creaked as she rested her chin on the steering wheel. In fact, she couldn't remember seeing a single car since the detour directed her off the state route.

Was this her punishment for lying to her mother?

"Meow," Nutz complained. He stretched and padded over to her lap.

"Wait or walk?" Her fingers disappeared into his soft fur. His pleasure rumbled against her palms. "What do you think?"

"Meow." He wiped his cheeks on her steering wheel then hunkered down.

Cold air swept goose bumps across her skin, leaching the warmth from her sweater. She shivered and reached for her jacket. Pillows of down filling stopped the loss of body heat. Stiff fingers dove into her pockets. Wool blocked her progress. She tugged. Purple mittens tumbled across the seat. She dug deeper in her pockets. A pack of stiff Juicy Fruit gum and a hat joined the unearthed booty. Nutz batted at the pom-pom on the hat.

"Not a bad haul but not very conducive to a long stay in the car." Egypt stuffed her hands in the mittens and tucked her ears under the hat. The temperature in the old Volkswagen dropped to match the outside. Still no car in sight. "Guess I forgot something after all." Her winter survival pack was safe on the top shelf of her closet. Her mittens shifted as she rubbed her hands together. "I suppose this wouldn't have happened if I had made a list."

She was going to have to walk. Stitches burrowed deeper into his pine bedding. *They* were going to have to walk. The animals would freeze if she left them in the car. Egypt glanced in her rearview mirror. She hadn't spied a single building after the turn-off or another vehicle. Fear shot adrenaline into her blood. The waterproof matches rattled in their box. She would have to go out there, into the unknown, and find something to burn.

Metal clattered as she opened the hamster cage. Stitches poked his head out of his nest and blinked up at her.

"Come here, sweetie." He scrambled along the back of his cage to his food bowl. Tiny paws rifled the contents, selected sunflower seeds and dried corn kernels before stuffing them into his mouth. He squeaked as her hand closed around his body.

"Don't worry, I'm not taking your food. I'm moving you to a warmer bed."

She eased him into her coat's breast pocket. Tiny paws tickled her breast as he explored his new home. Seconds later his head poked out. Nutz sat up straighter, his gaze fixed on the rodent. Stitches chirped and disappeared.

"Well, that's settled." Egypt dusted bits of bedding off her gloves then reached for the door handle. Nutz stared at her.

"Are you up for a walk, boy?"

Egypt lifted the cat from her lap and scooted off the seat. Snow crunched under her pink hightops. Very gently, she lowered the cat to the ground. Nutz yowled and spat. Orange streaked in her vision as he leapt into the car. He shook the ice from his paws, spun about and glared at her. A low growl filled the car.

"I know we're not supposed to leave the car. We're only going up the road a bit, and I'm not leaving you here."

She lunged for him. Nutz clawed up the seat back and launched himself over the presents. He skidded into the rear window then faced her, fur bristling. His tail twitched faster than her windshield wipers on a good day. She snapped the front seat forward and reached for him. Muscles stretched along her ribs. Metal bit into her hip. The cat swatted at her hand, snagged the yarn of her gloves.

"Sheesh. Helen wasn't kidding. You certainly don't like the snow. We can't stay here, Nutz. We'll freeze to death."

The cat pressed himself further against the glass.

"We're going to have to leave the car to find something to burn."

Nutz blinked and tucked his paws under his chest. His tail wrapped halfway around his body.

"Whatever is wrong with the engine can't be fixed with duct tape and garbage ties."

He blinked at her.

"I know we're supposed to stay with the vehicle but no one's come along in forty-five minutes. Which means we only have a few hours of daylight left. If I'm going to burn the spare tire I need kindling."

The cat stared at her pocket. His whiskers twitched.

Understanding knocked around Egypt's skull.

"All right, you big baby, I'll carry you." She unzipped her jacket. Cold air sucked the heat from her skin. Nutz streaked across the packages and perched on the driver's seat. She tucked him against her belly, tightened the drawstring of her jacket to hold his weight and slowly zipped up the coat. "And here I thought cats were the epitome of dignity."

Nutz stretched across her belly. He sniffed her pocket, stuck his nose in the hole of the lining. His taut muscles relaxed.

"Okay, Egypt." She shook her anxiety out her fingertips and stamped the tingles from her toes. "Stay in sight of the road. That way you won't get lost and you can see if help is coming."

She stuck a note of her intentions on the dashboard and slammed the door. Cold air burned her lungs. Her feet refused to budge.

Psychos used the woods for their nefarious purposes, just ask Hansel and Gretel or Snow White or Sleeping Beauty. So did marijuana growers and...

"Marauding monkeys, get a grip, will you?" One step, then another. Left foot, right foot. Her feet responded to her brain's command. She cleared the front of the car and stopped. If she did encounter help she would need to know where her car died. She shuddered at her poor choice of words. "Broke down, not died. No one is going to die today."

Her gaze traveled along the side of the road. A small green square hovered above the mound of snow.

Mile marker 1225. What road in Arizona had that many miles? None. The state wasn't that many miles across. She stomped onward. One of the road crew must have decided to be cute. Hadn't the sign said to expect road delays until Christmas?

She rounded the curve. Her car disappeared behind a curtain of evergreens. Fingers closed around the stale gum. She pulled it out, unfolded the foil. She poured the chunks of gum sliding across the surface into her mouth. Sugar sweetened her tongue. The pieces softened in the rush of saliva.

"Now would be a good time for Prince Charming to make his entrance." No one appeared. Not that she actually expected a rescue. Still, anything was better than the oppressive silence.

"One hundred bottles of beer on the wall..."

Chapter V

"Alone at last." The leather reins tightened around Cade's hand. Numb fingers wiggled inside his gloves. Before him, Goodman and Holiday's hooves punched holes in the blanket of snow. Frigid air filled his lungs; the knots inhabiting his shoulders eased their grip.

"I should have thought of this sooner." He relaxed against the bench, nestled in the faux sheepskin covering. The whoosh of the sleigh's runners cut into the silence of the forest. He crested the hill. No more being hunted like an eight-point buck on the last day of deer season.

He was free.

Cade guided his team around a clump of pine trees. The forced gaiety of "ninety-four bottles of beer on the wall" reached him seconds before turquoise flashed in his peripheral vision. He braced his feet against the runners and yanked on the reins. The back of the sleigh swung left, thumped against the snow-covered log edging the trail. The abrupt stop shuddered up his frame.

"Of all the stupid, hair-brained, empty-headed..." He yanked the swinging brass lantern off its hook. Light invaded the dim forest, pushed aside the shadows cast by the towering pines.

Purple-clad hands wiggled above a cavity punched in the snowdrift. Frustration rumbled from Cade's throat. Damn, he hadn't imagined it. Metal scraped metal as he returned the lantern to its home. He could leave her here, pretend he hadn't seen the blue coat and purple mittens or heard the bellow of "ninety-four bottles of beer on the wall" ricocheting around the forest.

Grunts and thumps echoed from the silhouette in the snow. This was his brothers' fault. Cade lifted the reins, ready to slap them against the reindeer's rumps.

"If you're finished gawking, do you think you can help me from the snowbank?"

Her voice ignited a fire in his gut, like a dose of French brandy on a winter's day. Potent. Intoxicating. Cade gently lowered the reins. Goodman sidled closer to Holiday, urging her forward. Cade stretched the leather taut.

"Are you certain you wish my help?"

"Gee, let me think. I'm stuck in snow that thinks it's quicksand. My behind is numb. I can't feel my lips. And I am most definitely not in the mood to make snow angels." The mittens transformed into sock puppets, mouthing her words while her message abraded his conscience. "Yes, I think I would like your help."

She was cold. Cade studied the ice glistening on his boots. His shoulders rolled against the lamb's-wool lining his jacket. Why should he feel guilty? He hadn't intended to run the woman down; and, damn it, a man had a right to his privacy. He dipped his right ear toward its shoulder. Tension popped along his neck. Hell, he'd better help her. If word ever reached town or, God forbid, his mother...

With a sigh, he looped the reins around the front of the sleigh and dismounted.

"Are you going to help me or not?"

Demanding. Irritating. Interfering. What kind of woman walked around snow-packed woods? He eyed the Nikon camera nestled on the quilt. He shouldn't. He really, really shouldn't.

The camera settled in his palm like the handshake of an old friend.

"Well?"

Sassy. Meddlesome. Light shot out of the flash, illuminating her hands waving above the mound of white.

"Snow angels, huh? Now, why didn't I think of that?" Hell, if the woman wanted to dress like one of the figurines he would use her as one. It just might get the rest of them to leave him be.

"Did you say something?"

Snow crunched under his boots as he stepped closer and snapped off a couple more frames. Battered pink sneakers arced above the ground before thumping against the snowdrift. Amusement trickled down his spine. Her predicament might very well end his torment.

"Your angel requires a bit more work. Try moving your arms parallel to the ground instead of perpendicular to it. That should plump up her wings."

Curses shot out of the hole. A purple pom-pom bobbed on a sea of white. Two more pictures captured the moment.

"I didn't quite catch that."

"Do you think you could hurry? That lightning means a storm's coming."

Cold stung his gums. He forced the smile from his face and snapped off a few more frames. He should plaster her vulnerability over the town hall, let those hunting their fifteen minutes of fame know the price. His protective instincts flickered on. He mentally stamped them into oblivion. She had no right to be here, no right to own a silky voice that wrapped around a man and tugged him closer.

"I'm not here to make a snow angel!" The sock puppets disappeared. Seconds ticked by while his lens zoomed in on her location. "Hello? Are you still there?"

"I'm still here." Cade snapped the lens cover in place and stepped closer. "So, if you're not here to punch designs in the fresh powder then what brings you to my forest?"

Flakes dotted the blue jeans hugging her shapely legs. Nice, very nice. His gaze bumped over her lumpy turquoise jacket and settled on her face. Cold stained the flesh above her violet scarf. She would make a perfect figurine, especially since her mouth would remain permanently shut.

"You own the entire forest?"

Leave it to a woman to latch on to his slip of the tongue while avoiding answering his question.

"No."

"Are you going to help me or not?" Exasperation wrinkled her forehead, contradicting the humor twinkling in her amber eyes.

Cade resisted the urge to suck in his gut as her gaze traveled over him. So he lacked the washboard abs flaunted in the media—he wasn't exactly canned dog food. Besides, her opinion of him didn't matter. Not one bit.

"It's really not such a difficult decision. You big strong man. Me tiny stuck woman. Big strong man pull tiny stuck woman from hole." Her mitten-clad hands gouged the down stuffing covering her hips.

"Yes, ma'am." Okay, so she possessed a sense of humor. A day's growth of beard rasped against his glove as he wiped the smile from his face. He certainly wasn't going to let her know he found the quality attractive. Hell, the last time he smiled at one of the Blue Coats she had dashed to the printer to order wedding invitations.

"Are you alone?" Her gaze darted left then right before settling over his shoulder.

"Just me and the animals." He wasn't what she expected. His skin tightened in irritation. Not that he cared; his ideal woman was demure and soft, not some vulture-woman hybrid waiting to swoop in for the kill as soon as he showed any sign of weakness.

"I thought I heard you talking...Never mind." Her coat swelled with invisible courage before she slipped one hand into his palm and clasped his wrist with the other.

The camera slid over his hip. Cade ignored the electricity sparking along his skin. She was just another Blue Coat. There was nothing special about her. The purple scarf didn't prove anything. Too bad his body wasn't listening to his brain.

"Perhaps you would prefer someone else?"

"No, you'll do."

He'll do. Did the irritating woman think she only had to say "jump" and he'd ask how high? Anger scalded his insides. He yanked her to her feet. She slammed against his chest. Desire engulfed him, fueling his anger. She swayed on her feet. Her raspberry scent filled his lungs.

"Good heavens." Heat seared Egypt's flesh through her knitted gloves. Their clasped hands captured her attention. All that heat and no steam. How could that be? She glanced at her assassin turned rescuer. Leather bunched and rippled over his arms. His red flannel collar blurred with his black jacket. Hell's Angel driving a sleigh.

She slapped the mitten to her lips and watched as snow showered down like powdered sugar. Her amusement died at the disapproval bracketing his mouth. She coughed the giggle from her throat. He tugged on his hand, jerking her forward. Cold leather skimmed the tip of her nose. Her lids flickered closed. Pine. Animal. Man.

Him.

Her heart bumped inside her breast. Desire vibrated down her arms and legs. She wanted his scent on her skin. Wanted...

His strong hands cupped her shoulders, forcing her back a step.

"Are you hurt? You're a bit unsteady on your feet." Fingers massaged her scalp through her cap.

Her head followed his touch, just like Nutz did when she scratched his cheeks. Nutz. Egypt patted her coat, felt the cat nestled against her belly. Tiny paws reached up her sweater. She rubbed the marmalade-colored feline through the down filling. His purr rippled up her chest.

"No bumps. How many bottles of beer have you drunk?"

Beer? Drunk? He had heard her singing yet he still ran her down. Egypt's eyes flew open. Two faces stared at her, one from each of the mirrored lenses of his sunglasses. "None, thank you very much. The singing was for your benefit. So you would know I was here."

His eyes narrowed. "How did you know I'd be in the woods?"

"Not *you* you. *You* as in *someone*. Anyone." She smacked the snow off her mittens. "I started following a road then poof, it disappeared. I was getting ready to turn back when you mowed me over." His full bottom lip twitched. Anger withered her budding attraction. "I hardly think this is funny."

"Didn't think you would."

She batted his hands away. This was all his fault. Running her down, smelling like that. Egypt spun on her heel. The soles of her sneakers skidded on a patch of ice. The snowbank rose to embrace her once more. Air whooshed out of her as his arm snaked around her waist. Nutz yowled and clawed his way up her chest.

"I thought you didn't come here to make snow angels."

Sensations crackled along sleepy synapses. Her back blazed with his warmth. Winged anticipation fluttered in her belly. Her feet dangled six inches off the ground. Slush dripped off her shoes. "A woman has a right to change her mind."

"Then I'll leave you to it." He set her firmly on the ground and stomped away.

"Wait!" Her cry bounced off his back as he climbed aboard his sleigh and gathered the reins. Apparently, he wasn't her knight in shining armor but a devil sent to tempt her with the hope of rescue. "Please?"

His sigh fogged his glasses. He ripped them off his face and cleaned the lenses on his scarf.

"Do you have a cell phone?"

He hooked his glasses around his ears and faced her.

"Nope."

"So much for an easy solution."

"Anything else?" His index finger rubbed the white line scarring his left cheek.

Familiarity zipped through her.

"Have we met?"

"Lady, if that's the best pick up-line you have..."

"Pick-up line! I am definitely not hitting on you." She crossed her arms and kneaded her biceps. Though, if he continued to be disagreeable, she might just hit him. "Should have known such a gorgeous package would contain a mountain of attitude."

"You'd skin a man who said that about you." His lips curled in amusement at her expense.

"What?" Dread skimmed its icy fingers down her spine. Please, please don't let her have spoken her thoughts out loud.

"Don't worry, Princess, you're not the first to succumb, although 'gorgeous package' is a new one. Most just call me handsome." Wickedness twisted his lips. "A few even called me a hunk."

Her mitten pressed against her forehead. She should have known her prayer would go unanswered. If God had been listening she would be tooling along the freeway instead of traipsing through the snow looking for a mechanic.

"I never said anything like that."

"No? Then drooling must be your natural look."

"I am not drooling." Egypt resisted the urge to dab at the corner of her mouth.

"So, it *is* my 'gorgeous package.'" His left eyebrow rose, daring her to challenge his conclusion.

"I have more important things on my mind then your... package. Gorgeous or otherwise." Rope bit into Egypt's sides as she jerked on her coat's drawstring. The conceited oaf. Did he actually think women followed him into the forest to gawk at his tight backside?

"Like what?"

"World hunger. Peace in the Middle East. The weather." The weather. She glanced at the gray clouds scuttling across the sky. The lightning may have stopped, but those clouds spelled snow.

"We're a little past small talk, don't you think?"

"I wasn't making small talk." Egypt tossed back her shoulders and glared at the man. Apparently, he couldn't think beyond himself. She ignored the drop of disappointment trickling down her spine. His love affair with himself wasn't her concern. Finding a phone was.

"Then, why don't you thank me for rescuing you."

"Rescuing me?" Crimson tinged the edges of her vision. Egypt stomped over to the sleigh, ripped off her glove and poked his thigh. "You're the one who landed me in this spot in the first place."

"So, you admit you weren't just out for a walk."

"I...You..." Coherence melted in the cauldron of accusations. Her skull throbbed from the crush of her fists.

"Elocution's not one of your assets, is it, Princess? Don't worry, I'm certain batting those golden eyes normally gets you anything you desire."

"Elocution?"

"Coherent sentences. Putting thoughts into words."

"I know what elocution is, I'm just surprised you do." Pain needled her chest. Nutz squirmed, mirroring her agitation. Egypt rubbed her coat, coaxing the cat to retract his claws.

"What's the matter, Princess? Did reality shatter your porcelain dream man?"

"*Dream* man? You're not good enough to be the warts on the Frog Prince. You overbearing, conceited, rude, self-centered—"

"Good." A smile curved his lips.

Egypt blinked, wiping the anger from her thoughts. Why should his failings make him happy? Her gaze traveled over his face. More importantly, why did he have only one dimple? Except for an old scar, his left cheek was smooth. His canine teeth flashed. Predatory. Dangerous. Exciting. She patted her hands together. Good thing she wasn't interested in such things.

"You with me, Princess?"

"Of course." Egypt grabbed a stick of gum from her pocket and jammed it into her mouth. The light spilling from his lantern gilded the silver foil. Sugar oozed across her tongue.

"You sure?" His left eyebrow arched.

"Absolutely." She wrapped the foil around her thumb. Her collar cushioned the back of her head as she gazed up at him. He was so tall and...and wide.

"Then, what were we talking about?" With great care he wrapped the reins around the scrollwork of the sleigh and slipped off the seat to stand before her.

"Hmmm." Her palms itched to touch him, to see if any man could be so solid.

"You've got that look again."

"Look?" She would love to look, to strip away all that leather and watch the dip and rise of sinew and muscle.

"All soft and kissable."

"Kissable?" Her breath stilled in her chest. Leather creaked. His arm moved. He was going to touch her. Her eyes flickered closed. Pink flashed on the screen of her eyelids. Once. Twice.

"What the..." She opened her eyes. A camera lens stared at her. His camera lens. It wasn't lightning she had seen after all. The rat had taken pictures of her flopping around like a landed fish. "You lousy, no-good, son of a—"

"Careful, Princess. No man likes to hear his mother slandered."

"You were taking pictures." Her knuckles popped as she drilled her fist against his chest.

"You wanted to be a work of art."

"You're insane." Egypt clutched Nutz closer to her chest. She was alone in the woods with a lunatic.

"That's rich. I wasn't the one who traveled all this way, dressed like that, to pick up a complete stranger."

"There is nothing wrong with the way I dress " Egypt tossed her scarf over her shoulder. She should never have abandoned her car. Someone would have come along eventually. Someone who wasn't a madman fixated on her clothes. Snow crunched under her feet. She would just go back to her car, lock herself in and wait. She glanced over her shoulder. Good, he wasn't following her.

"Where are you going?"

Where was she going? The truth could sign her death warrant. *People*—the word of salvation snapped inside her skull. If he thought someone waited for her, she would be safe. Please, God, keep her safe.

"Home." Egypt cleared her throat. Her answer sounded almost normal.

"No one lives that way."

"Lots of people live this way. Hundreds." One step then another. She would follow her tracks right to her car. Footsteps crushed the snow behind her. Oh, God, he was following her. Moisture evaporated from her mouth. "I'm fine. Just fine." Her heart raced, matching the tempo of her stride. And she would be as soon as she reached a crowd. "You can go now."

"You want me to leave?"

"Yes." Panic shattered the normal timbre of her answer. Egypt swallowed. She needed to appear unruffled—predators always sensed weakness. "Go wherever it is people like you go."

Snow crunched, then stopped. A growl hummed in the air, the crunching started again. Louder with each stomp.

"I can't, in good conscience, leave you alone out here." His gloved hand rested on her arm.

"Yes, you can." Electricity crackled across her skin. How could she have confused desire with fear? He moved in front of her, blocking her path. Evergreen boughs stretched alongside her. The only avenue of escape lay behind her. How could she ever have thought his arrival was a godsend? "Leave me here, I mean. My friends will find me soon. I have lots of friends." She nodded, an affirmation, not a nervous tic. "All of them are nearby. Definitely within shouting distance." Hysteria choked the last word from her throat.

His left eyebrow arched. "No."

"No?" She stepped to the side, knocking snow from the bough. Icy water trickled down her back. He shadowed her. Nutz dug his claws into her skin. The pain sharpened her thoughts. He wasn't going to let her go so easily.

"Look, Princess, you're obviously lost."

"I'm not lost. I know exactly where I am."

"Where are you?" He crossed his arms; annoyance beat against his cheek.

"In the forest, near a road." She backed up a step. Slow movements. Any head start was better than none.

"Nice try. Now get in the sleigh."

"No, I'll walk." Bark snagged her mitten as she darted around a pine tree.

He jumped over a fallen log and pounced in front of her.

"Look, lady, either you get in under your own power or I'll put you in."

"But—" *Think, Egypt, think.* Self-defense lesson number one: her brain was her best weapon.

"No buts." He stepped closer. She moved back, reacting to his movements like partners in a dance. "It's an open sleigh.

Hell, you can even sit in the back and scream at the top of your lungs if it makes you feel safer."

An open sleigh, not a van or dark alley. Birds twittered and darted through the trees. Sunlight burst through the clouds and dappled the ground. She watched too many crime shows. Embarrassment scalded Egypt's cheeks. Fear had cast her in the part of the fool. And the only thing worse than being a fool was being an idiot. Only an idiot favored hypothermia over rescue. She stomped to the sleigh.

"Fine." Her gum snapped. Heat zipped up her thigh as her sneaker slipped along the runner.

"Easy."

Warmth radiated from the hand pushing against her back. Nubby sheepskin covers cushioned her palm as she scrambled into the front seat. The scrollwork dug into her hip as she scooted away from him.

"Are you hurt?" His jaw clicked shut as if he wanted to recall the words of concern.

"No. No, I'm fine." She grimaced as Nutz climbed up her chest and butted his head against her chin.

Her rescuer shook his head. "Then hang on."

He snapped the reins. Sinew bubbled under the reindeer's coats as they dashed forward.

Air whooshed out of her lungs as her spine knocked against the wooden seat. Her mittens slipped on the brass trim. Hang on. What kind of warning was that? Annoyance replaced her earlier fear. Leather slapped the animals' rumps. He certainly seemed to be in a hurry.

"Where are we going?"

Chapter VI

Where are we going? Her question ricocheted inside Cade's skull. From the corner of his eye, he watched her. Arms hugged her waist while her jaw worked feverishly to pulverize her gum and her chin burrowed into her scarf, hiding those kissable lips. Her eyes sparkled, shoving aside the fear that had been there earlier.

She had been afraid. Afraid of him? The thought rankled. Who wanted a wife who was afraid of her husband? Husband? Wife?

"Who the hell said anything about marriage?"

"Marriage? I didn't propose marriage. I asked where we were going."

The woman twisted on the bench to stare at him. Her amber eyes glistened, not with anger but amusement. She was enjoying the trip. Cade forced his jaw to relax. Damn. He'd been suckered by a sense of humor, a shared appreciation of the absurd.

Of course, her shapely body hadn't hurt, either.

"Well?"

He slanted her a look. Uppity wench. His index finger traced the curve of his bottom lip. He knew where he was going—right to the nuthouse on insanity road. He would be crazy by the time they were finished with him.

For the last two months, those blue-coated harpies had kept him a prisoner in his own house. Another month of confinement and he'd be locked in a room papered with mattresses wearing a white coat and holding crayons between his toes.

"To town. Isn't that what you wanted, Princess?"

"Actually, I asked for a phone, but a town will work."

He just bet town would work. Cade urged the reindeer faster. What better way to get rid of the competition by showing up with the prize dangling on her arm? Get rid of the competition...

An idea swirled inside his skull. His muscles tightened. Goodman and Holiday slowed. If all those women thought he was taken, they would leave. One bride-to-be would be easier to deal with than twenty.

But was he willing to toy with the woman's heart?

Hell, she hadn't any problem playing fast and loose with his freedom. Besides, one date wasn't a proposal. With any luck, she'd realize how mismatched they were before dessert arrived.

"It might just work."

"Why wouldn't it?" She tilted her head and regarded him with her amber eyes. "I mean, what town doesn't have a phone?"

Familiarity echoed within his chest. The world shifted from the solidity of routine to the shakiness of undiscovered territory. Which had he sculpted with his hands and heart: the skating figurine or the woman before him?

"Shit." Cade's snort clouded the air. He couldn't do it. The attraction between them was too potent. She'd have him down the aisle, standing in front of a priest, before his brothers could say "told you so." He ripped the baseball cap off his head and scratched furrows in his hair. He'd swallow his teeth before he'd allow any of his brothers to be right.

"You're angry again."

"Damn right."

"Look, it's obvious you don't want to take me to town. Why don't you just let me out here, and I'll walk the rest of the way." Annoyance hummed along her straight back. Her stranglehold on the seat strained the fabric of her mittens.

White flashed on his lids as he rubbed his eyes.

"I can't do that."

His foot jumped along the floorboards in a dance of annoyance. He glared at her. Hell, he should leave her. Isn't that what he wanted in the first place? Holiday snorted and tossed her head. The woman was trouble.

"Why not?" Her pink tongue poked through the gray gum.

A groan rattled up his throat. Lust roared to life, inflaming his lower body. He shifted on the bench. Leather constricted his swollen flesh. He forced his shaking hands into his lap. Why not? Because a masochist liked to be tortured.

"I'm waiting." Her fingers thumped the cushion between them. "Why can't you drop me off here?"

"Hypothermia." Cade held up his index finger. "Frostbite. Blizzard. Wolves. Bears." Like good soldiers, his remaining digits straightened with each reason. He raised his thumb before waving his splayed fingers at her.

"You forgot the 'oh, my.'"

"I'm out of practice."

"I noticed the tarnish on your armor." She smiled.

His breath lodged in his throat. She was a perfect duplicate. Perfect? The cold must have affected his brain. She was annoying, demanding and too funny for his peace of mind. She wasn't any different than the others. He'd remember that as soon as he dropped her off at the hotel.

"I swear to God—"

"You do that a lot."

"Hell, yes. Twenty times in the past week—"

"The past week? You've sworn more than that in the few minutes since we met."

"I've taken twenty 'lost' women to the phone. One was in my house, fondling my stuff."

Compassion flickered in her tan eyes. A dream of a smile played with her lips.

"I meant swear."

"Hell, yes. A man likes to—"

"It's rude."

Cade tugged the baseball cap over his eyes. She thought he was rude. Laughter shook his shoulders. He swallowed his amusement.

"Never deterred the others."

"Stop the sleigh. I won't ride with a rude man."

Cade groaned. After two months, he had finally mastered the art of rejection. So, why wasn't he happy?

"Sorry. Okay? Geez. I swear I won't swear again."

"You'd be more convincing if you weren't smiling." She winced and patted her stomach.

"Hell—" She raised an eyebrow. "Er, heck, woman. You're hurt."

"Am not." Her words preceded them down the road.

Cade pressed the heel of his hand against his temple. His brain throbbed from the increased pressure. Maybe his skull would crack open and eject his brain into the snow. Maybe then he'd figure out what language she spoke. From the corner of his eye, he saw her lips quirk. Then again, maybe not.

"God damn infernal women—what man ever understood a one of them?"

"I can hear you."

Cade cleared the expletives from his throat.

"I promise to take you directly to the hotel without uttering one single profanity." He touched his hand to his chest. "Honest."

"Yeah, right," she snorted.

He swallowed his groan. The only double positive in the universe that made a negative was undoubtedly invented by a woman. Cold air burned his lungs.

"Look, Princess—"

"Egypt."

"What?"

"My name is Egypt. Not 'lady.' Not 'woman.' Not 'Princess.' And definitely not 'wench.'" She ticked them off against her gloves. "Egypt, like the country. You know, the land of pharaohs and pyramids."

"Bossy, uppity," he muttered.

"I can still hear you."

Cade rubbed his eyebrows and pinched the flesh puckered between his eyes. The woman had the hearing of a bat. No, not "the woman." Egypt. He glanced at her. The name fit. Her tan eyes warmed a man's soul. Her golden skin heated a man's flesh. Of course, she was also harsh and unforgiving as the desert sands.

"I wasn't swearing." He ground out.

"No, but you were being rude." She scooted to the side. One foot dangled over the edge. "And I am neither uppity nor bossy."

"Who said I was talking about you, Prin—Egypt?"

Her eyes narrowed for a second. The chewing slowed.

"Who were you talking about, then?"

"Could have been talking about Holiday." At the mention of her name, the reindeer shook her head. Bells jangled. "She doesn't like the cold."

"Uh-huh." She snapped her gum at him. "Is this the part where you mention the oceanfront property for sale?"

"Miles of beach, very little ocean." He offered her his most charming smile. She scowled back at him. The woman was impossible to please. God, he loved a challenge. "May I take you to town, Egypt?"

He amplified the wattage of his smile. Cold stung his gums. Her scowl deepened. Didn't she realize the risk involved in such a simple expression of good will? Hell, any second now his frozen lips would shatter and crumble to his feet.

"Put your teeth away. I'll stay with you."

"Thank God." Cade worked his jaw. His lips unrolled, tingles burst across his cheeks.

"No swearing." Her eyes narrowed as she waited for his reaction.

"That was a heartfelt prayer."

"I'll bet." She raised her chin and focused her gaze somewhere over the reindeer's heads. "You wouldn't happen to be related to those bears you mentioned."

"We're in the same family."

"Thought so." Egypt stamped her feet, forcing the cold from the flesh. Pain needled her toes before scaling her legs. Hypothermia. Frost bite. Neither was a pretty picture.

The sleigh glided over the snow blanketing the forest floor and slipped between the gray-and-black shadows of the overcast day. Bells dotting the reindeer's harnesses jingled in the crisp air. She hid her nose behind her jacket collar as they crested a small hill. Her stomach floated to her throat as they sped down.

Not a bad way to travel. In fact, it was rather pleasant. No wonder those Currier and Ives prints sold so well. Egypt slammed the door on her thoughts. She refused to allow her feelings about Christmas to spoil her winter's outing.

"You know, riding in a sleigh pulled by two reindeer is a lot smoother than I thought it would be. I suppose you make a mint, charging unsuspecting tourists for the pleasure of a ride. I mean, those Santa pictures at the mall cost fourteen bucks a pop and that sleigh doesn't move."

A muscle ticked in his jaw. He kept his gaze forward.

"If you like my sleigh so much, then why are you trying to punch a hole in her floor?"

"I'm not." Warm air filled her palms before she shoved her hands between her thighs and squeezed them together.

"There's a blanket in the back."

"I can take it." She bit off the words before her chattering teeth cut her tongue. Frigid gusts of air abraded her cheeks, burned her eyes. She blinked, only to wince as the moisture seemed to freeze.

"You're stubborn."

"And your point is?"

Her reflection glared back at her. Those sunglasses. Her fingers twitched with the need to rake them off his face and look into his eyes. His eyes. Who cared what color they were? She only wanted to know what he was thinking. Her gaze dropped to her shaking knees. Emotions roiled within her, the strongest skimmed the surface and were quickly identified. Exasperation. Amusement.

Desire.

"My point, Princess, is that you are cold."

"It's Egypt, remember? And it's winter. I believe winter and cold go together."

She cupped her hands over her mouth and exhaled. He was definitely to blame for the amusement and desire but the exasperation? That was self-directed. How could she possibly be interested in another man so soon after Darrell's desertion?

"Pneumonia, influenza and colds also go with winter."

"Aren't you forgetting the plague?" Annoying. She had forgotten annoying, conceited and egotistical. He was deliberately being disagreeable. But why? He wasn't her type. What rational woman wanted a man who wore black leather tighter than his own skin?

"You catch the plague from fleas not the cold."

"Wow, you must be dangerous at Trivial Pursuit."

His eyebrows touched ends, puckering the skin above his nose. He wasn't the only one capable of using words as weapons.

61

"Use the blanket."

"Why? You don't need one." She patted her hands together, rubbed them up and down her arms then shoved them between her legs and squeezed her thighs together.

"Fleece-lined leather. Besides, I'm wearing boots, not soggy sneakers."

"So?" Nutz butted against her jaw. His low growl rumbled across her skin. Her teeth nicked her tongue, unleashing the tang of sweet metal across her tongue.

"Humor me."

"All right." With a sigh, she pulled the blanket from the backseat. The corner of the quilt slapped his cheek. "Happy now?"

"Deliriously."

Egypt tucked the blanket around her body. The quilt blocked the cold from snatching her body heat. Her limbs warmed. Much better, not that she'd tell him. He was conceited enough.

"So, why'd you do it?"

She blinked. Had she missed part of the conversation?

"Are you talking to the reindeer again?"

"No, I'm talking to you." He cracked the reins over the reindeer, urging them faster across the meadow. "Why did you wear that outfit?"

"There is nothing wrong with my clothes." Egypt gritted her teeth. How could she have been attracted to the jerk? Insensitive lout. She wouldn't set him up with her worst enemy. "How much further to town?"

"Not much." A dimple winked at her.

"Good." Her knitted mittens slipped over her flesh as her hands wrestled over her lap. Pink tinged his nose and cheeks, like lipstick from a lover's kiss. Lover? Kiss? The cold had obviously frozen the logical parts of her brain. "Are you sure you don't want some of the blanket?"

"I'm sure."

"Pneumonia, cold and flu don't scare a big man like you?"

"I find the weather...bracing."

"Bracing? I guess all that leather makes you rather hot." Her gaze dropped to his boots. He had big feet. Did that mean...? Muscles rippled across his thighs, pulling the leather smooth except for the bulge...

Egypt forced cold air into her lungs.

"Yes, bracing. I can see what you mean." Good heavens, all this time she thought the relationship between a man's shoe size and his endowment was an old wives' tale.

"Are you all right? You seem a little flushed."

"Fine." She quickly forced her eyes on to the kaleidoscope of colors marching across her lap. "Red and green. Christmas colors." Everything made sense now. This was her punishment for decking the store with Christmas cheer in August. Since she escaped death by way of a sleigh and reindeer, she would be done in by another Yuletide mishap.

"Yes, Christmas colors for Christmastime." The husky timbre of his voice washed over her. "You don't like Christmas?"

Egypt blew air into the fruity gum until the bubble splattered over her lips. There was something in his voice. Something other than his usual annoyance. She chewed the gum off her lips. If she didn't know better she would say he was actually interested in her answer.

"I like Christmas fine." Or, at least, she had before working retail, where the amount of Christmas spirit is tallied in dollars and cents not kindness and goodwill.

His lips lifted. The dimpled flashed. Her heart stopped then filled her chest. There outta be a law against such a surly man having such a gorgeous smile.

"You don't like Christmas," he whistled. "You'll be rather out-of-place in Holly, then, won't you?"

"Holly?" Thoughts flipped through Egypt's mind like Rolodex cards in a windstorm. She never remembered passing through the town before. Her memory conjured the orange construction signs dotting the highway. Somewhere along the serpentine detour she must have made a wrong turn. "How far is Holly from Route Eighty-nine?"

"Eighty-nine? Not far..." He winked at her. "...if you're flying."

Egypt moved her gum from her left cheek to her right. When had she made a wrong turn? More importantly, how far from home was she?

"I grew up in Dragoon's Springs. As teenagers we bumped over every service road and state route. I don't remember any Holly. How long has it been there?"

He switched his reins to one hand.

"Seems like forever. Of course, the sign says it was established in eighteen-eighty-eight."

"That's pretty old for Arizona." She reached under her scarf and scratched Nutz's head. "I am still in Arizona, aren't I?"

"Eastern Arizona, to be precise." He frowned, "Unless the town has moved overnight." He winked at her. "Don't worry, Princess. Dragoon's Springs is just over those mountains. You could be home in an hour, if you could fly."

She relaxed. The detour hadn't led her too far astray. With a little luck, she'd find a mechanic and be on her way home in an hour.

"Is Holly one of those small towns where everyone knows everyone else?'

"Yep."

"Great." Egypt spat her gum into the foil wrapper and stuffed it into her pocket with all the other balls of spent nerves.

"Don't worry. Regardless of your attitude, you should blend right in." His Adam's apple bobbed in time with his chuckle.

"This has something to do with my clothes, doesn't it?"

"Could be."

Egypt played with the cuff of her mitten. His fixation on her clothes didn't matter; finding a mechanic did. She folded her hands on her lap as they burst out of the forest.

A town lay nestled in the valley. She blinked. The pitched roofs, sweeping streets and twinkling lights grew larger.

"Oh. My. God."

"Swearing, Princess?" he tsked. "Isn't that rather rude?"

She closed her eyes as a wave of nausea swept over her. He was right. She didn't belong here.

Chapter VII

Egypt counted to three, opened her eyes then squeezed them shut and counted ten Mississippis before peeking again. It was still there.

"I'm being punished."

"You probably deserve it," he chuckled.

"I...I..." Her jaw swung back and forth, as if broken from the confusion. Was this where weary clerks went when the coldness of retail sales leached the Christmas spirit out of them? Her hands slapped her jacket. Where was her gum?

"'Course, most consider Holly a treasure, not a punishment."

"It looks like a movie set."

"A movie set?" Puzzlement furrowed his brow. "Which one?"

"All of them. Every last one of them." Her hands dipped in and out of her pockets. "Like some mad director couldn't decide on one, so he tossed a country hamlet into a Victorian town and added a dash of Federalist architecture just to thoroughly confuse people. *A Christmas Carol, Miracle on Thirty-fourth Street, It's a Wonderful Life.*" She tugged the pack of Juicy Fruit from her pocket. All the wrappers were empty. "They're all here. Every sappy, two-tissue-boxes, heart-wrenching story."

"Something wrong with those things?"

"It's almost too perfect." Her whisper washed over her face. She crumpled the empty paper and foil. The hands continued her search while the brain reconciled her surroundings with reality.

Cottages dotted both sides of the road. In the front yards, tipsy snowmen greeted visitors, knobby arms thrown open in welcome. A few held boughs of holly draped across their icy bellies. Coal smiles beamed at her as they passed. Egypt twisted in her seat. Did their twinkling eyes follow their progress?

"All that's missing is a top hat and a Frosty parade-marching down Main Street with a hoard of children skipping behind."

"That's not until tomorrow."

Reality slipped. She could see it. She could actually visualize animated characters waltzing down the street to Burl Ives music. Egypt shook her head, praying sense rose above the flotsam of fantasy.

"You're joking, right?"

"I don't know..." Broad shoulders shrugged, "Strange things happen during the Christmas season." He leaned closer. "Magical things."

Egypt shivered as a waft of warm peppermint washed over her.

"Very funny."

They bumped down the center of the cleared street; clopping hooves heralded their arrival. Egypt leaned out of the sleigh. Cobblestones. Where in the world had they gotten cobblestones?

"Careful, you might fall. Or are you planning to jump head first?" He tugged on her jacket.

She straightened on the seat, her spine resting against the seat back. Why was he being nice?

"Do you have a split personality?"

"No. Why?"

"You can't seem to make up your mind whether to be angry or entertaining."

"It's all part of my charm."

She blew her bangs off her forehead. Yes, his charm was the problem. When he was charming she forgot how irritating he was. Focus on your surroundings, Egypt. Anything but him.

Snow edged the street like frosting on a wedding cake. Icicles dripped from the black lampposts. Egypt blinked. There were no cars. She checked left then right. A few horses dozed next to a post, cherry-colored blankets protecting their hide from glossy ebony saddles. Two more steeds waited while a couple climbed aboard a white carriage.

"Where are the cars?"

"Most visitors park in the lots outside of town. Helps to preserve the movie set feel." His sarcasm misted on the air.

"What about the residents? Or does everyone drive a sleigh?"

"Some do; others have carriages. Most prefer to walk, visit with their neighbors."

Gossip about their neighbors. *Still single, dear? Yes, we heard about your latest break-up. Is this number fourteen or fifteen?* Fourteen.

Not that anyone needed to be told. Everyone always knew. In small-town America rumors stuck tighter than flies to paper. Flies? Roaches. A regular roach trap. The innuendo never left.

"People come and go all the time." He frowned at her.

Her companion's deep baritone brought her back to the sleigh. At least, Holly wasn't her hometown. No history followed her here.

"How? You said no one has a car."

"No, I didn't. You asked about sleighs, not cars." He nodded to a couple strolling along the sidewalk. "Besides, a car is only one way to get from here to there. Surely, you've heard of buses and planes."

"Yes, but—"

"Holly's a small town. A five-minute walk will take you from one end to the other. Why would you need a car?"

He was angry again. Was it her questions or her presence?

"I guess you wouldn't."

Egypt picked a loose thread on her mitten. He had avoided her question. Maybe he hated cars. That would explain the sleigh. She'd ask someone else. After all, if there were cars nearby there would have to be a mechanic or, at least, a service station. She glanced around hoping to find evidence supporting her theory.

Swags of evergreens connected opposite sides of the streets. Huge crimson bows marked their point of attachment overhead. A couple in matching plaid sweaters crossed in front of them. They strolled under the thousands of twinkling lights strung from the lampposts to a flagpole rising high in the air of a courtyard. Red, blue, green and yellow light filtered through the town square. Wrought iron benches circled the Christmas tree decked in scarlet balls and gold lights.

Where was she?

There was no way she could have forgotten visiting here before, yet it all seemed familiar. Egypt shifted on the bench. Had she fallen through the looking glass when she pitched through the snowbank? Maybe she was still stuck in the snow, hallucinating from exposure. That's it—she was still stuck in her car. None of this was real. It couldn't possibly be real. She pinched herself then rubbed the sting from her thigh. Okay, so she was real, but what about everything else?

"Doc Hausen's office is the next building."

"I feel fine." She glanced at the man by her side. He hadn't introduced himself. Maybe her brain hadn't conjured up a name for him.

"You sure?"

"Yes." One purple mitten emerged from the warmth of the blanket. Maybe she should pinch him. If he screamed then she would know he was real.

"Then stop fidgeting and stay covered."

"Yes, sir." Egypt forced her hand under the quilt before she saluted. Maybe some things were best left in her fantasies. Like him.

"Do I have something on my face?" Cade asked.

"No. Why?"

"You're staring." They stopped at the corner and waited as another carriage jingled past. He leaned closer. His leather-scented body heat warmed her nose. "Doesn't that fall under the rude category?"

Egypt blotted her forehead with her mitten. Hypothermia could be ruled out. Those hallucinations were supposed to be pleasant. There was nothing pleasant about getting one's words tossed back at you every minute.

"It's not too late to visit the doc."

"No," she said, contradicting her nod. "I'm fine. To the hotel, please."

"Whatever you say, Princess."

"Egypt, remember?" Icicles dangled from the eaves of the cottages. From this distance they looked to be of uniform length. How could that be?

"I remember."

"What?" Her gaze swung back to her companion.

"I remember your name."

"Then why do you insist on calling me Princess?"

His shoulders rolled in his jacket. "It suits you."

"It..." The scent of cinnamon and vanilla carried away her thoughts. Her nose twitched. Christmas cookies. Someone was baking Christmas cookies. Her stomach growled.

"Princess?"

Egypt pinched the temptation from her nose. She needed a mechanic not cookies. A mechanic would fix her car, allowing her to put this place far behind her.

"It does *not* suit me. A princess is a spoiled, demanding, helpless sort of female."

A trio of carolers stopped under a lamppost, spotlighting their Victorian dress.

"Exactly." With a flick of his wrist, the reindeer tugged the sleigh around the corner.

A growl rumbled up her throat. Why did she bother arguing with the man?

"This place looks familiar."

"Have you visited us before?"

"No. No, I would have remembered." Egypt blinked. In an instant, the memory surfaced. She snapped her fingers. "This place looks like one of those ceramic villages. You know, the ones everyone sells this time of year?"

"You don't say?"

Certainty filled her. "Yes, it is exactly like one of the villages. Not the cheap ones in the craft stores, but the high-end ones we sell at Winter's Wonderland."

"You sell them?"

"Yes." Egypt ignored the bite in his voice and bounced in her seat. "I even set up the pieces correctly. Yep, see there's the barbershop." She pointed to the twirling candy cane attached to a row of buildings. "This is too much of a coincidence. I wonder if the artist lives nearby?"

"I doubt it's a coincidence at all."

Egypt ignored him. Santa Claus's countenance beamed from the drugstore window while holly dribbled from the mortar and pestle adorning the sign. Tiny elves marched across the hardware store window, hammers pounding make-believe toys. The candy shop displayed regiments of chocolate truffles, covered nuts and caramels. Baskets of bread flashed in the bakery window—baguettes sprinkled with sesame and poppy seeds, wreaths studded with candied fruit.

A young boy stumbled from the bakery. A yeast-scented cloud rose from the roll in his hand. Her stomach growled. She set her hand over that grumbling organ and tightened her fist. Nutz squirmed and crawled up around her shoulders. She should have brought something to eat. Of course, she had planned to be at her parent's house not long after lunchtime.

Her reluctant driver pulled up in front of a two-story building. A white porch surrounded the house like a ballerina's tutu. Wrought iron twisted around the turrets. If she couldn't find the Christmas spirit in Holly, there was no hope for her. Would the whole thing melt back into the snow if Scrooge appeared?

"Bah, humbug." Laughter filled her mouth and bubbled against her lips. Guess it would take more than that.

"Did you say something?"

"No."

"This is the hotel." He scowled at her, the sunglasses still firmly in place.

She hated those glasses.

"What color are your eyes?" She flashed him her palm. "Wait. Don't answer that. I don't really care."

"The hotel has three phones inside."

Egypt carefully folded the blanket and set it in the back. No need to beat her over the head. He wanted her out of the sleigh.

"Thanks for the lift."

He grunted. The language of cavemen everywhere. She turned around then faced outward. The sleigh hadn't seemed that high when she climbed aboard. *You can do this. Just take it slow. Slow.* Egypt set her foot on the rail. Her sneaker lost traction and slid to the left. Pain zipped along her flesh as her elbow collided with the front end. Her bottom bounced on the floor, rattling her teeth in her skull.

"Stay there, Princess," he growled. Leather slapped the brass rails seconds before he leapt from the sleigh.

"Hmmm, okay." Egypt groaned. What kind of twit couldn't climb out of a stupid sleigh? Apparently, her kind. That didn't make her a princess, did it? One foot hovered over the ground. The other's toes were pinched by the fancy scrollwork.

"Ready, Princess?"

"Ready." Warm hands slid under her jacket and wrapped around her waist. Her temperature rose. *It's the down in your coat not his hands.* His *bare* hands. When had he taken off his gloves? She kicked free off the runners. "Thank you."

She continued to dangle in the air. For a man in a hurry to get rid of her, he wasn't willing to let her go. He may have eliminated multiple personality disorder, but that still left schizophrenia.

"I think I can walk on my own."

He grunted, set her on the sidewalk and climbed back into the sleigh. Leather snapped. Snow squished as the sleigh pulled away.

"'You're welcome' is the appropriate reply," she yelled at his back.

Her thank-you brushed over Cade like a wool blanket on chilled skin, warm and welcoming. He shook off the thought. He didn't need her thanks. He would have done the same for anyone.

Turquoise blazed in his peripheral vision. He turned. A handful of blue-coated women were clustered by the Ice Cream Shoppe. Why hadn't they left? What was it going to take to get rid of them?

At least, her act had failed to convince him. Only a fool would believe she'd worn that jacket purely by coincidence. Good thing he wasn't attracted to her.

I wonder if the artist lives nearby?

Her syrupy voice poured in his ear. Humph. Like she hadn't known exactly where the artist lived. She was just like the others, dreaming of a partner that existed only in a pewter figurine. And the scarf...

"Cade. Yoo-hoo, Cade."

The bevy of blue coats turned in his direction. Great. Now they'd seen him. Two broke away from the pack and hustled toward him.

"Sorry, Mrs. Crumbie can't stop. Holiday doesn't like to be kept standing."

"Cade Dugan, you stop by the hotel for supper, now, you hear? Patience and I wish to thank you for all those referrals you've given us these past two months."

"Yes, ma'am." He waved and cracked the reins, dodging the blue coat that darted across the street. "Just as soon as you empty the hotel of guests. Especially the last one," he muttered.

He needed to stop thinking of her. And he would, just as soon as all the icicles in Holly melted.

Cade drew the reindeer to a stop beside his parents' Victorian house. Holiday rolled her eyes.

"Don't worry, girl. I'll take you home as soon as we pick up Pete." He offered her and Goodman a carrot from his pocket then opened the wooden gate.

Pete's face appeared in the window. His pink tongue glistened against his gray fur before his head dropped and his ears flattened. The wolf/husky hybrid pressed his nose against the corner of the pane and barked. His whole body shook in greeting.

Cade's older brother sauntered across the veranda to lean against the railing edging the porch. The three youngest Dugan boys quickly joined him.

"Thought he was trying to scare them women off?"

"Nah, that's just an act." Sloan, Cade's fraternal twin, stopped next to Todd. "Isn't that right, Jay?"

"Dunno. Seems to me he got tired of the starving artist routine and is going for Mr. Macho." Jay, the baby of the family, crossed his arms over his chest.

"Seems like only kinky women would be attracted to a man in that much leather." Nick leaned against another post.

"Go soak your heads," Cade growled. His right foot rested on the first porch step. This was not his day. First the Princess now his brothers. At least, he knew how to deal with his siblings.

"Looks like our sensitive brother's scared of them women."

"Come running home to Ma for protection, Cady?" Sloan asked.

"Laugh while you can, Sloan. I just mailed the latest figurine out today. Some women really go for redheaded men. Why, I'm guessing several plus-size women will be arriving in Holly hours after it hits the store."

"Son-of-a—" His red-haired brother leapt from the porch. Cade stepped aside and watched him slip down the walk. Planks creaked under his remaining brothers' weight.

Todd exchanged worried glances with Nick and Jay.

"You know you're not supposed to model any more figurines after townsfolk."

Cade grinned at his brothers. His mother had issued that particular edict after the mayor complained.

"Who's hiding behind Ma's skirts now?"

"It's not funny." Sloan braced his feet in the snow. "Mayor Browning was a confirmed bachelor until you cast that figurine."

Nick nodded. "He seems happy with his new wife."

"So do the baker and Doc Hausen," Todd glared at him.

Three couples. Three matches made after he had modeled his figurines after local townsfolk and paired them with women from his imagination. Cade would be number four if the streak held. If the Blue Coats had their way.

"What—you boys don't want to be part of a legend your gossip created?"

"How many cornered you this time?" Nick, the peacemaker, halted his brothers' attack with a fist on their chests.

"What's it to you?" Cade glared at his siblings. Two months was long enough to be the source of their amusement.

"Well, I'll be. He's finally lost track of them all."

"I bet it was Denise from up the road." Jay braced his feet shoulder-width apart.

"How about Michelle from Noel?" Sloan ran his hand through his red hair. "If you had to match me up with someone at least you could have made it resemble her."

"Knock it off," Cade growled.

"Oh, come on, Cade." Sloan cracked his knuckles. "You know we're going to get it out of you one way or another."

"Ma is busy talking over the fence to Mrs. Crumbie." Todd jerked his head to the side of the house.

"Yep." Nick shoved his hands in his pockets. "She said you were tooling around with some little darling wearing a magenta scarf and sky-blue jacket."

"Her scarf was purple."

"You don't say. Purple." Nick winked at him.

"So, you did pick her up." Todd stepped down one riser.

"Where is she from?" Sloan circled closer behind him. Cade removed his glasses and set them on the newel post. Another alliance had been formed, and this time he was the odd man out.

"Was she dressed like Maybelle?"

"Maybelle wasn't dressed." Cade turned slightly so his back was to the railing. If he was lucky, he could hurl Sloan into the rest of them then he could dash for the back door.

"She was wearing the blue coat—"

"But not a blue scarf."

"Back off." Cade forced his arms to his side.

"Well, see, now, there are four of us and only one of you." Todd curled his four fingers into a fist.

"She is none of your business." Every muscle in his body tensed, waiting for his eldest brother's signal to attack.

"He's getting a little hot under the collar." Sloan backed up, as if sensing Cade's intent.

"Maybe we should cool him off." Jay pushed back his long black locks.

"Since Mom is busy getting the juicy details from Mrs. Crumbie, we'll just take our little conversation over to the snowbank."

Todd slammed into Cade's side, pushing him off the stoop.

"Don't you think we're getting a little old for this?"

Sloan wrapped his arm's around Cade's waist. "Must be true love, he's starting to talk about age."

Nick and Jay exchanged wicked grins before they captured Cade's kicking legs. The five brothers slipped across the front yard with all the grace of a drunken spider.

Cade stopped squirming and crossed his arms. Yet another mark against the Blue Coats.

"Do you guys have any idea how stupid you look?"

"Not as stupid as you."

With one mighty heave, all five feet, eleven inches of Cade became airborne. He landed with a thud. Teeth rattled and bones crunched from the impact.

"Can we grow up now?" He spit out the snow. Copper exploded on his tongue. He touched his lip and winced. Crimson glistened on the tip of his glove. "Son-of-a—"

"Watch how you speak about our mother."

"I'll be her only son in a minute." Cade lurched forward. The snow sucked him back. Egypt would have a fine time if she saw him now.

"Ice is good for a cut lip."

A snowball splattered against his cheek. Flakes slipped between his collar and skin. A shiver twitched up his frame. Snow crunched under his gloves. He could dig himself out and fight back at the same time. A large snowball sailed toward Todd.

"Daddy!" Ten-year-old Candance's voice pinged against Cade's tingling ears. Pete's barking filled the air.

"Don't let that damn mutt out!" Pete sprinted across the porch and launched himself at Sloan, knocking him to the ground.

"Grandma, Grandma! They're at it again." The storm door slammed shut behind her.

"Damn. Where is that girl's loyalty? From the way she acts, you'd think Cade was her father, not me." Todd sprinted after his daughter while the other three scattered in various directions.

Cade sat up and dusted off his pants. Pete loped over and sat down next to his master.

"They were right about one thing." He slipped his hand under Pete's collar and pulled himself free. "That dunking definitely froze whatever thoughts I had about her."

Chapter VIII

Cade glanced up as the storm door hinges screeched. The pencil gouged his flesh before snapping in half. His brothers better not have decided to bring their wrestling match inside. Not that he wasn't capable of kicking all of their collective butts; he simply had enough women trouble without adding his mother to the list.

Mrs. Dugan stomped her snow-crusted boots on the green welcome mat in the mudroom. Cade's sigh mixed with the gust of frigid air snaking into the room. His neck popped as he dipped each ear towards its respective shoulder. His mother shook herself out of her jacket then stilled. Lines marred her skin as she squeezed her eyes shut. Her mouth moved. One. Two.

Counting. She was counting. Everyone knew Martha Dugan only counted when she needed to control her temper. Cade quickly dropped the shattered pencil into his lap and picked up his coffee cup. The ceramic handle pressed against the back of his hand. His fingertips throbbed. The bitter scent of fresh coffee stung his nose and warmed his lungs. Mrs. Crumbie. His mother had been talking to Mrs. Crumbie. The same Mrs. Crumbie whose sisters ran the hotel where he had dropped off Egypt. What lies had the latest Blue Coat told?

"Mother, I—"

"That woman can talk longer about nothing than a politician at election time." Mrs. Dugan snapped her coat flat then slammed it on a peg. She stepped out of her boots and swatted at the snow speckling her brown hair.

"Yes, about the latest—"

"She doesn't mean any harm, Cade. She's just lonely." His mother whisked an apron off the dryer, slipped it over her head and tightened it around her trim waist. "You really shouldn't get angry at the old gossip. She wasn't blessed with children whose lives she can interfere in."

Cade felt his lips curl in answer to his mother's smile. She squeezed his shoulder then ruffled his hair.

"Is that her?"

One pink fingernail tapped the drawing on his napkin.

"That's the pain in the—"

"Cade."

He swallowed the swear word. The napkin tickled his palm as he wadded up the illustration.

"She's no different than the rest of them."

"Did you draw pictures of the rest of them?" Her left eyebrow cocked, pleating her forehead.

"What difference does that make?" His chair's legs bumped over the linoleum as he pushed away from the table. The pencil pieces bounced twice before rolling under the oven.

"None, I suppose."

Cade stepped on the garbage can pedal, and the lid clanged open.

"Exactly. No difference whatsoever." He chucked the crumpled napkin on top of a clutch of broken eggshells then released the pedal. His distorted face glared at him from the chrome lid. Too bad Princess Egypt couldn't be ripped from his thoughts as easily.

He stomped to the counter. Pain rattled up his shins and out his skull. Egypt. That was the name of a country not a

80

woman. Her tan eyes winked at him from his memory. Cade snatched the coffeepot off its resting place.

"Still, she is rather pretty."

"I hadn't noticed." He spun around and faced his mother. The amber brew sloshed inside the glass pot. Brown dotted his hand and burned his flesh. The woman was a damn nuisance. Good thing she hadn't gotten to him. His full cup of coffee mocked him.

"Coffee?" He yanked a mug off the shelf before his mother could answer and slammed it down in front of her.

"Thanks," she said, mopping up the wave of coffee oozing toward her. Sloan's face flashed in the window above the sink. He drew his finger across his throat then pointed at Cade.

"So, you didn't tell them anything, huh?"

"Nothing to tell." Cade toasted his brother and took a seat at the table. The metal frame creaked as he leaned back. His mother stopped stirring her coffee. Her blue eyes narrowed. Embarrassment burned his skin. Two of the chairs legs hit the ground; the breech of manners shook his teeth. "Sorry."

"They're waiting for you, aren't they?"

Cade shrugged. He could handle his brothers. The ceramic mug warmed his lip seconds before the taste of French roast coffee exploded on his tongue. Pain rocketed around his mouth as the liquid invaded his cut.

"Perhaps you should put something on your split lip." The words dispersed the steam dancing over her coffee.

"Already did."

"So...what did you tell them?" His mother tilted her head to the left.

"Nothing to tell."

"You got a black eye and a split lip for nothing?"

"They were rather piss—er, perturbed at my..." Cade cleared the confession from his mouth. His mother didn't need to know he had spent his months in hiding crafting his revenge. He blew the steam across his mug. If he was number four, then his brothers would be five, six, seven and eight. He had already carved them in wood; all that remained was a suitable mate.

"Your...?" Suspicion clouded his mother's eyes.

"My gentlemanly reticence."

With a sigh, Martha rose from the table and began stacking dirty dishes in the dishwasher.

"You should have seen your brother come flying around the corner chasing Candance."

"I did hear him mutter something about loyalty before taking off." Cade gently set the cup on the table and reached for his niece's colored pencils. The tan one settled in the callous on his middle finger. Seconds later a face and a pair of eyes stared back at him. His hand hovered over the purple pencil.

"Mrs. Crumbie thinks she wore the wrong color scarf."

"It was purple." Cade watched the color bleed from his knuckles. Damn. He had done it again. Couldn't she have found someone else to haunt?

"Candance won't thank you for breaking her pencils."

His palm tingled as the pencil rolled into the pile.

"I like this one much better than the first." She picked up the scrap of paper and held it up to the light. "Although I have to wonder if you haven't embellished it a bit."

Cade lunged for the paper but she stepped away.

"Embellished." The word squeaked through his tight throat.

"You know you've always been an excellent artist but, well, this is even more sexual than those you did of Angela Mayfield your senior year." Martha tucked the picture in his breast pocket and returned to washing dishes. "And she was nude."

Sex. Nude. Angela Mayfield. Flesh slid under Cade's hands as he tried to reshape his face by brute force. His mother had known about his first crush. His mother knew about sex and a naked Angela Mayfield. His intestines twirled around his stomach like spaghetti on a fork. What other secrets did his mother know?

"They were quite good, even if a little generous in her proportions."

His heart thumped against his mouth as he slammed into the chair. Surreal. The whole day had been surreal, and now he was talking about sex with his mother over coffee. Where were the pink elephants?

"Wh—"

"I mean, if she was that well-endowed she would either walk hunched over or need an entourage to carry her breasts around."

Laughter gurgled in his throat before hopping across his tongue and slipping past his lips. Angela had an army of boys willing to carry her breasts.

"I worry."

He blinked and wiped away the image.

"Worry?"

"You idealize women. Life, too, but especially women." Suds slipped off her hands and floated to the floor. "How can any flesh-and-blood woman live up to your fantasies?"

Cade plucked the picture from his pocket. Idealize women. His snort fluttered across the paper. The illustration didn't even capture Egypt's spirit. The tan color couldn't match her golden skin. As for her hair?

"That woman cornered me again."

Burl Dugan strode through the laundry room without bothering to wipe the snow from his boots. Cade watched disapproval reshape his mother's face.

"After forty-two years, you'd think he'd have learned to wipe his feet by now."

"If I kicked all my bad habits, what would you do for the next forty-two years?" Burl winked at his youngest son, quickly retreated and dragged his boots over the coarse straw mat.

"What could Mrs. Crumbie possibly have to say to you, dear?"

Burl kissed his wife on the cheek and plucked one of the pins from her bun.

"You mean, aside from what she already told you?"

She gave him a kiss then took the pin back. Unease slithered though Cade. His parent's open affection had never made him uncomfortable before, yet today...

He smoothed the leather over his thighs. Today, their obvious love made him feel empty. He reached for the sugar.

"Are you saying I'm a gossip?"

"Never." Burl placed his hand over his heart. "You are too busy being the light of my heart to chaw about the lights going out. After all everyone knows that when the lights fall dark in Holly someone's met his match."

Cade dumped half the contents of the sugar bowl into his coffee. The darkened lights had to be a coincidence. There was no way in Hell he would believe she was responsible. Absolutely no way.

"The lights?"

When his mother threw herself into her husband's arms, Cade saw his chance to escape. He eased from his seat and tiptoed toward the door.

"Burl Dugan, you had better not be teasing me."

"I would never tease about anything so important. Going somewhere, son?"

Cade gulped his coffee-flavored sugar.

"I was just...I thought..."

"Cade, you sit down this instant." His mother skipped to his side and ushered him back to the table. "Why didn't you mention the lights going out?"

"I didn't know." Cade tugged on his collar. Damn leather. No wonder he felt like he was sitting on a burner. Why did the lights have to burn out today of all days? Why did he have to live in a town so steeped in folklore? So what if a few strings of lights had gone out? That didn't mean his match had arrived.

Absolutely not. If Egypt was his match then Pete would sing "Jingle Bells" on Christmas Eve.

"So, she's not for you?"

"No. Absolutely not."

"Well," Burl squeezed his wife's hand, "Mrs. Crumbie seemed to think it had something to do with that little girl our son brought to town."

Cade eased his legs to the side of his chair. Five steps, six at the most, and he would be out of the kitchen.

"Little girl." His mother chucked the dishtowel into his father's belly. "Then she certainly doesn't have anything to do with our boys. They're only interested in women." She grabbed a cookie sheet off the counter and plunked it into the sink. "Cade, sit in that chair right. Do you want people to think you were raised in a barn?"

"Candance is probably..." Cade felt his backbone melt into the quivering mass of jelly the rest of him had become. With any luck he'd drip off the chair and ooze out the door. Unfortunately, luck had abandoned him today.

"Stay and chat awhile, son. Give your brothers a chance to finish that trap they're rigging out front." Burl smiled at his wife. "Of course, Cade wants a young wife. They're easier to control."

Martha jabbed him in the side with her elbow.

"Just for that, Burl Dugan, you don't get any cinnamon rolls." She yanked the towel out of his hands and rammed her fists inside the terrycloth.

"You're my girl, aren't you, Marty?"

"You sit right down in that chair, mister. We will talk about your deplorable linguistics later."

The cinnamon buns bounced as his mother slammed the plate down in front of Cade. His fingers sank into the warm bread.

"I better be leaving. Goodman and Holiday have been kept standing long enough." Cinnamon and sugar sashayed around his mouth and two-stepped across his taste buds.

"Your brothers have seen to the animals." Burl snatched a bun off his son's plate. "Now, about them lights."

"I'm sure an electrical failure caused the lights to go out."

"Checked that." A blob of white icing splattered on the table. His father cleaned it off with a swipe of his finger. "Checked the bulbs and the fuses, too. Everything seems to be working just fine." He popped the rest of the bun into his mouth and pinched another off Cade's plate.

Stubble sanded the tip of his fingers as Cade stroked his chin.

"She could still be responsible for the lights."

Spoons clattered as Burl pounded on the table.

"So, there is something about her."

"Definitely." Cade crossed his arms and leaned back in the chair. Guilt pinched him as hope beamed from the faces of his parents. He shoved the useless emotion into a dark corner of his mind. He would marry one day. and when he did he would be the pursuer not the pursuee. "She doesn't believe in the magic of Christmas." He forced his lips into a solemn expression as he dropped his next bomb. "She even said 'Bah, humbug.'"

"What?" Color fled his parents' faces as their raised voices rattled the windowpanes. Unspoken communication passed between them before they turned on him. "How could she not believe in Christmas and be in Holly, son?"

"Don't know."

"But you did talk to her." His mother drilled his shoulder.

Snippets of his exchange with Egypt hounded Cade. He cleared his throat of the wad of cinnamon bun. If his parents ever found out what he'd said...

He would just have to make sure they didn't.

"It wasn't a conversation."

"Too busy doing other things to talk, eh, son." Burl beamed at him.

"No. I...I just dropped her off at the hotel."

"Where is she from?"

"She didn't say."

"Well, what did she say?" His mother glared at him.

"Nothing. She was rude, obnoxious and ordered me about like I was her personal flunky." Cade shoved away from the table.

"I don't think that snow dunking cooled you off enough, son." Burl rubbed his hands together.

"I'm going to check on Candance." Cade deliberately ignored his mother's concerned look and marched from the room.

"Don't keep your brothers waiting too long. The cold is making them downright ornery." His father's words pelted his back.

He forced his fists to his side. At least with his brothers he could fight back.

Nutz poked his head out of Egypt's jacket. Fur tickled her chin before his rough tongue cleaned her jaw.

"Stop that." An impatient meow filled her ear. "Nutz, behave." She grabbed his head. His skull slipped under his fur as he pulled away. "I have enough problems with the car. I don't need a cat's tongue frozen to my cheek."

Nutz sneezed before slipping under her scarf to chew on his claws. Egypt patted his head then pulled open the maple doors of the hotel. Her nose tingled from the assault of peppermint and evergreen. Horns tooted and bells pealed. Hidden speakers unleashed Christmas carols throughout the reception area. She cleaned her shoes on the straw mat at her feet then tiptoed onto the gleaming wood floors.

"Oh, dear, oh, dear." A welcoming smile beamed at Egypt from a face as tanned and wrinkled as a withered apple. "We weren't expecting you."

"Yes, I know. I—"

"Come in. Come in." A cranberry apron toned down the scarlet-and-white stripes running over a massive chest that would have made a cooing pigeon proud. A frothy cap wobbled atop a mass of gray curls swirling around her head. "My, you must be chilled to the bone."

Her hostess flicked the white ruffle out of her eye.

"It is rather chilly out." Egypt unwound the scarf from her neck and inhaled the warm air. Sensations crackled across her cerebellum. Pain. Warmth. Heat. Her teeth bit into her mittens as she pulled them off her hands. Of course, she would feel heat. Her flesh had practically been flash-frozen. None of her body's responses had anything to do with the touch of his hands on her skin. Not a one.

"Who is it, Charity?" Another woman bustled into the room. A score of gingerbread men and women sunned themselves on a glass platter. Flour dusted the green-and-white striped apron protecting her evergreen dress. "We're full up."

"I wasn't expecting her, Patience." Charity fished a snowman mug out from under the counter and filled it from the ivory carafe sitting on the counter. "How many marshmallows would you like, dear?"

"You weren't expecting her?" Patience slid the tray onto the counter then lifted silver tongs from a tea service. The tines chinked together before plucking marshmallows from a nearby sugar bowl. "Why do you continue to ask our guests, sister? Everyone loves a fleet of marshmallows floating over a sea of cocoa."

The mug scraped the counter before it nestled in Egypt's hands. She blinked as the warmth spread along her fingers. Maybe she really had fallen into an alternate universe. One where twin elves inhabited a porcelain village. She caught the chords of a Christmas carol. "Walking in a winter wonderland." Well, that certainly fit her afternoon.

"Um, yeah. As I was telling your sister, I'm not looking for a room but a phone."

"She's wearing the wrong color." Patience's lips traveled to the side of her face, aiming her words at her sister.

"I know, Patience." Charity tapped her gnarled finger against her pursed lip. "Maybe purple will bring her the luck the others didn't have."

Chocolate blanketed Egypt's tongue. Her toes curled in her sneakers. Vanilla infused her palate as the creamy marshmallow dissolved in her mouth. Why was everyone obsessed with her clothing?

"You were right about the marshmallows."

"Your scarf is supposed to be blue, dear, like the figurine."

"Purple was the best I could do." Her defense rippled across the brown liquid. The white pillows bobbed in the disturbance. She swallowed another gulp then set her mug on the counter. She had enough of the mad hotelier's cocoa party.

"Never mind, never mind." Charity's hands fluttered around her head like one-winged doves. "What can we do for you dear?"

"I just need the phone."

"Over there." Patience sliced the air with a gingerbread man then bit off his head. Egypt followed her direction. A groan raked the moisture from her throat. Jackets dripped from the coat tree like turquoise leaves in a Dali painting.

"Thank you." The counter felt smooth and solid under her palms. What could blue coats possibly mean? Air dried her tongue as her lungs expanded then deflated. Metal bit into the pad of her thumb as she unzipped her coat. Nutz tumbled onto the floor. His tail twitched before he captured it and began smoothing the bristling fur with his tongue.

"Oh, my." Charity scampered around the front desk. "It's a cat."

"What a sweet puss." Patience ran her hands over the marmalade tabby.

"This won't do. This won't do at all." Charity wrapped her apron around her fists. "She's got a cat."

"No, sister, not at all."

Egypt stumbled towards the phone and collapsed on the seat.

"That's right, dear. You make your phone call. We'll take care of your tom." Patience scooped Nutz into her arms and waddled out of the room. "Would such a sweet tom like some milk?"

Nutz blinked once at Egypt before licking Patience on the chin.

Numb fingers fumbled with the phone before Egypt caught the receiver between her ear and shoulder. The dial tone hummed in her eardrum. Five-two-zero-nine-three—her finger slipped and hit the two-button.

"Great." Her digits stung as she slapped the cradle and started over. Five-two-zero-nine-three-one. She managed to dial the rest of her parent's number.

Click. Click. Click. Nothing.

She stared at the receiver, tapped the flash button then hung up.

"One more time. Phone card number. Good. Good. Parent's number. Yes. Yes."

Click. Click. Click. Nothing.

"What the heck?"

"Sorry, dear. You can't call long distance today." Charity set a bowl of cream on the floor and blotted the spilled milky drops with the tip of her apron.

"True. True." Patience ran her hands down Nutz's body and curled his tail around her fingers. "We thought you were going to call someone in town."

"I don't know anyone in town." Egypt smoothed her throat, hoping to ease the tightness.

"No one? That is a problem."

"Of course, you don't know him." Patience winked at her.

"Can you recommend a mechanic?" Egypt's fingers bumped over her forehead. Her veins pulsed over her temples. Great, now she was getting a headache. Where was the blizzard to top off her horrible day?

"A mechanic?"

"Yes," Egypt hissed, "my car broke down outside of town."

"Oh, dear. That is a problem."

"Yes, indeed." Patience nodded.

"The perfect ploy." Charity winked at her sister.

"Why, yes. Absolutely perfect." Patience patted Egypt's arm. "Very clever."

"Excuse me. I don't believe it is particularly clever to break down in the middle of nowhere." Egypt uncurled her fists.

"Of course not, dear," Charity winked again.

Egypt rubbed the half-moon shapes from her palms then forced her hands flat against her thighs. Either the woman had a tic or she had missed something. Something to do with a blue coat, a blue scarf and a figurine. Her neck popped as she turned her head from side to side. Would she have caused this much of a sensation if she had worn a Santa suit?

"Holly doesn't have a mechanic."

"You don't have a mechanic." Egypt pinched the bridge of her nose. Worse than a blizzard. A rather harsh lesson in daring the Powers That Be.

"No, indeed," Charity beamed, "but we do have a tinker."

"My, yes. The tinker is who you need." Patience winked.

Good heavens, the tic was spreading. Egypt scooped Nutz off the floor.

"If anyone can get your car started, he can."

"Don't you mean get her motor running, Patience?"

"Motor running." Patience clamped a hand over her mouth, muffling her giggles. "Very clever."

Egypt settled the cat against her belly. With a drawn-out meow, he climbed to her shoulders and draped himself around her neck. She patted his head. At least, he hadn't jumped out of her arms. She never would have gotten him back then.

"Where can I find this tinker?"

"Well, he's not in his shop."

"No. No." Charity nodded. "I saw him turn the corner not more than five minutes ago."

"Faith called. She said he was at his parents'."

"I thought the phones were out." Egypt tucked the scarf around the cat and zipped up her jacket.

"Local calls only, dear. The slightest blow cuts the valley off from the outside."

"So, I can call him?" Pain burn Egypt's scalp as she freed her hair from under Nutz's body.

"Call? No, no, dear. These things are better handled in person."

"His parents live just up the street." Charity nodded

"Thank you." Egypt backed toward the door. She should leave the hotel. If she didn't she might end up as loopy as they were. "Which way?"

"Turn right then go past the square." Patience brushed the crumbs from her bosom.

"Under the burned-out bulbs." The sisters exchanged looks. "Then another right at the corner."

"That would be Yule Street. It's the third house on the left."

"Thank you." Egypt opened the door and stepped outside. A bevy of blue-coated women surrounded her. Silence perfumed the air like cheap cologne, heavy and offensive. "I see everyone else likes a good sale."

A few women smiled; two nodded. Everyone else glared.

"You're new." The crowd parted before her. Their gazes dissected her as she passed.

"Tea is in fifteen minutes, ladies." Charity and Patience joined them.

"Plenty of time for her to return."

"Did you see her scarf?"

The closed door trapped the answer. Egypt nodded and trudged down the sidewalk. Curiosity sparked across her brain. A blue coat, a blue scarf and a figurine. She would solve the mystery after she contacted the tinker. A tinker. Laughter rumbled across her tongue. Her steps lightened. What kind of man called himself a tinker and lived with his parents? Her imagination conjured a bent and gnarled man with wisps of gray hair and magnifying glasses perched on the end of his nose.

She scratched Nutz's chin.

"At least, I won't have to deal with the leather menace."

Chapter IX

Egypt stopped in front of the third house. Pristine snow trimmed the Victorian's sunny yellow facade. Blue lights outlined the pitched roof and rounded edges. A cast iron Santa and team of reindeer leapt over the turret's spire, heading east. She wrapped her hands around the white slats of the picket fence.

"And I thought I had it bad. I only have to endure Christmas for four months; these people have to breathe it in every day of the year. No wonder they're all lunatics." She shook her head. "And here I am talking to myself. Must be in the air." Cold tingled down her nose and across her cheeks. "All that cinnamon and vanilla didn't make Santa jolly. It made him nuts."

At the mention of his name, Nutz butted his chin against her jaw. His purr rippled over her chest.

"Easy, boy. We're almost there."

Egypt rolled the rope between her thumb and finger before tugging. The latch lifted and the gate swung soundlessly open. Unease itched down her spine. Someone was watching her. She looked left then right. Every house had people in the front yard. The men sported shovels and stood on cleared sidewalks. Clusters of women and children huddled on their porches. All eyes were trained on her.

Nutz growled.

"Great, I'm stuck in Peyton Place with an attack cat. That should provide plenty of conversation at the dinner table." The latch jingled as she slammed the gate shut. Her observers jammed elbows into neighboring bellies. Men nodded and grinned. "Norman Rockwell meets the Twilight Zone."

What were they staring at? It certainly couldn't be her jacket. Everyone seemed to have one. Egypt picked her way across the yard. Branches stuck out of lumps of snow. A carrot leaned against the front step. Another pointed at a bare tree. A few scarves snaked across the ground while black dotted a patch under the pine tree.

"Looks like someone slaughtered an army of snowmen. Figures the holiday spirit would be all for show, even in Holly." She spat her gum into its foil wrapper and shoved it in her pocket. "Here goes nothing."

She eased open the storm door and lifted the brass knocker encircled by a pinecone wreath. The thud of metal against the plate echoed in the house seconds before the door was thrown open.

A strawberry blond elf regarded her with indigo eyes while a herd of black moose circled her green sweater. A red ribbon fluttered from the front pocket of her blue jeans. "It's been tried before, you know."

"Isn't that why it's there?" Egypt looked at the knocker. "I'm looking for the tinker."

"He's not going to be happy to see you." The little girl crossed her arms and narrowed her eyes.

Egypt blinked. It looked like her bad day had skipped *worse* and gone straight to *terrible*. Obviously, the people of Holly fell into three categories: those drunk on the Christmas spirit, the professional voyeurs and those individuals completely lacking in manners. While the pint-sized pixie fell into the last category, Egypt had gone through too much to stop now. "I—"

"Haven't you caused enough trouble already?"

Egypt crammed her hands into her pocket. The foil-wrapped balls of gum rolled across her palms like dice.

"If you could just get the tinker." She forced her lips into a smile. She would be pleasant to the little troll, even if it killed her. "Please."

"All right, but don't say I didn't warn you." Her long po-nytail slapped the doorframe as she turned and stomped away, leaving the door open.

Egypt stared down the hall. Red and green candles laid siege to a marble-topped table. Swags of evergreens strangled the oak banister. Red bows pinned a hall mirror in place. White exploded on her lids as she ground the heels of her hands into her eyes. Tendrils of cinnamon teased her nostrils. She held her hands out in front of her and rubbed them together. At least the front of her body was warm.

Thump.

Egypt glanced to her right. Four male faces grinned at her from beneath the lacy drapes. A woman's voice snapped and the curtain dropped.

"Look..." The menace in leather charged around the corner. Excitement crackled across her skin like static electricity. She had forgotten how good-looking he was, and his eyes...

His blue eyes snapped with anger and...interest. Her tongue stuck to the roof of her arid mouth. He was interested in her. Her heart stilled for a moment before battering her breastbone, trying to reach him.

"It is not enough that you run me to ground in the forest, now you track me to my parent's house."

"I...I..." She was attracted to him. No, nothing so lame as mere attraction. She wanted him, wanted to rip off his clothes and throw him to the ground. Her heart settled into her chest to beat not with a civilized lub-dub but with an elemental staccato.

"You, you, you..." He loomed over her. Tall. Powerful. Stimulating. His hot breath washed over her, heating her blood. She could have him. Here. Now. "The world doesn't revolve around you, Princess."

Princess. The hated epithet. Numb legs stumbled across the porch. Air whooshed out of her lungs as she slammed into the post. Pain drove off the desire. What was the matter with her? She had almost ravaged a stranger. A stranger she didn't particularly like. Frigid air filled her lungs, leaching the heat from her blood.

"If you could just get the tinker," she whispered.

"You want the tinker, huh? You've got a problem that needs fixing, Princess?" His eyeteeth winked at her.

Anger jerked her muscles. Her spine popped as she straightened. Her reaction was no laughing matter.

"I don't know what your problem is buddy, but I need the tinker." She crossed her arms and glared back at him. Obviously the insanity infusing this place had gotten to her. The jerk wasn't even that good-looking. The split lip and black eye he'd acquired since she'd left him were proof of his nasty disposition. "If you could just get the tinker, I'd be on my way that much faster, and you could slink back under that rock you call home."

Her tormentor crossed his arms and leaned against the doorjamb.

"Why do you want the tinker, Princess?"

She opened her mouth but her answer lodged in her throat. Nails scraped wood. A ball of fur and teeth leapt off the oak planks. Two massive paws harpooned her shoulder, shoving her backwards. The rail cut across her spine. Air cooled her left foot as her sneaker flew in the opposite direction. She was going to die, murdered by a hairball with teeth.

"Down, Pete."

Pain flared along her neck and cheek as Nutz scratched his way free. Something gripped her wrist. Her shoulder burned. The fur woofed. Nutz hissed. Noise ricocheted inside her skull.

Her attackers retreated, allowing the pressure to fade to a bruising memory.

"What the hell? Are you all right, Princess?" Naked hands swept over her cheeks, down her arms and squeezed her fingers. "Open your eyes, Egypt."

Egypt. He remembered her name. Her eyes flew open. Her breasts tightened. The insanity stirred once more. Stitches poked his head out of her pocket and clambered up her scarf to perch on her head.

"Son of a—"

"Cade Dugan, you watch your mouth. This is my house, and I will not tolerate swearing in it, especially at this time of year." A petite woman hovered in the doorway, drying her hands on an apron.

"But—"

"Not one word." She shook her finger at the leather nemesis.

"The woman's carrying an entire zoo, Ma."

Ma? Amusement restored Egypt's equilibrium. Her nemesis had not been forged from brimstone to spring fully formed from the bowels of Hell. He had a mother. A diminutive woman with soft brown hair who was smiling at her. Perhaps this woman was the rainbow after the hurricane.

"Ma'am, I—" Nutz dashed between the woman's legs, raced up Egypt and hissed from atop her shoulder. Pete's hind legs shot out from under him. He slipped across the oak planks on his rear end, blue eyes wide against his gray fur.

"Oh! Oh, my!" Cade's mother smacked her fluttering skirt against her thighs.

"Control your menagerie, Princess."

His words slipped under her collar and caressed her spine.

"Two animals do not constitute a menagerie." Egypt plucked Stitches from off her hat. His frail body trembled in her hand, vibrating fur poked through her fingers.

"Stay, Pete." The dog dropped his head and stared at her leather-clad tormentor. "Woman, you are a menace. Not only do you hound me, but you bring a rat and a feline along for the ride."

"Stitches is not a rat." Fur tickled Egypt's cheeks. "He's a teddy bear hamster, and if you had half a brain you'd know that."

"I apologize for my son's rude behavior." Cade's mother laid her hand on Egypt's arm. "Believe it or not, I raised him better."

"She started it."

"Cade. Pet Pete so he knows you're no longer mad at him. There is nothing worse than a pouting wolf under your feet."

"Wolf." The word squeaked through Egypt's tight throat. Saliva dripped from Pete's pink tongue as he continued to stare at her. The eating scenario wasn't as far fetched now.

"Well, half wolf. Pete doesn't mean any harm. He was just curious, that's all. The boys never allowed me to own a cat. Guess they weren't manly enough." She stepped closer. "Hello, there." Cade's mother smoothed the cat's bristling fur. Nutz dug his claws into Egypt's shoulder but his purr betrayed his pleasure. "You're a sweet kitty, aren't you? Yes, you are. Here, now, you don't want to stay up there. You could fall and hurt yourself." She plucked the feline from his perch and held him against her chest. "What's his name?"

"Nutz."

Cade snorted. "Probably suffers from the same condition as its owner."

Egypt matched his glare.

"What woman in her right mind takes her zoo with her when she goes hunting for a mate?" Cade stepped next to his mother.

"Mate? I'm not hunting for a mate. I just need the stupid tinker." Mother and son blurred from the tears swimming in her eyes.

99

"Cade, stop badgering her." His mother stepped inside and down the hall. "Come inside, dear. Everything will look better after you warm up a bit."

"Mother, I don't think—"

"Cade, bring her into the kitchen. Can't you see she's half-frozen?"

Egypt wiped her nose on her sleeve. "If you could—"

"Will you get inside, already?" He glanced over his shoulder then back at her. "Please."

His hand motioned her forward, her feet obeyed. Traitorous body. She turned as she reached the threshold so her shoulder wouldn't brush him. "I just want the tinker."

He leaned forward, crowding her with his heat and irritation. "How can you want and need the tinker but not be looking for a mate?"

"I need help, not sex."

Air hissed past her ear. His pupils dilated. His gaze settled on her lips. "A mate provides more than just really, really hot sex."

"Get her a cup of coffee, Cade. I just put on a fresh pot."

"I don't want any, thank you."

His hand cupped her elbow, steered her across the foyer. Every nerve ending in her body jingled to life, overloading her brain with sensation.

"You have something against my mother's coffee."

"I don't like coffee, but I thank you for the offer."

"My mother made the offer."

"Right, your mother." Egypt shook her head, hoping to clear the haze clouding her normal thought processes. Why was he unaffected? It wasn't fair. She didn't want to be the only human-shaped gelatin wobbling about.

He propelled her through an archway, and she found herself surrounded by lemon-yellow walls and ceiling-high white cabinets. The scent of cinnamon, baking bread and fresh coffee teased her senses.

"Cool, a hamster." Hostility evaporated from her adolescent greeter. The girl sprang from her chair and skipped the distance to Egypt. "Can I hold him? Please?"

She clasped her hands together and bounced on the balls of her feet.

Egypt smiled. Animals always softened the most hardened hearts. She glanced at Cade. Almost always.

"Sure." She placed a quick kiss on Stitches' head and opened her hands. "Just be careful. He's had quite a scare today."

"I will. I will." Stitches' whiskers twitched as he scampered across the bridge of hands. "Ooh, he's so soft."

Aluminum scratched linoleum as Cade pulled out a chair. Sunflowers stared up at her from the plastic seat. Egypt's fingers skimmed the silver top of another chair. She should refuse his offer, take a seat of her own choosing and show him he couldn't push her around. His left eyebrow cocked. A dimple flashed in his cheek. The jerk. He actually dared her to refuse. She spun about and plopped down in the seat.

"Thank you."

"Don't mention it." He tossed himself into another chair. His full lips compressed to a thin line.

"What brings you to our little town...er, um..." Cade's mother set Nutz on her ironing board then placed a saucer of half-and-half before him. The cat crouched before the offering, one green eye trained on the archway and the dog filling it.

"Egypt."

"Pardon?" After one final stroke along Nutz's body, Cade's mother cleaned her hands in the sink and dried them on her apron.

"Her name is Egypt, like the country." Cade plucked a pencil from a nearby can and tapped the eraser against the table.

"What a lovely name. Are you from there?"

A plate of cinnamon rolls slid in front of Egypt. Her stomach growled. Her fingers sank into the warm dough, sugar oozed down the golden crust.

"No, ma'am. I'm originally from Dragoon's Springs, but I live in Phoenix now."

"What brings you to Holly, Egypt—and you must call me Marty."

"Yes, ma'am, er, Marty. As I was trying to tell Cade..." His name teased her tongue and filled her mouth. He slid a mug towards her then snatched one of her cinnamon rolls in payment. "I was looking for the tinker."

"Look, this is getting old." White furrows appeared along Cade's scalp as he plowed one hand into his ebony hair. "If you don't want or need a mate, why do you want the damn—er, darn tinker?"

"My car broke down, all right?" Egypt flung her half-eaten bun onto her plate. Her insides twisted around the lumps she had swallowed and threatened to squeeze them out of her stomach.

"You have a car?" Marty leaned against her counter.

"I thought you were visiting friends." Cade snatched her half-eaten pastry off the plate and took a bite. "No, wait. You were making snow angels, right?"

"Cade, stop eating her food." Marty snatched Egypt's plate and filled it with sugar cookies.

"That's what she said." His Adam's apple bobbed as he gulped his coffee. "Isn't that right, Princess?"

"Yes. No." Embarrassment burned Egypt's cheeks. Leave it to the jerk to make her look like an idiot in front of his mother.

"So, you admit to lying in the past. How do I know you're not lying now?" He leaned back in his chair, hands clasped behind his head.

Egypt's palms itched with the need to slap the smug smile from his lips. Her hands throttled her mug instead of the oaf's thick neck. "If you could just tell me where the tinker is, then what you know or think won't matter."

"But Cade *is* the tinker, dear." Marty's smile belied the concern in her eyes.

A chill swept over Egypt's skin. Trudging through the snow, praying for a mechanic, bargaining for a reprieve. She shook her head. Her hearing was off. Fate would never answer her prayers in such a twisted manner.

"That's not possible. You—"

"Yes. Me." Cade leaned across the table and freed the mug from her grip. "Nice acting, Princess. I'd almost believe you didn't know."

"Look, hon—mistletoe."

Egypt glanced up. The hallway was clogged with men. Their leader, a gray-haired, barrel-chested man, dangled a snip of green from his fingers.

"Where should I hang it?"

"Not now, Burl."

Burl looked at Marty then shrugged.

"Can I warm up my coffee?" His gaze slipped off her to focus on Cade.

"Take the pot into the other room." Burl tiptoed into the room, tossed the mistletoe at Cade then grabbed the coffeepot. "And your sons, too."

"Can't I just—"

"No."

"Just an introduction."

"Burl, as much as I love you, your enthusiasm can be a little frightening and Egypt has been through enough for one day." Marty flapped her apron at him.

"Egypt. Such a lovely name. Welcome to—"

"Dad!" Cade yelled.

"Holly. What did you think I was going to say, son?" Burl winked at him.

Her nemesis shifted in his seat. She would enjoy his uneasiness more if she didn't think it could be turned on her just as easily.

"Egypt's car broke down, dear."

"So she says," Cade challenged.

"That's because it's true." Egypt folded her arms across her chest and glared at him. Glee, amusement and exasperation bobbed on the undercurrents flooding the room. Something was afoot. Some mischief in which she played an unknowing part. She snagged Cade's eye. He knew. He *knew*, and he wasn't telling.

"So, she's not from around here?" Burl remarked.

"Take the coffee and your sons in the other room, dear. I'll fill you in later."

"All right, boys." Burl brandished the coffeepot at his sons. "Show's over. Back into the living room with all of you. Don't want to scare her off too soon."

Cade shoved away from the table. "I'll look at your vehicle. Come on, Pete."

"Wait. I'll come with you." In her haste to leave bedlam, Egypt tripped over the table leg. Pain rocketed up her elbow as it collided with the tabletop.

"I can handle it."

"You don't know where it is." Rubbing her elbow, she stumbled after him.

"Mile marker twelve-twenty-five." He yanked his jacket off the peg by the back door and rammed his arms in the sleeves.

"How did you know?"

"It's always marker twelve-twenty-five." He slammed the back door in her face.

Egypt's hands slipped on the knob. Her heart pounded in her ear. The latch gave. She tumbled out the door, stumbled down the steps and slammed in his back.

"Just a minute. It is my car, and I am not going to leave it for you to...to tinker with."

"Don't you think you've caused more than enough trouble, Princess?" Cade scooped her into his arms and carried her inside. Once there, he unzipped her jacket and spun her about, removing her coat as he went. "Now, stay," he ordered. Pete sat by his feet and whimpered. "Not you. Her."

The dog darted out the door seconds before it slammed shut behind him.

Egypt looked from the door to her pets.

"You go ahead, dear." Marty smiled, handing Egypt a coat and scarf. "We'll watch the animals until you get back."

Chapter X

Dumb. Dumb. Dumb. Recriminations hounded Cade's every footfall. God, how could he have been so stupid? She was lying, deceitful and manipulative. His blood iced in his veins.

And she was alone with his parents.

His baseball cap plopped to the ground. Leather puckered as he jerked the reindeer to a stop and scooped up a capful of snow. Icy water trickled behind his ears as the blob of snow melted.

"My car broke down," she had said.

He yanked on Holiday's reins. No doubt about it, the woman was clever, very clever. None of the others had thought of pretending to be an outsider. And for a moment, one wild crazy moment, he had actually believed, wanted to believe she was the one. What a chump.

Flannel warmed the nape of his neck as he tugged on his jacket.

He wouldn't have been such a sucker if it hadn't been for her hair. He plucked a couple of strands off her scarf draped over his shoulder. The honey-colored lengths furrowed his black gloves. And the scarf. How had she known about the scarf?

Someone must have found out. But how? The true version of his dream woman was locked in the safe in his studio. No one knew it existed except his mother.

Pain burned his thigh as his boots skidded on an icy patch. He glanced left then right. No one had witnessed his clumsiness. At least, that was something to be thankful for.

Of all the Blue Coats, she was the worst. How had she known? A wild notion surfaced and banged against his skull. Maybe she was his mate. Maybe the dark lights actually meant something.

And maybe pigs pulled Santa's sleigh instead of reindeer.

Cade flung the strands to the ground and watched the wind carry them off. He never should have taken that bet, never should have created his fantasy woman.

Who the hell knew she would appear?

He stopped in his tracks. Egypt was not his Miss Right. His mate was kind and giving, gentle and soft-spoken.

Goodman butted his back, shoving him forward.

"Okay, okay, I'm walking." He stumbled forward. "Must be my day for bossy females."

Pete whined, a high-pitched arrow of disagreement. Cade glanced over his shoulder. Streaks marred the glass on the driver's side of the Volkswagen. His dog raced across the front seat to press his nose against the passenger window.

"Traitorous mutt." Pete's ears rotated from the side to the front. "Yeah, I'm talking to you. You should be out here picking ice out of your toes. Not in there, snuggling in her chair."

Wind gusted, sanding his cheeks. Her scarf slapped his face and stuck to his tongue. Her scent filled his head. Messages jumped nerve endings, turning his muscles to rubber bands. Bones ground against joints as his skeleton was pulled in unnatural directions. Cade spat out her scarf.

"You had better not smell like her." Pete's tongue lolled out of his mouth. Great. Now, his own dog was laughing at him. "Laugh it up, you mangy mutt. You're getting a bath when we

107

get home." The dog barked then rested his chin on the steering wheel, his ears flat against his head. "Nice try, but you're still getting a bath."

My car broke down.

Everyone's car broke down at mile marker 1225. Twelve twenty-five. December 25th. Few grasped the significance. If his Princess had taken the turn-off a half a mile up the road from her car, she would have reached the service station and parking lot. But she hadn't. She had missed the turn and followed the road.

Waves of air crashed over his face as his hand batted at her haunting voice. The damn car probably lacked an engine. Car, hell. He bet all the clay in the world he'd spent the last forty-five minutes towing an enchanted cranberry around and not an ancient Volkswagen Beetle. He kicked at a patch of ice coating the road. A satisfying crunch echoed in his ears. Not that he could find out. Her engine had been sealed behind the red metal. And her keys...

Frustration clouded the air. Why weren't her keys in her jacket?

"Because that would make my life too easy." His snort clouded the afternoon air. Cade shook off the self-pity.

So, what was he going to do with her?

Not a damn thing. One fat snowflake landed on his cheek. Cold leather fingers scratched his skin as he brushed it away. Silence pressed against him as other flakes drifted down from the gray clouds.

She had ceased being his problem the moment he spied that wedding dress.

The pristine silk and frothy veil obscured the back passenger window like an expensive window shade. No wonder she had sprinted outside, eyes snapping. She hadn't wanted him to find the proof of her perfidy. Had she thought she could hide the diaphanous fabric before he had seen it? And what about the wedding gifts overflowing the backseat?

"The woman's just plain nuts. Mentally unstable. What man could possibly want her?" The wind snatched the question out of his mouth and carried it into the towering pines. "Not me, that's for damn sure. My woman will be colorful and vibrant, like Christmas. Not driftwood bleached out by the warm summer sun."

Bleached out? Damn. Now she had him lying to himself. Hell, who would have thought there could be so many shades of tan? From her streaked hair, tan eyes and golden skin, every angle had been kissed by sunshine. And what about the skin under her clothes? Cade unzipped his jacket. The frigid air snatched the heat from his body. He was warm enough by himself. He didn't need a living sunbeam to warm his day.

She was a fraud, pure and simple. Hell, the woman hated coffee. That alone should be enough to kick her out of his thoughts. It had been more than sufficient for the others. Unease twitched along his skeleton.

Egypt was different from the others.

And not in a good way. She had hunted him down, armed with a wedding dress. Were the invitations far behind? Anger stormed his frame, jerking his muscles like marionette strings. Holiday complained at the harsh treatment. The reins slipped in his grasp.

"Sorry, girl. Women trouble." Holiday rolled her eyes and nudged Goodman.

"I pity the man who gets stuck with her." Cade loosened the reins. "No wonder she had to trap a mate. What man wants a woman as prickly as a saguaro and twice as poisonous as mistletoe?" A picture of her full lips flashed in his mind. Soft. Alluring. Kissable. "Okay, so kissing her might not be so bad. But spending the rest of my years wrapped in the poisonous vine? It's enough to choke the life right outta a man." Pete woofed and scratched against the window of the car as they turned down his street. "She didn't feel that good in my arms."

109

"Lights are still out." Sven King crossed his beefy arms and glared at Cade. "More so than before."

"It's probably just the generators."

"Yeah, and Kris Kringle is just a fat old man." He dismissed Cade's explanation with a wave.

"Another five strands went out since you left." Sven's wife Helga stood beside her husband, handing him Christmas bulbs.

"You don't say?"

"Not only that, but our whole street is dark." Helga prodded her husband to continue his task. "And this only two days before Christmas."

"Anyone check the fuses?"

"Do you think I'd check thousands of lights before I checked the blasted fuses?" Sven glared at him.

"You were never known for your brightness, Sven."

"I seem to have caught on a bit faster than you." Sven caught his wife around her waist, hauled her to his side and planted a kiss on her lips.

Envy shot through Cade at the love sparking off his neighbors. So, he was jealous. Hell, he was thirty-two years old. More than old enough to know he didn't want to spend the next thirty-two years with only himself and a traitorous dog for company. But that still didn't mean she was his mate.

"I just love it when a man finds his match. Sets all the men folk to feeling a bit more amorous." Helga fanned her rosy cheeks.

"Oh, for the love of Pete."

"Pete? What you talking about yer dog fer, Cade?" Old man Henderson yelled from his front porch.

"I'm not talking about my dog, Mr. Henderson."

"Ye just said fer the love of Pete." Mr. Henderson stabbed the air with the gnarled branch he used as a cane. Popping and creaking filled the air as the old man pushed his way to his feet. "I may be old, but my hearing's as good as any."

110

"We were just telling him about the lights being out, Mr. Henderson," Sven yelled. "Cade thinks it's a problem with the power."

"Ye can bet yer fancy britches it be a problem with the power."

"See, I told you." Cade grinned at the Kings. Finally, someone agreed with him—and Mr. Henderson, of all people. Cade ignored the stab of disappointment and focused on the victory pumping through his veins. Yep, if Mr. Henderson agreed then it had to be true. The man was older than the first Christmas tree and almost as enlightened as Saint Nick himself.

"The power of love ignored and wasted be mighty powerful."

"Damn it to h—"

"You're cursing don't help none, either. Best mind your tongue if you hope to win yer gal. That one will lead you on a merry chase afore ye catch her."

"Better run, Cade," Sven urged with a wink.

"I don't think Helga would love you nearly as much with your lips someplace behind your teeth, Sven."

"Ohhh, I'm so scared." Sven taunted as he tiptoed behind his wife. "Protect me, Helga. Protect me."

"Will it be a Christmas wedding, Cade? I love Christmas weddings."

"There *is* no Christmas wedding," Cade growled.

"'Course not. He may not be able to win her a-tall, let alone afore Christmas."

"Win her?" Cade straightened his back. "I don't have to win her. She came hunting me, if you recall. If I wanted her, and I don't, all I would have to do is crook my finger and she would come running." Knowing grins twisted their faces. Damn, it was like looking at a bunch of snowmen. "Win her, hell!"

"Stop yer swearing, boy. Now git home." Mr. Henderson's cane thumped on his porch. "Go on, git. And decorate yer house. Naked thing like that is an abomination this time of year."

Crazy old man. Cade tugged on Holiday's reins and started the last leg of his trip. He obviously doesn't know what he's talking about. Five more strings of lights had fallen dark. Eight out in all.

"Hell." Cade glanced over his shoulder. "Er, darn."

Maybe he was at fault. Not his love life but his swearing. He turned into the driveway. The reindeer picked up speed, anxious for their dinner of oats and hay.

Pete barked. His nails scratched the window.

"Calm down. Calm down. Serves you right. You could have taken care of business if you had walked beside me, but, no, you had to take refuge nestled in her scent."

The dog barked and howled. He climbed into the backseat. Cade could hear paper shredding in Pete's frenzy. A bell bounced against the window.

"Hey, stop that. What are you thinking, giving her another reason to stick around!" He tossed the reins to the ground and stomped to the car. The woman was so ornery, she would probably demand he re-wrap all her presents.

"Get out." Cade yanked the door open, and the dog tumbled out. Pete leapt to his feet and started sniffing the ground. "You know you're getting a bath for this."

Santa's cheery countenance beamed at Cade from its home in Pete's paw. Christmas paper? Cade's gaze followed the trail of red-and-green confetti. There were Christmas presents under the wedding gifts. Seven. Eight. Nine. Only three wedding gifts, but ten Christmas gifts.

What did it mean?

Had her friends wrapped the wedding gifts in Christmas paper or...

His heart hardened to a lump of iron in his chest. Or had he caught her in another lie? Bah, humbug. Was the woman even capable of telling the truth? Didn't she know her falsehoods could hurt someone?

Pete's bark changed to a high yip. Awareness teased the hair on Cade's arms and neck. Someone was there. The wind whisked over his features. Sunshine and warmth surrounded him. Air stagnated in his lungs. His heart stilled before slamming against his chest.

Egypt.

"No. No. She wouldn't have." Cade scanned the yard and porch while unharnessing Holiday and Goodman. The reindeer trotted across the snow to wait by the barn door. Goodman pawed the ground. Pete sniffed the air, howled once then headed for the barn. "You smell the coat, boy."

Cade dangled the turquoise jacket in front of the pawing dog.

"She wouldn't have followed without her jacket. She would have froze before she went a hundred yards." He wrenched open the barn doors. The musky sent of used straw, warm animals and dry oats greeted him. The reindeer raced to their stalls. Goodman butted Holiday aside and lapped at the water in the trough. Pete dropped his nose in the dark-brown dirt then sneezed.

"See, I told you."

"It's warmer in here than it is on your porch."

Cade's bones pushed against his skin as Egypt stepped from behind a wooden camel. Pete dashed to her side.

"Sorry, didn't mean to startle you."

He yanked on his jacket, glad the leather had kept his skeleton in place.

"You didn't startle me. Pete warned me of your presence."

"I suppose women are always hiding in your barn." Egypt strolled out of the stall. Hay stuck out of her hair.

"Only the desperate ones." Cade nodded. At least his voice sounded normal; but if she was the desperate one, why did he have to resist the urge to grab her and never let her go?

"Hey, at least I didn't touch your stuff. And the only thing I am desperate for is my car."

"You should have waited at my parents'."

"Is that why you took my jacket? To force me to obey your orders?"

"Obey?" he snorted. "I'm sure you've earned every millimeter of that stubborn chin, Princess." He tossed the jacket over the nearest stall and yanked a pitchfork off the wall. Bits of straw dribbled from the lump speared in the tines.

"So why did you take it? Are you afraid you'd like my company?"

"Not likely." Great. Now he was lying to himself. So he hadn't wanted her to go with him. What did that prove? Nothing. Not one blessed thing.

"Then why take my jacket? Turquoise really isn't your color." She smirked at him.

Damn woman. She thought she had all the answers. Well, she didn't know him. He had a darn good reason for taking her jacket, and as soon as he thought of it he would tell her.

"Well?"

"Your keys."

"My keys?" The certainty left her face, leaving only confusion furrowing her forehead.

"Yes, you know—to your supposed car." He lanced another forkful of hay and carried to Holiday's stall.

"My *supposed* car?" Her eyes narrowed. She advanced on him, stopping his return. "You didn't find it, did you?"

"I found it." He sidestepped then slammed the pitchfork against the wood.

"Then where is it?"

"Outside." He speared the pitchfork into the bale of hay then turned to go outside. His unadorned lawn chided him. He should decorate for Christmas. The Blue Coats had interfered in his life long enough. His hands closed around the nearest wooden cutout. Today was the winter solstice. Today Cade Dugan took back control of his life.

"Is it fixed?" The tip of the horse blanket brushed his leg.

"Nope." Animal sweat fouled his nose. At least, she wouldn't smell so appealing now. The thought flashed in his mind before he shoved it away. She wasn't appealing, period. Snow squeaked under his boots as he stomped across the yard. He slammed the Wise Man onto the ground and kicked out the back support.

"Are you going to fix it?"

"Yep." He stepped around her and headed back to the barn. He refused to feel guilty. She and the other Blue Coats had robbed him of a month of Christmas spirit. She could wait for him. He tugged another wooden figure out.

"When?" She stamped the ground and stood, arms akimbo, blocking the exit.

"When I'm finished."

"And when will that be, precisely?"

"Depends on how long you stand there." She glared at him, her right foot transmitting her annoyance along the earthen floor. "You know, Holiday is going to be very upset that you're using her blanket."

"Holiday? And I suppose the other one is Christmas."

"Nope. Goodman."

"I thought reindeer were supposed to be named Dasher and Dancer or such." She shrugged the blanket off her shoulders, slipped off his mother's jacket and reached for her coat.

"Not always."

"But you have to name them something Christmasy." She forced the words through her teeth as she stabbed her arms into her sleeves.

"Nope." So, the mighty Princess hadn't done all her homework. Cold dried his teeth, freezing his smile. He forced

115

his lips together. The second Wise Man joined the first. A six-legged camel tottered out of the barn.

"Holiday and Good Man sound pretty Christmasy to me."

He took the camel and stood it up near the wise men.

"Billie Holiday and Benny Goodman."

"You listen to the big bands?"

"Yep." He reached for the last Wise Man and carried it out.

"Figures," she muttered, "but that doesn't mean he can swing dance."

"I can dance."

"Great," she growled and set the donkey on his boot.

"Don't you swing, Princess?"

Waves of crimson crashed over her face. Her mouth opened and closed twice before she answered.

"No. I do not swing."

Cade watched her rigid back as she stomped to the barn. Now what had he said to upset her? He stepped into the barn. His nose slammed into the Virgin Mary. He wrenched the wooden figure out of Egypt's hands before she flattened him.

"Why are you here?"

"I need my car fixed." She spun on the ball of her foot and scooped up the Baby Jesus.

"My mother never should have let you out of the house."

"I'm an adult. I can do what I want."

Air whooshed out of his lungs as the edge of the manger jabbed him in the gut.

"Next time I'll take your shoes."

"What?"

"I said I'm surprised one of my brothers didn't offer you his coat."

"If one had, I wouldn't have stopped to warm up in your barn."

"How'd you know it was my barn?" He hefted the last cutout onto his shoulder and left. So, she had helped him set up the Nativity—that didn't mean anything.

"The sleigh tracks turned into this drive." she shrugged. "Well, that, and your name is on the mailbox."

He glared at her. "So, why didn't you wait inside? Make yourself at home."

"I didn't want to intrude."

"Woman, you've been intruding since the moment you walked in front of my sleigh."

"I did not walk in front of your sleigh." Her knuckle popped as she drilled his shoulder. "You tried to run me down. A rational person would be able to see these bright colors you keep obsessing over. Admit it. You did it deliberately. Don't deny it. You accused me of public drunkenness, so you must have heard me singing."

"I'm not obsessing over anything about you. You should have known better than to wear that outfit."

"Oh, you're impossible." She tossed up her hands before fisting them against her hips.

"Where are your animals?"

"Your mother and sister were kind enough to watch them."

"Candance is not my sister; she's my niece."

"Well, your niece and your mother are watching Nutz and Stitches. Now, are you going to fix my car?"

"I need a drink." A shot of whiskey would be nice. Something strong to pickle his brain so he wouldn't have to think about her.

"A drink?" She squeaked as she followed him up the front steps.

"Yes. You know, liquid that goes down your throat and into your gut." His boots scraped the porch as he climbed the stoop.

"Yes, I know what a drink is, but do you have to get one now?" Her voice rose on the end as she preceded him inside.

"Yes, now." Pete sprinted by Cade and leapt onto the couch. Embarrassment burned Cade's cheeks as he surveyed the front rooms. What a sty. Irritation straightened his shoulders. So, his house was a mess. She wasn't exactly an invited guest. Besides, maybe the disorder would put an end to her marriage plans. "The bathroom is through there."

"Pardon?"

"The bathroom. First door on the right." Confusion wrinkled her forehead. He leaned closer, inhaling her fresh scent. Her spine straightened but she held her ground. Aw, hell, the contrary woman probably thought to save him from himself. Well, she might be able to clean his house, but she was powerless against a surly attitude.

"You smell like a sweaty reindeer."

"Ohhh." Egypt stomped into the bathroom and slammed the door.

Amusement rumbled out of his chest. Pete whined and stared at him. "Don't look at me like that. You're still getting a bath." He ripped the lid off the coffee can and studied the dust coating the bottom. Not enough for a decent cup of coffee. Unless...

He grabbed a half-full mug of cold coffee and added the grounds then popped it into the microwave. The machine whirled to life.

The microwave pinged. Warmth seeped into his fingers as he lifted the mug to his lips. Bitterness exploded along his palate. Grounds rolled across his tongue. Revulsion shuddered along his frame as he drained the cup. Swilling vile coffee and wallowing in garbage. How had his life come to this?

The Blue Coats.

Muttering echoed in the bathroom. She was a Blue Coat. Thoughts cascaded along his cerebellum. His Princess needed to be taught a lesson. And he was just the man to do it.

Chapter XI

"*I* smell like a reindeer. *I* smell like a reindeer. *He's* the one that smells like a reindeer, damn his leather hide." Egypt scrubbed her hands. Knots of irritation bubbled along her jaw. Her reflection's light-brown eyes stared at her. "And now he has me swearing. As if I don't have enough bad habits."

She spun the taps off then snatched a towel off the counter. Terrycloth cushioned her fingers.

"I can do this. He's just a man."

She stuffed the damp towel into the brass rung and turned back to her reflection. Lengths of straw protruded from her hair like antennae.

"Okay, so I'm wearing a reindeer's dinner," she said, pulling the straw from her hair. "That doesn't mean I smell like one, does it?"

Her reflection remained as enigmatic as the portrait of the Mona Lisa.

"Fat lot of help you are." She sniffed her jacket. "Hamster, maybe. Definitely a bit of a cat." She lifted the hem of her sweater. Yarn tickled her nose. "But absolutely no horse or reindeer." She tugged the knitted material over her stomach and smiled at her reflection before exiting the bathroom. "And I would tell him so if I were speaking to him."

She stepped into the great hall. Information bombarded her senses and ricocheted inside her skull. Thoughts fizzled. Egypt closed her eyes. Maybe if she focused on one sense at a time, her brain wouldn't liquefy and seep out her ears. One calming breath then two. Synapses chugged to life, deciphering the scents. Pine. Stale coffee. The fermented-orange scent of turpentine. Other chemicals, tantalizingly familiar yet unnamed. And him. Her gut clenched. Her skin tingled.

Focus, Egypt. Don't think of him. His image wavered in her mind's eye. The cocky smile twisted his full lips. His flashing eyes tempted as they mocked. *For crying out loud, Egypt, he's not that good-looking.* She mentally stuffed his image into a little-used portion of her brain. *Now, concentrate.* Her battered will hunted down the appropriate memory and forced it to the fore. The great room shimmered to life.

Honey-colored beams soared above the towering pine tree crowding the picture window. Naked green boughs stretched from the creamy wall to tickle the stone fireplace. The white marble mantle glistened under the mound of cut evergreen branches. A tower of crimson ribbon perched atop the heap. Pine needles sprinkled the stack of boxes crouching in front of the massive hearth.

Ornaments. Four boxes of ornaments should be sufficient to decorate the huge tree yet there were more stacked on the counter. Her mind's eye turned toward the kitchen. No, not ornaments. Strands of cherry red beads dribbled from the box labeled garland while ropes of clear lights circled one labeled illumination.

Her frayed cloak of indifference unraveled. The Christmas spirit swept along her skeleton. Her fingers itched to deck the mantle with boughs of evergreens, hang ornaments and string lights.

"Are you going to stand there all day?"

Egypt's eyes flew open. How had she forgotten about him? She hadn't. Not really. He had been at her side, helping her decorate, brushing her arm, stealing a kiss...

"Well?"

Egypt shook her head, hoping to knock such nonsense from her head. Stealing a kiss? She didn't even like the man.

Liar.

The accusation flitted across her mind like an echo of a memory.

"Get up, Pete." Cade shoved the growling dog off the seat and patted the cushion. Pete lumbered across the carpet to the chair. Newspapers crunched as he climbed into the recliner.

Her gaze slid from the loveseat to the chair. It would be cruel to force the dog to move twice. Egypt took a deep breath. He may cause her to swear and lose her temper but no one could cause her to be mean to animals. She stepped over dirty socks, a crumpled flannel shirt, a wad of jeans and a pair of black ice skates before reaching her required seat.

"Thanks."

"You're welcome." He glared at her then turned his attention back to the television.

Pressure dotted her back. Even his couch was disagreeable. Egypt shifted left. A box stuffed with wads of tissue plopped to the ground. The pressure built to an ache. She shifted right. An Irish chain quilt oozed out of the shrinking crevice between their thighs. Pain spread across her back. She kicked over an empty glass. It stopped with a chink against the coffee table leg.

What if a spent spring wasn't the cause of her discomfort? What if something else was digging into her back? Pete slipped off the chair. He pressed against her leg before snatching a crust of bread off a plate. Her gaze flitted from the dirty dish to the empty cereal box lying on its side, flirted with the brown paper cups dribbling from a box of chocolates and landed on the cellophane clinging to the afghan draped over the back.

"Oh, come on," Cade shouted.

Startled, Egypt sat up. The thing behind her slipped. Hundreds of tiny hands tickled her waist.

"A blind woman with a toothpick can play better than that. Get the puck. The puck, you idiot." He leaned forward, stabbing his finger at the screen. Red-and-white jerseys tangled as two men slammed into clear Plexiglas surrounding a hockey rink. "That's a start. Now get the puck before they score again."

Cade flung himself against the sofa back. Pete set his chin on the armrest and sneezed. Sad blue eyes regarded her. She'd be lucky if a dog bone was gouging her back. Either way, she'd have to remove whatever it was by herself. Mr. Hockey was obviously too engrossed in his game.

Her hand slipped behind her back. Something warm and hard pressed against her palm.

At least it wasn't alive.

It raked her skin as she pulled it out. Her bones jellied in relief. Hysterical laughter pushed against her lips. A brush. It was a brush.

"Want one?" Foam swirled inside the green bottle Cade offered.

"Thanks." Cold seeped up her arm upon contact. Great, a cold beer. He really had needed a drink. Egypt pulled her jacket closed then tried the cap. The heel of her hand burned as the jagged edges cut her flesh but the cap didn't budge. Awareness skimmed across her skin. He was staring at her.

"Give it here, Princess." He took the bottle from her hand, laid the side against the coffee table and slammed the top. The cap rolled under the sofa. He handed the open bottle back to her.

"Thank you." Alcohol burned her throat. Tears stung her eyes. A shudder tore through her frame. Beer. How could something that smelled like fresh bread taste like toilet water? Coffee would have been better—at least then she wouldn't have frozen from the inside out. "How long is the game on?"

"It just started."

She collapsed against the loveseat as if her breath had supported her bones. It had just started. A timer flashed on the screen: 10:59. The countdown stopped while the referee motioned with his arms. Trapped. She was trapped here as long as the ref held the puck, as long as the clock still displayed numbers. Her fingernail picked at the label on the bottle. Her efforts were rewarded by paper ripping.

"Any idea what is wrong with my car?"

"Nope." Cade set his empty bottle on the table. He looked from her to her beer and back again. "You don't like beer either?"

"Not particularly."

"Too good for coffee; too good for beer." He plucked the bottle from her hand and raised it to his lips.

Egypt pushed off the couch.

"Do you mind if I make myself some tea?"

"Nope, but then, I don't have any tea."

"Hot water, then. You do have water, don't you?"

"Yep."

Egypt stomped into the kitchen. The man liked being difficult. The wooden knob felt smooth and warm as she yanked the first cabinet open. Empty. She reached for the second one. Empty. Great—was there anything in this house that wasn't disagreeable?

After her fifth cabinet she leaned against the counter. Grape jelly coated her hand.

"Do you have any clean dishes in your house?"

"Check the dishwasher."

Her gaze dropped to the bottom cabinets. All the fronts looked similar but only the one by the sink had buttons. She yanked on the handle. The door fell forward, bounced twice then settled parallel to the tile floor.

"It's empty."

"Nope. No clean dishes."

The lout actually sounded happy about being a slob. Anger snapped through her. She could see his grin reflected in the television screen.

"When are you going to fix my car?"

"I'll look at if after the game."

"Can't you tape the game?"

"Don't want to," he answered.

"What a baby." She shook the anger out of her fingertips. "Tea. I need a cup of tea." Egypt grabbed a mug. Bile rose in her throat as the sludgy contents oozed out of the cup and splattered into the sink. She turned on the taps and shoved the mug under the hot water.

"Didn't your mother ever tell you not to mumble?"

"If you just fixed my car then I could leave and you wouldn't have to listen to my mumbling." She filled the mug then set it in the microwave.

Cade stood up. His flannel shirt stretched taut across his torso as he twisted left then right. She cleaned her hands of the grape jelly and the desire to touch him. If there was any justice at all the man would be covered in warts.

"You are not a very pleasant person, are you, Princess?"

"Takes one to know one."

"My ten-year-old niece invents better retorts." He yawned then sat down on the couch and stared at the TV.

"Is this a ploy to get more money?"

"I don't want your money, Princess."

"Then what do you want?"

"Peace and quiet."

"Peace and quiet." Egypt muttered, yanking the mug from the microwave. Hot water sprayed over the rim. Pain zipped up her arm as the droplets fell on her hand. "I hope he chokes on his peace and quiet."

"Stop mumbling and sit down."

She shuffled over to her assigned seat.

"You just want me away from all the sharp objects."

Cade grunted but refused to look at her as she flopped down next to him. Hot water scalded her tongue before sliding into her stomach. Warmth soon chased the chill from her limbs. She set the mug on the coffee table and picked up the brush. The metal bristles blurred as she twirled the brush in her hands.

Pete lumbered around the arm of the couch and plopped down on her feet. He glanced at her over his shoulder then nudged her hand with his snout.

"You want this, boy? You like your brush, huh?" Egypt stroked his fur from his collar to his tail. "What a good dog."

"Kinda overkill, don't you think?"

The bristles parted as Egypt raked the soft fur from the brush.

"Most sports are."

She set the fluffy mass on a pile of old magazines then groomed Pete's left side.

"Not the game. You and Pete."

Her hand stilled over the scruff of Pete's neck. Cade sounded angry. Was this his brush and not the dog's? Couldn't be. It had gray fur in it when she first picked it up, hadn't it?

"Me and Pete?"

"He likes you, all right." Cade crossed his arms and glared at her. "The damn dog likes you."

He propped his stocking feet on the pile of newspapers resting on the coffee table. His big toe poked out of the white fabric.

"I like him, too." Egypt scratched behind Pete's ear then continued brushing his coat.

"Yeah, well, he doesn't have any say in it."

"It?"

"My life." Cade's feet tapped together, an outlet for his irritation.

"Your life." Egypt scratched her head. Pleasure skittered across her scalp. Why did it always feel like she was missing part of the conversation? Her ears worked fine so that ruled out audio difficulties. That could only mean the glitch was in him.

"Yes. My life. I will marry who I want, not who the dog likes." He snatched a bottle of beer off the floor and raised it to his lips.

"Ooookay," she drawled.

"Don't."

"Don't?"

"Don't say 'okay' like you're humoring a five-year-old." Beer sloshed inside the bottle as he pointed at her.

"All right."

"You're doing it again."

"Am not." Her teeth clicked together. Now *she* was behaving like a five-year-old. She would have an intelligent conversation even if it was one-sided.

"Are, too."

"Perhaps if you just explained what you're talking about."

"You know perfectly well what I'm talking about." Cade shook the remote at her before switching stations. Cheering filled the air as Number 49 caught the ball and raced toward the end zone.

"You're talking about the dog and marriage."

"Exactly." He finished his beer in one gulp then set the empty bottle on the floor.

"And that makes sense to you?"

"As if you didn't know." His hand dropped over the side of the couch. A thump and a rattle later, another bottle of beer appeared.

Explanations swirled inside her skull.

"Are you drunk?"

"Is that your plan? Get me drunk then haul me to the preacher?" Cade straightened and glared at her. "I plan to be perfectly sober for the ceremony and the honeymoon afterwards."

His blue eyes raked her from head to toe. Finally, she was going to get her explanation. Unease itched across her skin. Why did she think she would be better off not knowing?

"Whose ceremony and honeymoon?"

"Ours." He raised the bottle in salute. Wickedness teased a smile from his lips.

"I am not marrying you."

"That's what I said." He nodded and turned his attention back to the television.

"You did not." Egypt stabbed the off button on the remote. Their conversation had definitely taken a turn down Bizarre Lane. Obviously, the man skated through school on good looks and not a working brain. "You just said you would be sober for our wedding."

"And honeymoon." He turned the TV back on.

"There isn't going to be a honeymoon or a wedding. I am *not* marrying you." She punched the off button. The television fell black.

"No, Princess, *I* am not marrying *you*."

"What's the difference?"

"The difference is that I didn't purchase a wedding dress or have all my friends give me wedding gifts for nuptials that will never take place."

"Wedding dress? Gifts?"

"Stop the innocent act, Princess. It was old before I hauled that enchanted cranberry over half the state. Did you actually think I wouldn't see them?"

Laughter rumbled up her throat and tickled her tongue before spilling past her lips.

"That's not my wedding dress, and those aren't my wedding gifts."

Pain stung her cheek as she slapped her hand over her mouth. No wonder he thought she was husband-hunting.

His eyes narrowed. "Oh, no? Then whose are they?"

"My sister's."

Red suffused his cheeks. "So, why do you have them?"

"She needed some last-minute alterations done on the dress."

Disbelief pulled his lips to the side.

"And you were altering it?"

"No, no. The woman who made the dress lives in the valley. She did the alterations. I'm just the courier."

"Uh-huh."

"The wedding's tomorrow." Loss tweaked Egypt's insides. At least it was a mild pinch and not the hold of vice grips. That was an improvement. Besides, she wasn't losing an ex-boyfriend, she was gaining a brother.

"Tomorrow. They're getting married on Christmas Eve. If you don't believe me, check the paper. The announcement was supposed to be printed today."

Cade grunted. His finger traced the scar down his cheek then settled in the cleft in his chin.

"So, why'd you wear the Blue Coat?"

Yes, the blue coat. She had almost forgotten. His catching sight of the wedding dress couldn't explain either the plethora of blue coats or his obsession with them.

"I've had it since high school."

"So, you didn't wear it to look like the figurine?"

Egypt stuffed her hand in her pocket. The packet of gum crushed inside her fist.

"What figurine?"

A groan escaped his lips as his head lolled against the couch.

"You really are an outsider, aren't you?"

"If you mean I'm not from Holly, then, yes, I'm an outsider. But that still doesn't explain the figurine."

He crammed his feet into his boots.

"I'll see to your car."

Pete crawled onto the warm sofa and curled up next to her.

"What about the figurine?"

"It doesn't matter." Cade slammed out the door.

Egypt watched him storm past the window, his anger stamped on every board. Pete looked at her and whined.

Chapter XII

He was an ass. A talking, two-legged donkey, spewing nothing but fecal matter. Christ! Old man Henderson hadn't even come close. Egypt might lead him on a merry chase, but he would have to crawl through a field of land mines before kneeling on broken glass to even get permission to chase her.

Hopelessness washed over him, knocking the strength from his knees. He slammed against her car. The cold metal roof sucked the warmth from his skin. She was the one. The reason the lights had fallen dark.

She was his soul mate, and he had blown it.

If God truly looked after fools then maybe he'd be given a second chance. His numb fingers plowed furrows into his hair. And a third. Hell, he'd probably need twenty chances before she'd even smile.

"Holiday's looking fit. Word is, she's been picked for the Christmas relay." Burl Dugan stepped from the barn, Egypt's marmalade cat stretched out on his arm and her hamster's tiny head sticking out of his collar.

"Hey, Dad."

"Not exactly the standard reaction when a fellow's reindeer has been chosen to pull the sleigh on Christmas." Burl tilted his head as he regarded his son.

"Yeah, well, I have a lot on my mind." Snow flew through the air as Cade swept his hand across the roof of the VW.

"Eight more strings are out. That makes one-quarter of the town square."

"You don't say?"

"Just did. Given any thought to our power problems, son?"

"You could say that." Red flesh chided Cade's lack of gloves. Red. How appropriate. His hands felt like they were on fire. He could get his gloves, but he would have to talk to her. Egypt. What was he going to say to her? *Sorry I was such an ass, but, hey, let's get married, anyway?*

"Well, son, it's not the generator, the bulbs or the fuses. Mr. Henderson thinks it could be your swearing—"

"It's Egypt, Dad." He needed help, lots of help. Cade met his father's eyes.

"That little girl?"

"She's the one."

"You don't say."

"She's not even from around here." Cade's heart pounded in his ears. Invisible bands squeezed his chest. Was this love or a fatal illness?

"That would explain the car." Burl nodded to the Volkswagen.

"She had the coat before I even made the figurine. And the hair. And the scarf. There's no way she could have known." This couldn't be love. No one fell in love that quickly. Lust. He understood lust. She was a beautiful woman, in a feisty, ornery way. What man wouldn't lust after her?

"So, you finally stopped running from the truth, eh, son?"

"Guess so."

"Seems to me you might have your work cut out for you." His father scratched his head and grinned. "She didn't seem to like you much."

"I know."

"This might go a ways toward mending fences, if you know what I mean." Burl nudged the picnic basket at his feet.

"What is it?" Hope spurted through Cade's chest. Perhaps someone had taken pity on him and sent a magic elixir. Hell, at this point he wouldn't turn down an aphrodisiac.

"Dinner. Your mom asked me to deliver it along with the animals." Burl looked from the purring cat to the basket. "Down you go, Puss."

Nutz stretched and extended his claws before leaping nimbly to the ground. Burl clicked his tongue while scooping the hamster from his collar.

"You better take this one. He'd get lost in the barn."

Cade glanced at the grooming cat.

"Or eaten."

His father lifted Cade's collar and slipped the furry creature inside.

"Keep him in your shirt. He's sensitive to the cold."

He turned to go.

"Thanks." Cade shifted his weight to the balls of his feet. The hamster squeaked as he explored his new home. Whiskers tickled Cade's skin. He resisted the urge to scratch.

Inspiration pinned him in place. His father should be able to help. After all, a man couldn't be married forty-plus years and not learn a thing or two about women.

"Dad?"

"Yeah?" Burl turned and regarded him.

"About Egypt..."

"You've dated women before, son."

"Yes, but she's her."

"That's a fact." His father winked.

"How did you win Mom?"

"Oh." Burl winced and shook his head. "You don't want to go there, son."

"But Mom said—"

"She was being kind."

"You didn't—"

"Son, your mother was closer to Death when I was courting her than she's been in the forty-two years since."

"Death?"

"Four times." Burl wiggled four fingers in the air. A frown pulled his lips. "Unless you count the baked Alaska fiasco. Which I don't, but your mother does."

"Baked Alaska?"

His father rocked back on his heels, smiling as he gazed into the past.

"Had to redo your grandparents' living room before the wedding. Delayed the big day three whole months, what with the fire and water damage."

"Fire and water damage?"

"The Curse of the Dugans, your grandpa called it."

"Curse of the Dugans?" Terror twitched along Cade's frame. No one had ever mentioned any curse before. Leave it to his father to mention it when his courtship was already firmly in the Land of Not Flippin' Likely.

"Yep. I got off lucky with your mom. Now, my father..." Burl shook his head and whistled. "Well, let's just say your grandma had white hair long before I was born. Yep, the Dugan women have to be strong and quick-witted, otherwise...well, let's just say they wouldn't be wives."

Cade dropped his head into his hands. White dotted his eyelids from the pressure of his palms. He had already experienced the Curse of the Dugans.

"I almost ran Egypt over with the sleigh."

"Already tried to kill her once, eh." His dad smiled. "That's good, son. Very good. If our luck holds you only have two more attempts left."

"Two more?"

"Want a little free advice, son?"

"About trying to kill her?" Hysteria jumped on his tongue. He could see it now. *Why, yes, sheriff, the dead woman is my fiancée. You see, I loved her to death.*

"What? No, no—about courtship."

"Uh, no, thanks."

133

"Women like romance," Burl rushed on. "You got to romance her. Candlelight. Wine. Flowers. The works."

"Romance?" That sounded harmless. Romance. Cade nodded. He could do that.

"Just avoid flaming desserts. And skiing—avalanches happen all the time." His father shuffled towards the fence, scratching his chin. "And cooking, definitely cooking. One little mix-up in boxes, and before you know it you're rushing to the hospital to get your stomach pumped."

He waved as he reached the gate.

"Fires, avalanches and food poisoning." The Dugan Curse. His courtship was doomed before it even started.

"That's a rather unique Christmas carol you're singing."

"It's not a carol." Cade spun around. His gaze roamed over her face. Such a beautiful shade of tan. How many years until he could duplicate her coloring with his brush?

"I know."

Why did she have to be so beautiful? Egypt, his soul mate. He would protect her, cherish her and woo her. He opened his mouth then snapped it shut. His tongue remained glued to the roof of his mouth. How the devil was he to win her if he couldn't even speak?

"I—"

"I thought you might need these." Her keys glistened in the fading sunlight.

"Thanks." His fingers brushed hers as he took the keys. Her lips parted. Her eyes widened. Her body was interested even if her mind urged her to run away. Perhaps he hadn't blown it after all.

One step closed the distance between them. Her warmth filled his lungs. Her pupils dilated. Her chest rose and fell. Physical attraction. An excellent starting point. Seduce her body, and her heart will follow.

"I have something for you." His words conjured goose bumps across her neck.

"You do?" Her throaty voice pulled on his aroused flesh. She turned her face to his. Passion weighted her lids.

"Yes."

Her lips parted, taking in his words. Anguish pinged inside him. He was jealous of his words, resented their entrance into such a coveted location. *Kiss her*, his body screamed.

Stitches squeaked and scampered onto his shoulder.

"Stitches! Where did you come from?" Egypt snatched the hamster from Cade's shoulder and hugged him to her cheek. Yet another reason to dislike the little rodent. Her cheek should be pressed against her future husband's.

Cade's vision blurred as he shoved his eyebrows up his forehead. And now he was jealous of a hamster. How much lower could a man sink?

"My father brought him by."

"And Nutz?"

Nuts. He was definitely crazy. His index fingers swirled over his temples, stirring his thoughts.

"Oh, the cat. He's in the barn."

"Thank you." She bounced at his side then skipped across the yard. She reached the barn door just as the cat sauntered out. He meowed once, sniffed the basket then rubbed his cheeks against the woven wicker. "Guess I should put Stitches back in his cage."

Eyes sparkling, she beamed at him.

He stopped breathing. His heart turned over; and for the first time in his life, Cade knew he was in love.

"Guess I should look at you."

"Me?"

"Your engine. Yes, your engine." In love and a complete idiot. He wrenched open the door. Her scent enveloped him as he slid behind the wheel. Cavemen had it easy. Just grab a woman by her hair and drag her to your cave. His gaze glided over Egypt's face. With that stubborn chin, there was no way she would stay put even with a saber-tooth tiger guarding the exit.

"Do you think you could hand me the cage?"

Rattling metal filled the car as he lifted the cage off the seat. He judged the distance between the steering wheel and his chest. It wasn't going to fit. A sigh huffed past his lips. Maybe this time he wouldn't make a fool of himself. He stepped from the car and held the cage out to her.

Egypt lifted the latch. Stitches' whiskers twitched before he walked across her open palm and scampered inside.

"Thanks."

"My pleasure."

She leaned forward. His heart picked up speed. Was she going to kiss him? Did she feel the attraction? Metal scraped metal.

"The cage." She bit her bottom lip as her gaze slipped from his.

"Yes, the cage." Cade collapsed onto the bucket seat. Of course, she wasn't going to kiss him. That would have been too easy. We couldn't have that. He stabbed the key into the ignition and cranked it. The engine sputtered then died.

"Well, I guess I should leave you to it." The skin between her eyebrows puckered before she turned and shuffled away.

Was she reluctant to leave him or confused about the energy crackling between them? Adrenaline jerked his muscles. He couldn't let her leave. Not yet.

"What was it doing before you broke down?"

"Running." She turned and took one step toward him. Her left foot paused by the right as if uncertain whether or not to proceed. Finally, she shrugged and took another step. "I was driving along when the dash lit up like a strand of Christmas lights and the engine died. I managed to pull to the side of the road before the car stopped rolling."

She leaned against the door. Her breasts rounded between the bars as she clasped Stitches' home against her chest.

"What happened when you tried starting the motor?" Cade resisted the urge to rip the cage away from her chest and massage away the abuse. The steering wheel creaked as he twisted his grip.

"Nothing."

"The starter didn't click?"

"Hmmm. Maybe. I don't remember. Why?"

"It's easier to recharge a battery than to replace a starter."

"Oh. Well, it could be the battery. But I know it isn't the oil. I just changed that before we left."

"You changed the oil?" An image flashed inside his skull. Inches of tan skin glistening with oil. Egypt moaning as he slicked more across her back, over her buttocks, between her thighs...

"Yes, I changed the oil. I'm not completely helpless."

Her irritation swept aside his erotic thoughts. He could seduce her later. First, he needed to persuade her that not all of his comments were insults.

"So, why do you need a mechanic?"

"I need to be home by tomorrow, and I thought a trained mechanic would get me back on the road tonight."

"I see." He twisted the key in the ignition. This time the engine clicked.

"I heard it click that time."

"Sounds like the battery, but I'll check the engine just in case." He eased around her and strolled to the back. Egypt followed on his heels. *Focus on the engine, Cade. You don't know if her presence indicates distrust or a willingness to be close to you.* His gaze drifted to the snowdrifts. That would cool him down, but then he'd have to explain why he was shoving snow down his pants.

He lifted the hood and blinked. Duct tape wrapped all the visible hoses, clumps of electrical tape were stuck to wires and a few garbage ties were standing in for clamps.

"Did you do this?"

"Do what?"

"This..." Cade swallowed the word *mess*. He needed to woo her not insult her. "This feat of mechanical artistry?"

"Most of it. Darrell taught me to wrap the leaking hoses in duct tape. This popped off on my way to work." She tapped a blackened hose attached to the radiator. "Luckily, I found a few ties in the car and wired it back on."

"Amazing."

"You think that's amazing—my dad suggested I use a paper clip to keep the valve open so the carburetor could get enough air."

Her presence was a Christmas miracle. How else could she have made it this far?

"Simply amazing."

"You said that." Her eyes narrowed and her lips pursed.

"So I did." Pleasant. He must remain pleasant. He suppressed a shudder. God only knew what other discoveries awaited him. He pried the cap off the battery. "There's no water in the battery."

His jaw ached. Grinding teeth filled his ear. His princess needed a keeper.

"I thought I purchased one of those no-fill batteries last time."

"I'll just add a bit of water and put it on the recharger."

"How long will that take?"

"A couple hours." Cade ran his hands over his clenched thighs. "You should be ready to go after dinner."

"Dinner?"

"My mother made it." He nodded towards the barn. "It's in the basket your cat is nuzzling."

"Oh."

"Why don't you take your animals inside while I degrease the engine?"

"Uh, sure. Come on, Nutz."

Cade watched the sway of hips as she walked away. If her battery wasn't dead then God had taken pity on him. Figuring out what was wrong with her engine could take a long time. Maybe even a lifetime.

Chapter XIII

"The figurine." Egypt leaned against the door as it snicked into its frame. "Can you believe it? I forgot all about the stupid figurine." She raised the hamster's cage level to her face. "Good thing my hands are attached. Who knows where I'd leave them if they weren't."

Stitches stared at her for a minute before digging through his food dish. He latched onto a sunflower seed then jammed it into his lumpy jowls.

"Unbelievable." She fit the cage into an empty shelf in Cade's entertainment unit. "You'd think by the way he acted that I'd asked for the location of the Holy Grail." She pulled a pack of gum out of her pocket and picked out a foil-wrapped stick. Cinnamon exploded across her tongue. "What's so important about this figurine he keeps yammering about?"

Nutz stalked over to a plate and sniffed at a half-eaten slice of pizza. He smacked the crust with his paw then waited a heartbeat before repeating the action. Unimpressed, he licked his paw and surveyed the room. His tail curled like an orange candy cane as he sauntered over to the couch and rubbed his side against the corner.

"That figurine is the key—I can feel it." Pete raised his head. His jowls flapped as he half-heartedly woofed. "What's up, boy? You know, don't you?" His silky ear slipped under her palm. Her fingers disappeared in his fur as she scratched behind his ears. "Too bad I don't speak dog."

Nutz jumped onto the couch. He stopped, his claws poking the fabric. His tail twitched. His fur bristled. Pete sat up and stared at the intruder. Egypt's exhale bubbled her closed lips. Nutz hated dogs, even wolf-dog hybrids.

"Don't..." Nutz hissed, his back arched so high he had almost folded himself in two. Pete barked. The noise pealed around the ceiling two stories above. Her eyes seemed to ping-pong in their sockets. Bile burned her throat; bitterness heated her tongue. She swallowed and closed her eyes. The world steadied under her feet. "...fight."

Papers crashed to the ground. She opened her eyes in time to see orange streak up the stairs; the gray dog lagged two risers behind. Bumps and yowls rent the air.

"Stop it!" Egypt's yell echoed back to her. Nutz's low growl rumbled through the air. Pete barked then yelped. A gray head appeared. Blue eyes stared at her through the honey-pine railing edging the loft. His pink tongue flicked over his nose, once then twice. "No more fighting, do you hear?"

The dog lumbered down the steps and trotted to her side.

"He scratched you, didn't he?" Pete whimpered as he shuffled closer and dropped his head below his shoulders. "Here let me take a look." He nudged her hand away from her side. "Aw, that's not too bad." He tucked his nose under her arm while she scratched both sides of his body. "You'll forget all about it in no time."

Nutz poked his head over the balcony and meowed.

"Mean kitty. He just wanted to play. This is his house, you know." The cat stuck both paws over the edge of the loft and rubbed his head on the post. "You best behave, Nutz, or you'll find yourself out in the cold barn." The cat blinked and rested his head on his outstretched forelegs. "It's okay, boy. He'll be nice to you from now on."

Nice. Egypt straightened and shook the fur from her hands. Balls of gray skimmed the crowded coffee table then floated to the carpet. Come to think of it, Cade had been nice to her. Too nice. His image flashed in her mind. Her heart thumped a few extra beats. Tingles raced across her skin to converge in her belly. The full lips, the tempting blue eyes and the vein throbbing at his temple. His congeniality had almost burst a blood vessel. So, what was the cause of this outbreak of pleasantness?

The figurine. Everything revolved around it. But how to get him to confess? Her hands fluttered about her sides before settling on her hips. Skin slipped under her thumbs as she traced the bony curve. Dinner. He had promised her dinner. Her gaze landed on the dirty dishes covering the counter.

And just what were they going to eat off of?

Well, if he was going to be nice to her she could rise above his past behavior, especially if it would put him in a more talkative mood.

Egypt strode into the kitchen. Dirty dishes covered every counter like a three-dimensional tablecloth.

"Just pick a place. Any place." She turned left then right. Her gum snapped as she faced the counter nearest the sink. "And we have a winner."

She slapped on the tap, rinsed dishes then loaded them into the dishwasher. One-and-a-half counters later the dishwasher was full. She set a blue-and-white detergent tablet on the bottom of a glass, shut the door and punched the on button. The sound of rushing water filled the air.

"Well, that's done, but we still don't have any clean dishes." With a sigh she shoved her sleeves up to her elbows then filled the sink with hot soapy water. Foam shot into the air as a stack of plates plopped into the solution. A handful of glasses gurgled before settling atop the plates.

Warmth seeped under her skin as she whittled away the grime. She would have all the answers when she left tonight. Today would be a memory, and Cade...

Loss twisted her insides. She would put him far from her mind. Her fingernail bent as she scratched at the dried yolk adhering to the plate. The blob scratched free.

Well, he would have to be resurrected when she told of her adventures. Indeed, her family would need to know about his part in the whole breakdown fiasco—and then there was the wedding. With any luck, days would pass before he was relegated to a memory. Maybe even weeks. No doubt her parents would demand she retell her story at their New Year's party.

Her parents. Egypt slapped her forehead. Suds sprinkled her shirt. Pain tingled across the skin and pricked her temples. She had forgotten about her parents. Her gaze flew to the clock. Three hours late. No doubt her mother had called every hospital from Phoenix to the New Mexican boarder. And her Dad...

A shudder rippled along her spine. Her father had probably undertaken some major household renovation in the midst of the chaos caused by Paris's impending wedding.

Her mother would never forgive her.

The green scouring pad blurred as it circled. Water sluiced over the plate and her hands. She had to find a way to get in touch with them before she had to exchange her first-born child for forgiveness. Water raced down her hands. Droplets splattered against the stainless steel sink. Egypt reached for the nearest towel, dried her hands then tossed the damp towel onto the counter. Grape jam streaked her palms.

"Great, just great." Her wrinkled flesh disappeared into the water. A few quick rubs and they emerged jelly-free. She eyed the towel. "I'm not falling for that again."

Her faded jeans darkened to indigo as she dried her hands on the denim.

"Now what?" Her mind went blank as determination pursued her last thoughts. "I needed clean hands toooo..." Her right hand twirled in the air like a beater. Frustration clawed at her resolve. "Something to do with...ahhhh."

She scooped pots and pans into the sink. Her hands hovered over the bergs of bubbles floating in the coppery dishwater.

"Think, Egypt, think. You were standing here, washing a plate and plotting about the figurine." The recent past replayed in her mind's eye. "Yes. It had something to do with the figurine and a story. Story? Oh, my God, my parents and the phone."

The pine cabinets blurred into one long streak of amber as she spun on her heel. Cade had to have a phone. But would it work when the ones at the hotel were out? Knuckles popped as she milked her fingers. Her gaze drifted to the window.

Pristine snow glistened on pine boughs. Weak light bounced off the individual slats comprising the barn's siding. Not one snowflake flitted through the air. The day seemed to be clear, just as the weatherman had forecast. Had the hotel women lied to her? No, the phone had definitely been dead, but it had worked for the local calls.

Hope fluttered inside her breast. Maybe the lines had been fixed. She scanned the walls and counters. No phone.

"It doesn't have to be in the kitchen." Her gaze traveled to the living room, and she groaned. The place was such a mess her car battery would be recharged before she found the phone. Unless...

Thoughts stumbled over themselves in their rush to reach her consciousness.

"Every phone needs a jack. And every jack needs a wall."

Egypt strolled into the dining room. No phone jack marred the wainscoting or the plaster above the chair rail. She stepped into the living room, surveying the dry wall. Nothing. Frustration mounted as she reached the stairs. Upstairs? She didn't want to go up there. No doubt his bedroom was there. She spit her gum into its wrapper. The warm gum oozed around the paper as she squeezed.

What choice did she have? The only room she hadn't searched on this level was the bathroom. No one put a phone in the bathroom, or did they? Nonsense. She had already spent time in there. Surely, she would remember seeing a telephone.

Her hand rested on the newel post. She wasn't snooping nor was she looking for anything to fuel her fantasies—er, story. So what if he had a big bed with satin sheets and mirrors above his mattress. Her breasts tightened at the thought of satin slicking against naked flesh. She wasn't interested in his sex life. Not one bit. Sweat beaded on the round post. She needed a phone, pure and simple. Her left foot rested on the first riser.

"You've cleaned."

Her heart slammed against her chest. Heat scalded her cheeks. Don't be foolish, Egypt. He can't know what you were thinking. She forced her gaze to meet his. Electricity snapped across his blue irises. His dimple winked seconds before he cupped his hands in front of his mouth.

"You didn't have to wash the dishes. You're a guest."

Her brain chugged to life. She needed to respond, needed to sound casual. She swallowed the lump of anxiety lodged in her throat.

"A...a guest?" There. That sounded almost normal—huskier than usual but not guilty.

"Yes, you know—someone invited to stay and visit for a bit."

"But, earlier—"

"Ah, about earlier." He quickly shrugged out of his jacket and slapped it onto an empty hook on the coat tree. "I owe you an apology."

"An apology?" Her thoughts fled as he unbuttoned his flannel shirt, revealing the white knit fabric underneath.

"I apologize most heartily for my crassness, not to mention rude behavior." He set his hand over his heart and bowed slightly. "Am I forgiven?"

His palm skimmed his flat stomach before brushing his thigh.

Desire exploded inside her belly. Her primitive self trampled the veneer of civilized behavior. *Touch him. Claim him. Take him.*

"Huh? Uh, yeah, sure." Great, Egypt. What's next—grunting and rifling his hair to pick out the bugs?

"Your cat should be safe upstairs. There's not much even an inquisitive feline can get into." Still holding her gaze, he tugged the end of his flannel shirt out of his jeans. One nonchalant shrug later, the shirt slid down his arms and joined the jacket on the coat tree.

"My cat?" Strong bones weakened like warm gelatin. The white undershirt had come free when he'd freed the flannel shirttail. If he would just raise his hands she would get a glimpse of flesh. Maybe even spy a trail of hair marking the way to unadulterated pleasure.

"Yes." He bent down to untie his bootlaces.

His shirt slipped forward. A rectangle of smooth flesh met her inquisitive gaze. Not bad, not bad, but if he just turned a bit she might get a nice view of his behind.

"That was why you were going upstairs, wasn't it?"

"Umm." Leather tightened across his flanks as he turned slightly. Who knew stripping could be this erotic?

"Egypt?"

"What?" She blinked, wiping away the sensual haze.

"Wasn't that why you were going upstairs?"

"Upstairs?" Cold reality froze the molten desire. She knew the answer to his question. "No."

She wrapped her hands around the banister to keep from clapping.

"Then why...?"

"The phone. I need to use the phone." She nodded, happy to be on firm ground once again.

"I thought you used the one at the hotel?"

"It was out." Like she had been out of her mind, but hopefully both states would prove temporary. Get a grip, Egypt. You don't even like the man. For all you know he has a split personality. Mean one minute, acting like her dream lover the next.

"If the hotel's phone is out, mine's probably out, too."

"Oh." Metal exploded in her mouth as her teeth nicked her lip. Her parents would be worried.

"You were supposed to be home hours ago, weren't you?"

"Yes."

"We can always try," he grinned. "The phone's in the studio."

"Studio?" Her gaze traveled up the stairs. If his studio was upstairs then where did he sleep?

"Yes, it's in the back."

"Out back?"

"No, not outside." He closed the distance between them. "In the back."

Egypt looked around. "Where?"

"Watch." He smiled at her. His lone dimple flashed before he tugged on the hall light sconce. The wall in front of her clicked and parted. The air filled with grinding as unseen wheels turned. "Pretty cool, huh?"

Trees and snow met her gaze. Had he lied? It looked like the outside to her. Light bounced off the floor-to-ceiling glass. Massive beams divided the see-through expanse. The gray afternoon light filtered into the room, washing easels, cabinets, shelves and tables in its pearly hue. A few stools hunkered over the shiny concrete floor.

"Amazing."

Brushes fanned around the lips of cups. Tubes of paint representing the entire spectrum lay in rows on the table. Wooden tools stretched across a tray next to a slab of clay wrapped in plastic. Pads of paper and rolls of canvas were stowed neatly into niches. Wooden dividers separated pencils, charcoals and pastels.

"It's so organized."

"Of course, it's where I work." He cupped her elbow. His fingers stroked her upper arm through her sweater. "Do you paint, draw or sculpt?"

"I can barely manage calligraphy."

"Well, here's the phone." He ushered her over to a large drafting table. A gold-and-cream antique phone squatted in the corner. He gently lifted the mouthpiece and handed it to her.

For a moment, Egypt stared at the receiver in her hand. How could such a mundane thing exist in an artist's wet dream? She held the receiver next to her ear then tapped the flash button. Nothing. No dial tone, no buzz, not even a crackle.

"It's dead."

"Hmmm." He stuck his hands in his pockets.

"I don't suppose you have a telegraph or a carrier pigeon somewhere around the house?"

"Nope." He stroked his scar. "Anyone in your family have email?"

"My brother, but I don't see how that would be of any use with the phone dead."

"Ah, but I have a cable modem not a telephone modem." He spun her about and shepherded her to an armoire. Once there he pulled open the doors. A computer monitor stared back at her.

Egypt blinked. A giant eye filled the twenty-four-inch screen. It blinked then resumed staring. The eyeball floated in the pixel socket as it looked up, down, left then right. As soon as Cade touched the mouse the eyeball blinked and disappeared. He clicked an icon then slid a chair over to her.

"Have a seat."

"This is great. My brother's online all the time."

"I'll leave you to it, then." Without a backward glance, he strode from the room.

Chapter XIV

"Everything all right?" Cade looked up from smoothing the quilt over the table.

"Yes." Egypt shoved her hands into her jean pockets. No wonder he had such beautiful hands. He was an artist. What would it be like to be one of his pieces, feel his hands running over her shoulders, down her breasts, skimming her belly—

"You sure?" He swiped three green pillar candles off the counter and set them in the center of the table next to a basket full of crimson poinsettias. "You were in there a while."

Insane, she had gone insane. Skin slipped under her fingers as she massaged her forehead. Desire hummed along her muscles. A flick of her wrist disrupted the notes of desire.

"My sister wanted to make certain I hadn't forgotten anything." At his look of puzzlement, she elaborated. "Instant messaging. My brother was online."

"Oh. Well. Dinner's almost ready. Care to take a seat?" He held out a ladder-backed chair and patted the red cushion.

She could do this. She could have a normal conversation with the man. Just don't think of his hands. Her wild gaze darted around the room. The now-clean room. Gone were the discarded clothes and the dirty dishes.

"You cleaned."

"Wasn't that my line?" His dimple flashed at her. "I hope you're hungry. Ma made enough for a small army." A bowl of garlic mashed potatoes chinked against a dish of green beans. Steam wafted up from a platter of roasted chicken and danced over the brown liquid filling the gravy boat. Butter glistened on the golden Parker House rolls heaped in a wicker basket.

"Everything looks wonderful." Her nose quivered in delight. Her stomach rumbled in jealousy.

"It should taste even better." His arm brushed hers as he took the seat next to her. He smiled as he took the wobbling bowl of potatoes from her hand. "No fire extinguisher or stomach pump necessary."

"That's the second time today you've muttered something about stomach pumps and fire extinguishers."

"Actually," he grinned at her, "I think it was fires, avalanches and food poisoning."

"Oh, my." A bit of roll absorbed her groan. He was doing it again, distracting her from her true mission. Frustration drained the color from her knuckles. Cheer up, Egypt, at least he's being talkative. Now, steer the conversation in the direction you want.

"My thoughts, exactly." He scooped a pearl onion and a chunk of bacon out of the green beans.

"About that figurine..."

"Will you be the maid of honor at your sister's wedding?"

"It was the least she could do, considering she's marrying my boyfriend, um, ex-boyfriend."

"Your ex-boyfriend." He whistled low in his throat. "Now, that sounds like an interesting story."

"It is." Egypt shoved a piece of chicken into her mouth. He wasn't going to turn this back on her. She controlled this conversation, and he was going to tell her what she wanted to know.

The roasted chicken dissolved on her tongue.

"And will you tell me about it?" He added more soda to her glass. Bubbles spiraled through the dark beverage, joining the foam rapidly popping on the surface.

"I might." She speared one green bean. The ends drooped as she twirled her fork.

"You might?"

Victory charged through her veins, slammed into her heart and shoved her lips into a smile. "If you tell me about the figurine everyone keeps mentioning."

"Deal."

"You go first." Unease itched across her skin. She hated it when she and a friend said the same words at the same time. That he had echoed her thoughts only made the matter much more disturbing.

"Ladies first."

"How do I know you'll keep your end of the bargain?"

"Scout's honor." Cade held up three fingers and laid his hand over his heart. "Besides, my story's boring. No doubt you'll be snoring before I'm even finished telling it, and I'll be cheated out of my part of the bargain."

"Well, mine isn't that exciting, either."

He cocked his left eyebrow and stroked his scar before sliding a few more slices of chicken breast onto his plate.

"You're right. Anything that gets Pete off the couch isn't exciting. It's downright miraculous." He tossed a piece of chicken skin to the drooling canine then trailed his fingers up his glass. "Well?"

"I don't know where to begin." Egypt forced the green bean mush down her throat. Reluctance drained from her weighted limbs to pool in her feet. Why had she agreed to this bargain? Nothing, not even learning about that stupid figurine, was worth revealing her secret.

"The beginning's a good place." Cade leaned forward and rested his chin on his steepled fingers.

Pursed lips aimed her sigh into her hairline. She would honor the pact. Candlelight glinted off the tines of her fork. He had better do the same.

"Darrell and I met at the mall."

"Darrell, of duct tape fame?"

"One and the same." Egypt laid her fork across her plate. Either Cade had a good memory or he wasn't happy with her "tampering" with the engine. Tampering. Her fingernails scratched trails around her lips. That's what Darrell had called it. Funny how hindsight twisted his joke into sarcasm.

"How'd you two meet?"

"At the food court." The cotton napkin pleated under her fingers. "He had taken a job at Snyder's during the semester break. I worked in the mall, too."

"At Winter's Wonderland."

"Yes." A very good memory. What else had she revealed about herself? Nothing too damning, she hoped. "And, well, you either ate at the food court or brown-bagged it. Anyway, one day, right in the middle of a particularly nasty week, he walked over and asked if the seat next to me was taken. I told him it wasn't and he sat down, even offered to share his french fries with me. We got to talking, and he confessed he'd been watching me for about a week and that today he'd finally gotten up the courage to ask me out."

"He stalked you?"

"No. He was just making sure Max was a friend and not a boyfriend."

"Max?" Cade pushed out of his chair. He yanked his plate off the table and stalked to the sink.

"He works in the candy store, next door to Winter's." Egypt set her silverware on her plate and joined him. "Sometimes, when business is slow, we stand outside our respective stores and chat. I think Max was a movie critic in another life.

"So, Max is a just friend." Popping filled the air as he dipped first one ear then another towards its respective shoulder.

"You sound just like Sam." Egypt watched as mashed potatoes dripped from the spoon and plopped into the plastic container. He sounded like Sam. What had she been thinking? Sam had been jealous, while Cade...

"Sam?"

"Max's boyfriend." She thumped the spoon against the edge of the bowl. Vibrations tingled up her finger. *Don't read too much into it, Egypt.* He was simply trying to understand the story. Nothing more.

"I see."

"Anyway, the night of our date, Darrell walks into the store with a single red rose."

"A rose. That's romantic." Cade flicked the petals of the poinsettia.

"He was really handsome in his jacket and tie."

"Jacket and tie?"

Egypt set the dirty bowl on the counter and picked up a towel.

"Are you all right? Your face is flushed, and that tic in your jaw is back."

"I don't have a tic." He squeezed the words through his teeth, slapped on the faucet and scrubbed at the finish on the clean plate.

"Okay." Egypt stuffed the towel into a glass, tugged it free then set the dry cup in the nearest cabinet. Cade was obviously the strong, silent type; no wonder he strained the words through his lips like he was verbally constipated.

"So, he dressed up for your date."

"Not exactly." Her red fingers throbbed as she unwound the towel from around her hand. "He'd just gotten off work."

He tilted his head and regarded her through narrowed eyes. "So, it was a spur-of-the-moment thing?"

"No. Maybe. Anyway, we went to see—oh, what is that movie's name? You know, Sandra Bullock's latest?"

154

"The chick flick?" The towel splattered against the counter. His biceps bulged as he scrubbed the grape jelly.

"Yeah, well, the title's not important. He actually said he liked it."

Cade's eyebrow soared towards his hairline. He opened his mouth then shut it again. His teeth clicked together. His lips thinned. Anger hugged his frame tighter than his leather pants. She clasped her hands behind her back. She refused to pacify him. He had wanted to hear the whole story, from the beginning.

"We talked about it over a candle-lit dinner and then he took me back to the store."

"The store?"

"Yeah. He had wanted me to feel comfortable."

He chucked the towel into the sink, leaned against the counter and crossed his arms.

"What kind of nut job wants his date to feel comfortable? Hell, er, heck, a real date resembles foreplay. The man wants his date to feel excited, beautiful and sexy. Comfortable describes a pair of sneakers or old jeans but never, ever a date."

Excited. Beautiful. Sexy. Foreplay. Her heart thumped against her breastbone. She could well believe those words would described a date with Cade. She took a step closer to him. Pete pressed against her thigh, stopping her progress. Fur swallowed her finger, tickled her palms. *The story, Egypt, focus on the story.*

"The movie theater and the restaurant were both in the mall. Neutral ground." Not exciting by any stretch of the imagination, and she had quite an imagination. "I had my car so I could leave anytime I wanted."

Strange. Darrell's chivalry now seemed self-serving, a safety net in case the date hadn't gone as he wanted.

"A clever stalker."

"He's not a stalker. He's sensitive, kind and thoughtful." If her defense of her soon-to-be brother-in-law sounded lame to her ears, how would it sound to Cade? Egypt draped the towel through the oven door handle.

"And marrying your sister."

"I never said he was perfect."

"So, how'd they meet? Him and your sister."

"We'd been dating steadily for about six months. The holidays were approaching and..." Anxiety twitched along her frame. Her hands pantomimed the scene, trying to convince both the audience and the storyteller.

Cade held up a hand. "Let me guess—no family."

"He has family. They just live back East, somewhere in New Jersey—or is it New York? They're coming out for the wedding. Anyway, we were getting kinda serious."

"Kinda serious?" He plucked her fluttering hands out of the air. The pads of his thumbs glided over her knuckles and dipped between her fingers. "You doubted his intentions."

"Yes. No." Synapses stuttered, trying to carry the sensations to her brain. Heaven. She was in Heaven, lost in a torrent of pleasant sensations. "It had to be serious."

"Had to?"

"I hadn't had any of the dreams."

"Dreams?"

Egypt yanked her tingling hands from his ministration and rammed them into her pocket. The Devil had seduced her into betraying herself. Her gaze shot longingly to her jacket. Her tongue flicked over her dry lips. Too bad she'd eaten the last stick of gum.

"What dreams, Egypt?"

Lie. Lie as if your life depended on it, so that hot look blazing in his eyes doesn't freeze to wary friendship.

"The ones where my boyfriends fall in love with my friends."

Skin slid over bone as Egypt tried to mold her face into another's. So, this is the punishment for being a basically honest person. The lying pathways atrophy and die, never to be used even when desperately needed.

"I can see why dreaming about your boyfriend loving another woman would be disturbing."

"Well, it isn't the dreams per se." Egypt shoved past him. *Keep your mouth shut. Pinch your lips together if necessary.* She was obviously in a truth-telling rut. "It's the fact that every one of them came true."

Tape. She needed tape. If her mouth refused to stay closed on its own she would help it.

"Every one?"

"Yes," she hissed.

"How many have there been?"

"Seven. Ten at the most." Egypt stopped at the threshold of the studio. Where had she seen that roll of masking tape? On the counter or in one of the drawers she had rifled.

"Ten?"

"All right, thirteen. Fourteen, if you include my sister Paris." She tugged open the armoire doors and stared at the shelves. No tape in sight. What would he do if she started opening the drawers? "I have a lot of friends."

"Boyfriend-stealing friends."

What was she thinking? Taping her mouth shut. She was an adult, for crying out loud. Surely a little self-control wasn't beyond her.

"Do you want to hear the rest of the story or not?"

"By all means, continue."

She eased the armoire doors shut and took a steadying breath. He had already heard the worst. What possible harm could the rest do?

"Anyway, I brought Darrell home last Christmas, and the two of them just clicked."

"Why did you bring him home if you dreamt about him and your sister?"

"It was too late to change our plans." She trampled her stirring conscience, refusing to admit even to herself that she had been testing Darrell's loyalty. "Okay, now spill."

"Spill?"

"The figurine." She spun on her heel and poked him in the chest.

"I made it." Cade caught her hand between his.

"And?"

"It's what I do. I'm the artist you mentioned in the sleigh. Holly is the inspiration for the Christmas Village you like so much." He laced his fingers through hers and tugged her to the other side of the studio. With his free hand he flipped back the lid on a cardboard box and removed silver statues. "These are pewter castings, once painted they become the figurines."

She stared at the army of gray people.

"I think I'm still missing something. Why would these make you angry?"

Cade pulled open a drawer and lifted out three boxes of figurines.

"This is the mayor and his new bride. The barber and his fiancée. Miss Hutchins and her new boyfriend."

"Yes, yes, I got that part. The Christmas Village is modeled after Holly and her inhabitants."

"None of these people met until after I crafted the figurines. In fact, only the barber, the mayor and the baker lived in Holly before I went to work. To top it off, their partners looked almost exactly like the figurines, even wearing the same clothing the first day they met."

"So, you're saying that you brought these people together because your statues depicted them as couples?" Who did he think he was? Cupid with a sculpting habit?

"Did you match your friends with your ex-boyfriends because of a dream?"

He had a point. Not that she needed to tell him. His gloating grin dared her to contradict him. If discretion was the better part of valor, then her retreat should be downright heroic.

"I don't see anyone wearing a turquoise jacket and purple scarf."

"That's over here." He lifted a catalog out of a drawer. The pages fanned the air before falling to the sides.

A man and a woman stared at each other, lost in a world of their own making.

"See?"

"Her scarf is blue. Mine's purple." Egypt's fingernail tapped on the woman's picture.

"But the original figurine's wasn't." He opened another drawer and lifted out a sketchbook. Faces winked at her as he flipped through the pages. "Originally, it was purple." He held the page open for her to see.

Egypt stared at the picture. A purple scarf fluttered behind her. So the woman had brown hair and light-brown eyes. That didn't prove anything. Her gaze shifted to the woman's partner. Blue eyes sparkled. A lone dimple winked.

"Is the man supposed to be you?"

"It *is* me."

"There's no scar on his left cheek, and he's smiling. I've never seen you smile."

"I smile." Cade glared at her then forced his lips back.

"That's not a smile. That is what Little Red Riding Hood saw before the wolf tried to eat her. A smile—his smile—is an expression of joy. And what's this?" Egypt tapped the white speck dotting the collar of the woman's jacket.

"A lift ticket. When she originally came to me, she had a lift ticket attached to her zipper."

A chill swept over Egypt's cheeks. Her palms felt clammy against her fingers. It was a coincidence, nothing more. Lots of people left their lift tickets on their jackets. She wasn't the only one. Besides, hers had been there since her senior year in high school, years before.

"Given the rather, er, overwhelming coincidences between your creations and reality, why would you..."

"Create my future mate?"

"Yes."

"I lost a bet with my brothers. I never expected Holly would be flooded with Blue Coats."

"Blue Coats?"

"Apparently, word has spread of the 'coincidences' and, well, some women are willing to do anything to keep the legend going."

"And have you met her?"

"I think we have a problem, Princess." Cade smiled and dodged her question. "It's seems to be snowing."

"Snowing?" Egypt followed his gaze to the window. A mass of swirling white consumed everything beyond the glass.

"You can't leave in the middle of a blizzard, not with your car acting up. You could end up stranded, and I wouldn't be around to rescue you. Besides, the roads hereabouts are the last to be plowed."

"What am I going to do?"

"If worse comes to worst, you can always spend the night here, with me."

Her mind supplied the pictures to his sound track. Satin sheets, mirrors on the ceiling, yards of naked flesh. Excitement surged in her veins. Okay, so maybe she wasn't so unaffected by the story of that stupid figurine. That didn't mean she wanted to be his future mate. Did it?

Chapter XV

Egypt had taken the news very well. Cade straightened the pencils in the coffee cup. Of course, he hadn't mentioned that he knew she was his soul mate. He could just imagine her sprinting through the glass window screaming, into the blizzard beyond. No, it was best if she became accustomed to the idea slowly. Fortunately for him, this snowstorm provided the perfect opportunity.

Today, he would either win his dream girl or get her killed.

Deer droppings. Why had his father picked today to mention the Dugan Curse? Cade's hair pricked along his scalp. Maybe the curse was a trick. Burl Dugan wasn't above the occasional practical joke. But that didn't explain the sleigh incident. He would have to be careful, very careful.

His gaze traveled down her creamy sweater to their clasped hands. She hadn't objected to his touch, hadn't jerked her hand out of his. Tangible progress from this afternoon's attempt to leap from the moving sleigh. She was attracted to him. He felt it every time her hot gaze flicked over him. Every time a blush crept up her neck to stain her cheeks. Unfortunately, he also felt her resistance.

Color bled into the tips of her fingers and out of his. Their clasped hands trembled. Spine straight and shoulders back,

161

Egypt glared at the latest impediment to her journey home. Tan eyes widened then narrowed, as if she could will the snow to stop.

She was afraid.

The certainty settled on his shoulders. But did she fear him, or her reaction to him? His body screamed its impatience. If she hadn't objected to a little hand-holding, how would she react to a brush of their shoulders? Easy, Cade. The situation required finesse not mauling by a human octopus. Just take it one touch at a time.

"You needn't break out the good sheets just yet. I mean, how long can the snow last?"

"Longest blizzard I can remember lasted two and a half days."

"Two and a half *days*!" Her cold fingers slipped from his grasp. She trudged across the room and rested her forehead against the dual pane window. "No. It can't."

Guilt gnawed on his insides. He had been selfish, thinking only of himself and his second chance. She needed to get home, and he would see that she got there.

"You know, this little blow is already losing steam. I can practically see that tree just beyond the deck."

"Where?" Her hand fogged a silhouette on the glass.

"Right there." He poked the glass next to her hand. What would it hurt to slip his fingers under hers and warm the chilled flesh next to his heart?

"I don't see it." Her fingers wiggled in his hand's direction before she jerked them off the pane and shoved them into her pockets. "Thanks for trying to cheer me up."

"Just being a considerate host." Cade forced his gaze to remain focused somewhere beyond the glass. If she noticed his elation she would obviously attribute it to less-than-honorable motives. "Everything ends eventually."

She spun on her heel and shuffled to the table. Her hair stirred as she thumbed through his drawing tablet.

"Eventually might not be soon enough. I have to be in Dragoon's Springs by four o'clock tomorrow."

"I'm certain your family would rather you remained safe than rush to their side."

"My parents would, definitely, but Paris..." Her lower lip disappeared between her teeth. "Her wedding is the day after tomorrow, and I have her wedding dress."

"She's already stolen your boyfriend. Surely, she wouldn't want you to risk your life over a silly dress."

"Well," Egypt shrugged. "It's not quite that..."

Anger shrank his muscles; his bones trembled instead of snapping. Crushed candy canes. He'd definitely accompany Egypt home and give her obnoxious sister an uncensored piece of his mind.

"What is it, then?"

"The first time this...situation happened, I kinda did something." Egypt twisted her ring finger and stared somewhere over his left shoulder.

"Who wouldn't? If a supposed friend purloined my lover, they should expect a bit of revenge." He stepped into her line of vision. "So what was it, Princess? Frogs in the punch? Salt in the champagne? An accidental step on the bridal train accompanied by the sound of ripping fabric or a falling bride?"

"No. Nothing like that." Amusement undulated across her lips. "We, Paris and I, just soaped up the groom's car windows, let the air out of a few tires."

Cade blinked. Had he missed something?

"Soaped up the windows?" He had stopped soaping windows at age eight.

"Hey, they almost missed their plane to Hawaii."

"And this horrendous action banned you from all further nuptials?"

"No. No one other than my sister and I knew who was responsible."

163

"I see. She's afraid you still have feelings for Duct Tape Darwin." Oxygen solidified in Cade's lungs. What would he do if she admitted being in love with her sister's fiancée? Change her mind, of course. She belonged with him.

"Not likely—I doubt exploding rockets could separate them. I was supposed to drive up yesterday, but Mr. Winters became ill, and I had to stay and help at the store. I mean, he was nice enough to give me a whole week off, including the two days before Christmas. That's practically a miracle in the retail world."

"And?"

"Paris wasn't happy with the delay, especially when she called and Mr. Winters answered the phone. He was there for all of five minutes, and only to give me my Christmas present, but, well, she might think I did this on purpose."

"Unless you're related to Jack Frost or Mother Nature, no rational person would blame you for conjuring a blizzard."

"No one is rational a week before a wedding." Egypt ran her hands down her chest, patted her pockets then chewed on her fingernail. "I guess I should let my brother know about the latest snafu."

"Instant Messenger to the rescue."

"Email. I'm not up to dealing with my sister's paranoia at the moment."

She looked so lost, Cade had to resist the urge to hug her to his chest and kiss away her worries. His blood heated at the thought. Flames licked along his frame. He forced his arms to his side, winced as the feeling returned to his uncurled fingers. He needed a distraction. They needed a distraction.

Outside, a pine tree materialized before being swallowed by white flakes. Someone was definitely looking out for him.

"Are you feeling up to decorating a Christmas tree?"

"A Christmas tree?"

"Yeah. My neighbors have reminded me of my dearth of Christmas spirit, and since I did chop down that tree I think it only fitting it should get all decked out in Christmas finery before being confined to the wood pile."

"Well," she said, tapping her lip, "that's one way to pass the time."

"I'll meet you in the living room when you're finished."

Cade sauntered into the great room. He would have to return the poinsettias to Mrs. Saunders' porch as soon as the storm died. He flicked the curtain and peered into the whiteness. He just hoped her romantic nature overcame her protectiveness about the prize-winning plants. Not that the poinsettias and candles had been as romantic as he had hoped. Still, he hadn't known he was competing with Duct Tape's single red rose and chick flick.

He smothered the surge of jealousy and lit the kindling in the fireplace. The newspaper curled as he blew on the spreading flame. He'd bet what's-his-name never had a roaring fire on a cold winter's day.

"Get a grip, Cade." He poked the smoldering log. "And not around Duct Tape's neck. She's with you now. She belongs with you."

The poker rattled against its holder. He had all night to convince her. His hand skimmed his belly before his thumb hooked around a belt loop. He should be thankful for this time. His dinner seemed to be digesting. No flaming desserts, stomach pumps or avalanches.

Maybe the Dugan Curse had skipped a generation.

The grandfather clock tolled seven times. Seven o'clock. Twelve hours to win fair maiden, or at least get her to agree to see him again. Decorating the tree should provide plenty of opportunities for meaningful conversation and accidental touches. His gaze swept the room. Six boxes of decorations.

Where should he start? Which job would she prefer? His father had always strung the lights while his mother...

His mother preferred her children to decorate the tree. Cade lifted the lid off a box of lights. He and Egypt didn't have any children. Yet. Would their offspring have the Dugans' blue eyes or Egypt's warm ones? Maybe they could keep trying until they had several of each. God knew he was willing.

"Do you think the buses are running?"

"Buses?" His heart jumped into his throat. Thank Holiday's horns he hadn't been speaking out loud. "They only come through on Mondays. I doubt even the shuttles are running during this."

Her shoulders drooped. "Just thought I'd ask."

"You ready?" Strands of clear lights waved from his right hand. The multicolored lights dangled from his left.

"It's a big tree." Her gaze raked the ponderosa pine as she sauntered into the room. "The storm might have blown itself out by the time we finished decorating it."

"It's possible." Cade thumped on his chest until his heart decided to beat normally. She wasn't anxious to leave him. She just needed to get home. Any help he provided in achieving her goal would make the introduction to his future in-laws that much smoother. A win-win situation. "Which job would you prefer? Lights? Ornaments? Or knick-knacks?"

"Lights," she answered holding out her hands.

He slipped the stands into her waiting palms, making certain her fingers grazed the backs of his hands as he pulled away.

"They should all work."

"Aren't you going to help?" The tiny bulbs gouged Egypt's flesh and dispersed the tingles waltzing up her arms. How could he be so unaffected?

"I thought I'd pop some popcorn."

"Popcorn?" Cade massaged his hand. He was acting indifferent. Egypt coughed a bark of laughter from her throat. Her touch affected him. "You're still hungry after that meal? After that incredible cheesecake?"

He pushed his sleeves up to his elbows. Black hair covered his corded forearms.

"It's for stringing. After the holidays, I set the tree outside and allow the birds to feast on the garland."

"I see."

Loss pinched her insides as he disappeared behind the kitchen island. He set a hot air popper on the counter. Was he avoiding her? Did he think she was like the rest of his Blue Coats? The clear lights clattered to the floor. She wasn't one of his groupies, and she would prove it to him before the night was over.

"I'm going to need some help. The tree is taller than I am." Pine needles scratched her arm as she laid the lights on the branches.

"Just holler when you're ready."

A short time later, Cade set two massive bowls of popcorn on the counter, grabbed a bag of cranberries out of the refrigerator and joined her by the tree.

"Perfect timing," Egypt said, stepping from behind the tree. Her arms ached from tucking the strand in the branches above her head.

"I aim to please." His palms cupped her hands before easing the lights from her grip. Branches bent against his chest as he leaned closer to the tree. "Is this acceptable?"

"If you could just work them a little deeper into the tree. No like, this." She climbed the stepstool and pushed the lights a couple of inches closer to the trunk. Cade stepped onto the bottom step. His warm breath swept over her neck. His scent invaded her lungs. "This way the, er, ornaments can hang from the edge."

"We'll need another string if you want to go all the way...." His indigo eyes studied her lips. He shifted closer, so close she could feel his words buffet her sensibilities.

"Oh, yes." Her lids became heavy, narrowing her view of the world to just Cade. "All the way." Pete yipped, breaking the spell. Egypt cleared her throat. "All the way to the top. The tree would look kinda silly only half-trimmed."

At least her voice had lost that wispy, breathless quality.

"Closer to three-quarters." He stepped off the ladder and motioned for her to slip around him.

"I'll get it."

Deep breaths stilled her shaking limbs. That had been close, too close. Instead of proving she was different from the Blue Coats she had almost become one of them. Egypt trailed her fingers along Pete's furry head. She would have to send the animal a couple of rawhide bones for saving her pride. She plucked the closest strands out of the box and spun about.

Nutz sauntered across the living room floor. He paused by the couch, eyed the paws stuck up in the air then crouched under the coffee table, his gaze riveted on something only cats found fascinating.

"So, you've decided to come down, huh?"

"It needs to come down?" Cade peered at her from around the treetop.

"No, no. It's just fine. Nutz has decided to join us."

"Nutz? Your cat?"

With a bark, Pete rolled off the couch and stuck his nose under the table. Nutz screeched and headed for Cade's boots.

"Watch out " Egypt shouted, racing after the fleeing feline.

The cat darted around the tree and sprinted out the other side. Pete wasn't as agile. He thumped against the wall then collided with the tree. Pine needles pinged against the floor. Green filled her vision. Tiny needles pierced her sweater and pricked her flesh. Her legs folded under the weight. Her lungs labored for air.

"Egypt! Egypt, are you all right? Can you hear me?"

The weight lifted. Cool air inflated her lungs. Cade's face hovered over her.

"I tried to warn—"

"Shh. Don't talk now." He brushed aside the smattering of pine needles before checking her arms for broken bones.

Tingles danced over her flesh. She was pathetic. The man was administering first aid while she panted for mouth-to-mouth.

"This is all my fault."

"No, No. You're the victim here." He turned his attention to her legs. "The Dugan Curse. Two attempts down, one to go. I won't survive. I just won't—"

"Curse? What curse?"

"There is no curse." His lips thinned as his gaze raked down her. "Nothing seems to be broken." His fingers inched under her legs and around her shoulders. "I'm going to move you."

"I can walk." Strange. His he-man attitude wasn't as irritating as it should have been. Her cheek grazed his cotton shirt. Of course, none of the others had smelled of pine and popcorn. Her ear rested against the bumpy fabric, anxious to hear his heartbeat.

"Let me do this for you." His gaze locked with hers. Concern bracketed his mouth. "Please?"

As soon as she nodded, he scooped her up in his arms and carried her over to the couch.

"Thank you."

The ride ended too soon. Pillows replaced his arms. A cool blanket embraced her. What would it take to get him to hold her again? Nutz leapt onto the back of the sofa. Fishbreath washed over her before his tongue rasped the tip of her nose.

"May I get you something? An aspirin? Ice? An ambulance?"

"Cade, I'm all right." Pete's belly swept the floor as he crawled over to her side. Silky fur parted under Egypt's hand. His tail thumped the coffee table leg.

"How many fingers am I holding up?"

"Four and a thumb."

169

"I'm calling an ambulance."

"It's a joke. You're holding up your hand. Four fingers and a thumb. Only two of the fingers were actually poking the air. I don't have a concussion, Cade. I just had the wind knocked out of me."

"Are you sure?" His fingers bit into his biceps.

"Positive."

"Maybe you should sit on the couch and string the popcorn and cranberries. That should be safe."

Safe. He wanted to keep her safe. Irritation twisted along her insides. The first time she felt like playing with fire and the keeper of the flame babbles about keeping her safe. Obviously, Cade needed to reconsider his position.

"I don't know..." His Adam's apple bobbed as she trailed her fingers up his arm. "I could prick my finger and fall into a deep sleep."

He leapt to his feet and grabbed the bowl of popcorn. White kernels fluttered to the ground. Fear leached the color from his cheeks. Was he actually considering the possibility of such a thing happening?

"I was just joking." She reached for the popcorn.

Cade stalked into the kitchen, taking the bowl with him.

"Let me make you some coffee, er, tea."

"You don't have any tea." Egypt tossed aside the blanket. The world tilted then righted itself.

"I found some while you were on the computer. The first time, not the second." His eyes narrowed as she approached. "It was my grandmother's."

"Your grandmother drinks tea?" She reached for the popcorn.

"She's English and can't seem to help herself." Cade moved the bowl to the counter behind his back then pried the lid off a tea tin and sniffed the contents. "Tea doesn't go bad, does it?"

"I don't see how it could."

He slammed the lid on the canister and pounded it in place.

"Maybe we should just stick to hot water."

"No. No way." Egypt shook her head. "You promised me tea and I want tea."

"Strong women. Strong-headed women."

"Now what are you mumbling?" Egypt traced the dent in the can then stroked his fingers.

His tongue flicked over his lips. "I don't mumble."

"May I have a cup of tea?"

"If you go and sit down. On the couch. Away from the tree."

"Yes, sir." She dodged around him, grabbed the bowl of popcorn off the counter and skipped into the living room.

For a while, the air filled with the whirling of the microwave and the drumming of his fingers on the countertop. Egypt rubbed the back of her scalp. Maybe she had been too quick to turn down that aspirin. She shook her head and bit off a long length of red thread. The caffeine would eliminate her headache faster than any aspirin.

A dainty porcelain cup wobbled in front of her face. "Sugar? Milk? Lemon? Honey?"

Egypt shook her head. Her fingers slipped around the fluted body. The warm bite of Earl Gray tea teased her palate.

"Don't worry. I'm not going to sue."

"I didn't think you would." He sat in the chair. His blunt fingers rolled and unrolled the arm covering.

"Aren't you going to finish decorating the tree?"

"No."

"You can't leave it like that."

"It looks fine." He glanced at her before concentrating on the cover.

"Fine? It has half a strand of lights hanging off of it." Egypt waited until he was looking at her before blowing the wisps of steam off the surface.

"There's no rush." He blinked and stroked his scar.

"I disagree." His left eyebrow arched. "Nutz just disappeared under the tree. If you don't string the lights correctly, he might just pull the tree over—again."

With a sigh, Cade pushed out of his chair and marched over to the tree. A minute later, he flopped back into the chair and drummed his fingers on the armrests.

"You're kinda cute when you pout."

"I do not pout."

"Well, since you've already gotten the ornaments down I certainly plan to hang them."

"No. Stay away from the tree. Next time you could get killed."

"Egypt Starr dies in a freak Yuletide accident."

"Don't say that. You are not going to die "

"Geez. I was teasing. Will you at least put up the ornaments?"

"I like the lights. I've never done just lights before."

"I like ornaments. Lots of ornaments." She set her drink on the coffee table. "Please, decorate the tree. For me."

"Why is it so important to you?"

"Because you cut it down. It deserves its moment of glory before being consigned to the woodpile."

"And what will you do while I'm decorating?"

"String popcorn and cranberries and direct your efforts."

"Direct my efforts?" He glared at her.

"At least allow me a little vicarious fun." She smiled back.

"As you wish, Princess." He bowed to her then lifted the lid off the box of red, green and blue balls.

"We prefer another strand of lights near the top before advancing onto the garland."

"Sour eggnog." With deliberate care, Cade balanced the tray of balls on the back of the couch.

"Sour eggnog?"

"I didn't swear, did I?" His eyeteeth glistened as he plucked another strand of lights from the box. Excitement coursed through Egypt's veins. The wolf was back.

172

Chapter XVI

"It's midnight." The remote balanced on Egypt's fingertips. She pointed it at the television and jabbed the button. The rolling credits crumpled into a brilliant line before disappearing. The screen glowed ghostly pale in the dim room.

"Is it?" Cade smeared gray charcoal over his scar before leaning closer to the sketchpad propped against his knees.

"Both hands are pointing to twelve."

Tapping vied with the darkness for space in the cavernous room. The remote careened down a mound of newspaper and into a crumpled towel. His perfect host routine had lasted until the first commercial break of *It's a Wonderful Life*. Maybe that was too generous. His gaze had tumbled around the room while he drummed on the arch of his left foot with his pencil.

"The clock even bonged twelve times. Didn't you hear it?"

"Yeah." He blew on the paper then placed the pencil between his teeth. "Sure."

Egypt pushed off the sofa and padded to the window. Snowflakes drifted down from the heavens. Her jaw swung open on a yawn. Fatigue fogged the window. C-A-D-E. Cold stung the heel of her hand as she blotted out his name. She turned back to her audience. Maybe he wasn't ignoring her; maybe he was simply immersed in his art.

"Santa's on the lawn. He's demanding carrots for the reindeer. Shall I give him some?"

"Uh-huh."

She glared at his bent head. *Look at me, Cade. Please don't ignore me.* Tears watered her straining eyes. Okay, so maybe she couldn't will him to look at her. That didn't mean his behavior would go unpunished.

"He's not happy. Oh, look, he's just taken out the Three Wise Men."

"You don't say?"

Scratch. Scratch. Puff. What was he doing? Constructing a plan for world peace?

What was wrong with her? She had never needed a man's attention before. She nibbled her thumbnail. Cade wasn't an ordinary man.

"He's heading for the camel. Nope, the angel conked him on the head with the star."

"That's nice."

That's nice. She had single-handedly pitted one Christmas icon against another, and that's all he had to say. Egypt dried her thumb on her sweater.

"Santa will undoubtedly spend Christmas in the hospital, and all those kids will be disappointed."

Nothing. Not even a blink. She plucked her glass from the coffee table and rolled it between her palms. Beads of dark cola swirled around the bottom, collided with the melting ice cubes. She hated being ignored. The glass dangled from her fingers. As the host, it was his job to entertain her. The bottom of the glass rested on his naked big toe.

"Holy sh—season " Papers crashed to the ground as Cade kicked off the coffee table. He cupped his iced toe and brought his foot to his lap. "What did you do that for?"

"You weren't listening to me. A good host always listens to his guests."

"I was listening."

"No, you weren't."

"It's like this, Princess." Cade carefully tucked the charcoal cylinder behind his ear and flipped the cover over the occupied pages. "Drawing involves the hands and eyes while hearing involves the ears. Being that I am a gifted individual, I can do both at the same time."

He jammed the sketchpad under the chair cushion and advanced on her.

"Then, what did I just say, Mr. Gifted Individual?" Egypt stepped back. His arms swung casually at his sides. His steps were measured but his eyes glittered. Adrenaline conducted her heart to a faster tempo. What was he up to?

His index finger skewered the air.

"First, you mentioned the time. Midnight. Twelve bongs." Another finger joined the first. "Then, according to your narrative, Santa landed on the lawn and took on the Wise Men. You gave a blow-by-blow description of the skirmish then yattered on about Christmas being canceled and the children being disappointed."

Another step back. The windowpane rattled. Cold seeped into the loops of her knitted sweater. He braced his hands on either side of her shoulders.

"You left out the carrots."

"And the snow."

His gaze roamed over her face. One blunt finger swept over her forehead and down her temple to trace the shell of her ear. Her tongue stuck to her teeth. She wanted to be his artwork, wanted to feel the sure strokes along her edges, to revel in gentle caresses as he filled in the valleys, softened the peaks.

"What have you been doing these last few hours, anyway?"

"Drawing." He leaned closer but didn't quite touch her.

A microcosm of heat swirled around them. She wouldn't have been surprised if the snowflakes sizzled when they hit the pane.

"Drawing what?"

"Oh, just an idea I have."

Cool air washed over her skin as he inhaled her scent.

"May I see?"

"No." He shoved away from her and prowled the room.

"Please."

"It's just a rough sketch." His hair formed sharp peaks as he tugged on it. "I'll show it to you when it's finished."

Instinct screamed through her veins. That sketch was important. One glimpse, and her life would change forever.

"But I may not be here then."

"You're kinda cute when you pout."

She blinked, wiping away the insanity. It was just a sketch. Of interest, perhaps, but not a matter of life and death.

"Does that mean you've changed your mind about showing me the picture?"

"No."

"I didn't want to see it, anyway."

"You are a very bad liar." He strode over to her side and clasped her hand.

"Am not."

Pencil smudged her flesh as he ran his thumbs around the backs of her hands. A deliberate gesture. He tugged her towards the stairs. His touch marked her as his; and in doing so he had left a piece of himself, an important piece, in her care.

"Cinderella's coach wasn't the only thing to revert to its true nature at midnight."

"Meaning?" Their ascent was silent. Had her feet even touched the risers? Her heart squeezed than expanded. Would he claim the rest of her now?

"I think it is time for all good princesses to be in bed."

Bed. The word filled the space between them. She wanted to be in bed, with him. "Good" played no part in her plan.

"I'm not a princess."

"Would you rather be the footman? Or perhaps one of the horses?"

"Weren't they a dog and a bunch of field mice?"

He leaned around her. His chest grazed her upper arm. Hinges creaked as the door swung open.

"We're here."

Egypt's gaze darted around the room. A crazy quilt covered the king-size bed. An oversized armchair squatted by the window. A small wooden bowl guarded the top of the dresser. Clean and orderly. Disappointment rattled along her skeleton.

"This is a nice guest bedroom."

"Actually, it's *my* bedroom."

"Yours." She looked around the room again. He slept in this ordinary room. Where were the satin sheets? The mirrors on the ceiling?

"Don't worry, the sheets are clean."

"Oh. Okay." Sapphire cotton winked at her from under the quilt. They were the same color as his eyes but lacked his vitality.

"Were you expecting something else?"

"No." Egypt waved her hands, dispelling her thoughts lest he peek inside her skull. "I hadn't given your bedroom a thought."

His hand flattened along the small of her back, guiding her inside.

"The bathroom is through the far door."

Funny, the room seemed smaller with him inside. Or maybe because she was just closer to his bed.

"I don't want to put you out of your own bed."

"Are you offering to share?" He placed his finger over her lips. His smooth flesh traced the curve before his hands sought sanctuary in his pockets. "Wait, don't answer that. My heart couldn't take the battering."

She had been about to offer him the bed and something more. Why had he declined?

"Actually, on a similar note..."

Uncertainty pinched her insides. Egypt glanced at him from under her lashes. Maybe he was afraid she was like the rest of the Blue Coats.

"Keep talking."

"I don't have anything to wear."

His Adam's apple bobbed. His gaze drifted over her curves before his lids blocked their view.

"My clothes are still in the car, undoubtedly frozen, thanks to the blizzard."

When he opened his eyes, he stared at a spot over her left shoulder.

"I have just the thing."

He stepped closer then took two steps back and skirted around her. He stopped in front of the dresser and tugged the top-drawer open.

"My niece is always giving me pajamas." Light bounced off cellophane. "Any color preference?"

Egypt trailed her fingers across his shoulder blades before joining him by the drawer. Inhaling sharply, he stiffened but didn't pull away. He was definitely interested in her. His reluctance must stem from the Blue Coats.

"You got all of those from one niece?"

"Blue. That's good. I have lots of blue."

His hands dove into the pile before surfacing with several packages. A pair of red pajamas dove for the floor. A purple, a green and a black pair skated across the dresser top. Cade raked them into the crowded drawer, pounded them flat then slammed it shut.

"They don't match my eyes."

"They match mine." Cade ripped the plastic off then dangled the shirt in front of her.

"Don't I get the pants?"

"In a way." The plastic wrap disappeared in his fist. White dotted his knuckles like the snow on the peaks of a mountain.

"Which way?" The satiny fabric shifted through her fingers.

"I'll wear them and protect your modesty." He gathered the pants to his chest. "Sleep tight, Princess."

He dodged to her left and strode to the door.

After all her suggestiveness, he was leaving. What would it take to seduce the man?

"If I'm a princess what does that make you?"

"Your humble servant." The doorway framed his broad shoulders.

"*My* humble servant?"

He stopped. Now was her chance. Egypt held the shirt against her. The material warmed as she stroked it over her breasts and down her hips. Cade watched the gesture before forcing his gaze over her left shoulder.

"I moved that blessed angel for you."

"It's still crooked."

She fingered the hem of the shirt. Cade looked, swallowed then returned to memorizing the bare wall. Her efforts might work better if she was actually wearing the darn thing.

"You're lucky it's still in one piece."

"Sheesh, ask a guy to move—"

"You *demanded* I move the damn, er, dangling thing five times."

"You're a prince." Egypt stopped in front of him and laid a hand on his chest. His heart hammered at the flesh under her palm.

"Only for you." Cade captured her hand and raised it to his lips. "Dream of me, Princess."

Without a backward glance, he disappeared down the stairs.

Dream of me.

Egypt's fist punched straight through the down pillow and collided with the mattress underneath. Her skin stung from the abuse. A red welt rose as a feather scratched the flesh. She raised her hand to her lips, kissing the exact spot he had earlier. Long-distance kissing, how unsatisfying. Dream of him. Why settle for dreams when she could have the real thing?

Dream of me.

Was she ready to dream of him? What if she dreamed of him? What if instead of becoming her fantasy lover he paired up with one of her friends?

Never.

She wanted Cade, wanted him for herself. Now and all of his tomorrows. Couldn't she have just this one man?

Unless...

Dream of me.

Maybe it wasn't her he doubted? Maybe he wanted her to find the woman he had created. Uncertainty pricked her desire. Nonsense. He wanted her. Besides, wasn't she his dream woman personified? Hadn't she shown up wearing the jacket and scarf? What more could the man want? A neon sign blinking above her head?

Egypt stuffed the blanket in her mouth to stifle her scream. The velvet fabric dried her tongue and scritched across her teeth. Ex-boyfriend number three had made signs. So what if they weren't neon? They were big and flashy. Besides, she could always whack Cade over the head with one if he refused to at least give them a chance.

Them.

Confidence lifted the corners of her mouth. Poor Cade. When she woke up tomorrow after a dreamless night, he'd really find out what it was like to be hunted.

Chapter XVII

"Egypt."

Her dream lover had returned, but this time he had a face. Cade's face. Fire blazed in his indigo eyes. Egypt nuzzled against the heat of his touch. His calloused fingers slipped over her skin like the finest velvet. Her back arched; need dampened her flesh with its dewy kiss. If he would just cup her breast like he used to...

"Wake up, Egypt, love. You're dreaming."

A dream? No, this was so much better. Her breasts tightened as his fingers skimmed her nipples. It wasn't enough. She wanted more. Wanted his length pressed against her. Needed to feel his heated flesh pulsing under her hands.

"Stop moaning like that." A hand encircled her wrist. A thumb stroked the sensitive flesh. Her free fingers dipped into his belly button before slipping under his waistband. "Egypt, for the love of Pete, stop that. God only knows what your parents are thinking."

Parents? Why would her parents invade her dreams? Unless...

Embarrassment burned across her skin. She had blended reality with fantasy. What must he think? *Don't give him a chance to think, Egypt. Push him off-balance.*

"You're swearing again."

She opened her eyes. Cade lay next to her, fully dressed and grinning.

"And your mother's on the phone."

Plastic cooled her ear as he slipped the receiver in place.

"Mom?"

"Were you having a nightmare, dear?"

"Uh, no, Mom. It was just a dream." Egypt's tongue stuck to her dry lips. So what if she panted her answer? She hadn't exactly lied.

"You're sweating, Princess." Cade flicked a lock of hair over Egypt's shoulder before trailing his finger down her arm.

"Dreaming? Was it about him?" her mother whispered.

"Him?" Egypt's skin tingled as she slapped his hand away. Amusement danced in his eyes.

"That man," her mother hissed then cleared her throat. Egypt visualized her back straightening. "You didn't tell me you were spending the night in his house, dear. I can understand not saying anything to your father—he's a bit old-fashioned—"

"It's not like that."

"It's not like you went home and stayed the night with a complete stranger?"

"No, I—"

"Do you want some candy, little girl?" Cade's eyebrows wiggled over his forehead before he settled for leering at her.

"Shhh!"

His forearm blocked the pillow Egypt smacked him with. Grinning, he plucked it from her hand and tucked it behind her back.

"He took you to a hotel?" Impatience crackled across the line. Margaret Starr had waited too long to get her answers.

"He would have, Mother, except the blizzard hit, and I had to stay over. He was a perfect gentleman."

"A prince among men." Cade nodded. He grunted as her elbow sank into his belly.

183

"Do they still make those anymore?" Doubt colored her mother's voice.

Egypt fidgeted on the bed. She hadn't felt this guilty since she stayed out all night after the senior prom. She rolled away from Cade and faced the wall. She had done nothing to feel guilty about. Dreams didn't count.

"How'd you two meet?"

"Cade's the mechanic who's fixing my car so I can get home."

"So, you didn't sleep with him?" Her mother's sigh filled Egypt's ear.

"No, Mother." Egypt scooted across the mattress.

"But you dreamed about him." The statement was flat and as bitter as dark chocolate.

The bed bucked. The headboard knocked into the wall. Egypt glanced over her shoulder. He was actually following her across the bed. Hadn't the man heard of privacy?

"Did you dream about me, Princess?"

"I never said that." Egypt faced her flesh shadow. His chest rose and fell under her hand. "Stay."

"Honestly, Egypt, you're a female Noah for all your friends. Don't you think you could keep one for yourself?"

"I didn't dream about him with someone else."

Cade beamed at her. His finger pointed from her chest to his then back again. A wolf's low whistle shot out of his mouth.

"Oh. Well, in that case, bring him to your sister's wedding."

"I—"

"Think of your poor mother, Egypt. This Cage—"

"Cade." Egypt set her hand over his mouth then jerked it back when he placed a kiss in her palm.

"—is a mechanic, so I know you will get here in one piece. Do this for your family, dear. Poor Paris is already in the basement stripping wallpaper with your father."

"She has a point, Princess."

"You see, even Craig agrees."

184

"It's *Cade*, Mother." Egypt's fingers glided over the mouthpiece. "Go away."

"But you're just getting to the good part."

The bed dipped as he inched closer. Tingles exploded like fireworks along her thigh. Egypt backed away from him. Either she'd get away from him or fall off the bed.

"He sounds nice, dear. And since I know he'll be looking after you..."

"I *am* nice." Cade thumped on his chest.

Egypt twisted the phone so the mouthpiece was level with her eye.

"How nice will my mother think you are when she learns you tried to run me down with a sleigh? Or squash me with a Christmas tree?"

"You sound like a coffee drinker before her first cup of joe."

"Egypt, I really don't want to talk to those rude hospital people again."

"Hospital people? Mom, tell me you didn't call the hospital." Egypt's gaze flicked to Cade, who shrugged in reply.

"A mother worries. You'll understand when you have children of your own."

"I'll think about it, Mom."

"Cade said the roads should be cleared after lunch. There should be plenty of food at the reception, so an extra mouth wouldn't be any trouble." Fabric swished down the line. "How does the weather look there? I mean, the weatherman predicted clear skies for the next couple of days...and yesterday, for that matter. Paris would be very disappointed if Darrell's friends couldn't make it. Well, no use borrowing trouble. Half an inch shouldn't keep anyone away."

"It came down pretty heavy here."

"How much snow did you get up there?"

"Eleven inches." Cade whispered.

"Eleven inches, Mom."

"Yes, dear, I heard Craig the first time."

"It's *Cade*."

"Cade. Is he as handsome as his name?"

"Handsomer. A real gorgeous package," he whispered.

"I have to go now, Mom."

"And modest. Regal, in a princely sort of way."

"I'll call before I leave so you'll have a better idea when to expect us, er, me."

Egypt rolled onto her back and stared at the ceiling. Pain pricked her scalp. The big lug was on her hair. Maybe if she just ignored him he would go away.

"Is something the matter, dear? You sound a bit annoyed."

"No, Mom. Nothing's the matter." Her fingers slid along a lock and tugged it free. "There's just a lot to do before I can leave this afternoon."

"Well, okay. Bring him with you, Egypt."

"Bye, Mom." Egypt punched the talk button and the portable phone went dead. "Was it absolutely necessary for you to eavesdrop on my entire conversation?"

"A man prefers his arm attached to his body." His fingers wiggled against her cheek.

"You could have said something."

She rose onto her elbow and he slid his arm out from under her. Heat swept across her scalp. Several strands of her hair waved from the clasp of his watch.

"I did." He rolled off the bed and stood up.

"About your *arm*, not my conversation." Egypt rested her hands on the warm sheets. Get real, Egypt. The room was not colder simply because he had moved away.

"Hungry?" He plucked the hairs off his watch and tucked them into his pocket.

"Starved." Should she pat the bed, urge him to join her? Fear pinned her arm against the sheets. Why had her courage fled at dawn's light?

"Then get dressed, Princess."

186

"What? No breakfast in bed?"

"Not if you want the best doughnuts in all of Holly."

"Doughnuts?" Her stomach rumbled.

"Danish, bagels, coffeecake, muffins. Whatever you want, I'll get it for you."

"I'll be right there." Cold air raised rows of goose bumps on her bare legs.

"Your luggage, milady." Her suitcase bounced on the bed.

"When did you...?"

"Whilst you slumbered. Your car is running, too."

"You fixed it?"

"I recharged the battery." A frown tugged at his lips before he forced a smile in its place.

"Cade." Jittery legs carried her to his side. Her hand fluttered through the air before alighting on his arm. He covered it with his own. "Thanks."

"Just hurry, will you." He winked then backed out of the room. "I need to get to Babbette's before all the good coffee is gone."

Cade stood on the porch and rubbed the sleep from his eyes. He had her. He had seen it in her eyes. Now all he had to do was make sure he didn't blow it.

"Brrr." Egypt stamped her feet on the porch and shook her torso. "It's cold this morning."

He coughed the groan from his throat. Every word, every gesture beckoned him closer. He forced his hands into his pockets. Either she was incredibly naive or the most seductive woman he'd ever met. Of course, lack of sleep and coffee could have made him delusional.

"You ready?"

"Aren't you going to lock up?" Confusion pleated her forehead.

"No."

She knew exactly what she was doing. Lost and kissed by sleep, she wanted him to ease her way. Heaven knew if he touched her she would never make it to her sister's wedding. Angel's wings, he would have a difficult time letting her out of bed for their *own* wedding.

"Boy, you're grumpy this morning. Did you get up on the wrong side of the bed?"

Cade forced his gaze to the mound of snow that once was his hedges. Bed. The woman could revive a martyr and make him renounce his cause. *Snow. Ice.* Cold thoughts, very cold thoughts.

"I didn't go to bed." *Get with the program, Cade. Erupting volcanoes are not cold.*

"Why not?"

Yeah, she acted all sweet and innocent. But if she ran her tongue over her lips one more time he would have to stuff snow down his pants.

"Inspiration struck." His gaze flicked over her. Glad tidings, she was beautiful. Hark the Herald Angels—she had even stopped him from swearing in his thoughts. He was a man who didn't want to be saved. Hallelujah, he'd probably kill the man who tried. "I spent all night working."

And thinking cold thoughts. Not that it worked. His body was hotter than a poker in a blacksmith's fire.

"So, when do I get to see it?"

"It?" The word struggled through the desire throttling his throat. The woman wasn't suggestive; she was downright randy.

"The drawings."

"Oh, the drawings."

"You said—"

"After my coffee, okay, Princess?" The caffeine had better clear his head, restore a modicum of sanity. He'd settle for a bit of control.

"Oh, dear, my prince has reverted back into the toad."

"Frog."

"Whatever." She waved her hand and marched past him.

"I believe the frog changed into a prince after the princess kissed him." Cade's heart stopped beating. He had lost his mind. If God really did watch over fools, there should be a whole platoon of angels surrounding him. "I have yet to receive such a token."

Unfortunately, none could still his mouth.

"Will one kiss be enough?" Egypt stopped on the edge of the porch.

"It's a start."

"Do you want me to kiss you, Cade?"

Yes. Yes. Yes.

"Do you want to attend your sister's wedding?"

"Can't I do both?"

"No."

Her eyes widened as his answer sunk in. Now that she knew his intentions, she could either stop teasing him or make good on her promise.

"I have her dress." Egypt pivoted on the ball of her foot and stared across the lawn.

"I understand." His arms trembled as his body argued with his mind. He couldn't touch her. Yet.

"It's just a perfect morning. The snow is white and smooth. The air is cold and clean. Even the icicles twinkle like diamonds."

"It's Holly, Princess." Cade surveyed the beauty he took for granted before focusing on her straight back. Egypt. He would never take her for granted; she was too precious. "Let's go."

"You are not a morning person." Egypt stepped forward just as the loud cracking sound reached his ears.

"Look out " He tackled her, twisting seconds before they collided with the step railing. The icicle shattered. Marble-sized chunks tinkled across the porch.

"What did you do that for?" Her head lolled against his shoulder. Her eyes were wide open. Gray tinged her chalky skin.

"Icicle."

Her gaze slipped from his face and locked on the shattered ice sprinkled across the porch.

"That could have killed me."

"Yes." Laughter bubbled across his tongue. Three. The icicle had been the third attempt on her life. No more worrying about the next impending disaster. They were free.

Tufts of cotton batting swayed in the air. He set her away from him. A giant gash bisected her upper arm. That had been close.

"You're hurt."

"Huh? Oh." Her fingers slipped inside the cut fabric. "Funny, I don't feel anything."

He gingerly removed her hand.

"It doesn't seem to have punctured the flesh. You were very lucky."

"I don't feel lucky. I feel hungry." She threaded her fingers through his and tugged him off the stoop and onto the freshly shoveled walk. "I refuse to sit inside while you do the manly foraging bit."

"No reason to now. The third time was the charm." The Dugan Curse had been broken. All it had taken was a bit of grit and all color from his hair. What a difference a slightly premature white head made. She had survived, and so had he.

"Good, because I really want a toasted bagel with cream cheese."

"Shall we?" He offered her his arm and helped her into the sleigh.

"Hey, Cade." Sven King, dressed in a pair of jeans and unlaced boots, vibrated across his porch and picked up the newspaper. "Lights are back on."

"Did you find the one that was burnt out?"

"You're getting coal for Christmas, Cade. A whole truckload."

"Today's Christmas Eve, young man." Old Man Henderson rapped his cane against his front doorjamb. "No time for dawdling. The lights are still out in town."

"I'm working on it, sir."

"Best get cracking. You're not as young as you were yesterday."

"No, sir." Cade saluted the old man and snapped the reins. When had his street filled with so many busybodies?

"Are you the only tinker in town?"

"Me?"

Egypt gobbled the white puffs of air almost as soon as she expelled them. He slowed the reindeer but kept alert. If one of his neighbors told Egypt the truth...

A shudder tore through his frame. He refused to think about it.

"No. My father is a tinker. So are all my brothers. Well, all of them except Sloan."

"Sloan?"

"He's an accountant. Takes after my mother's side." Her hand tightened on his forearm. He liked her touch. She never grabbed and held on to him as if her life depended on it. Instead, she used the contact to reassure herself he was still there, still real.

"So, why don't they get one of your brothers to fix the lights?"

Why, indeed? What did his father say about lying? Never do it? That wouldn't help him. Stick as close to the truth as possible.

"It's my responsibility this year."

"This year?"

"I plan on conferring that honor to one or another of my brothers next year."

"I see."

She didn't, but soon she would. He would explain it to her on their honeymoon. With any luck she would think Holly's traits endearing and not loopy.

"Egypt. May I follow you home? Just to make sure you arrive safely."

"That's not necessary."

She tried to pull her hand out of his. He held on tight.

"Actually, you'd be doing me a favor. I need to pick up a last-minute gift for my mother, and I need to do it somewhere she doesn't have spies. You're perfect."

"I'm perfect?"

Easy, Cade, or Freud may have to devote a whole book to your disorder.

"You'd be the perfect reason to leave town without rousing her suspicions."

"Oh." Her smile faded. She focused on polishing the brass rail. "Okay. Sure."

"Thanks." Cade forced the smile from his face. The road to victory had been short but sweet.

Chapter XVIII

Heaven. She must be in heaven. Giddy as a schoolgirl with her first crush, Egypt hovered above the seat all the way to town. He wanted her, desired her enough not to take her. Her tongue clucked against the roof of her mouth. Aching teeth was a small price to pay for such bliss. Her tongue could bounce words out of her mouth until it was numb and exhausted once she got home. The rest of her was determined to enjoy the moment while she lived it.

God bless her rattletrap car. Without it she never would have met Cade. Cade. He had held her hand the entire trip. She resisted the urge to hug it to her chest. Bells tinkled as he pulled open the glass door. Warmth and the aroma of expanding yeast washed over her.

Definitely heaven on Earth.

"I see you've been working on the lights." A heavyset woman winked at Cade as he entered the bakery.

Fabric squished between Egypt's fingers as she squeezed the area over her growling stomach. Pink teacakes rested on a silver tray. Veins of cinnamon shattered ivory coffeecakes. Eyes of raspberry, cherry, blueberry and lemon beckoned her from swirls of golden pastry. Saliva filled her mouth. She could start with the shortbread on her left, eat her way through the strudel then roll out the door.

"Morning, Babbette." Cade grabbed a cup from the dispenser and reached for the coffeepot.

"Frederick made the coffee." Metal groaned. Flesh rippled under her pristine apron as Babbette shifted on the stool. She leaned over the counter to stare at Egypt's sneakers for a moment then rolled backward.

"Frederick?" Cade's head dropped below his shoulders. His empty hand rapped against the Formica countertop.

"Yes. Lots of call for a caffeine jump-start this morning. I believe your ladies were commiserating until early this morning."

"They are not my ladies."

"Yes, but they all wanted to be." Babbette wiped her hand on her apron then reached for a knife. The blade winked before disappearing in a plate of sticky buns. "Patience and Charity should have an empty hotel come Christmas."

"No reason for them to stick around."

A man sauntered out of the back room. Flesh shone through the black hairnet. He tucked the zebra mittens under his armpit and reached for the recently liberated sticky bun.

"Looks like you've already culled the keeper from the herd."

"Not all the lights are back on, Frederick." Babbette cleaned the blade on Frederick's apron then set the knife on the counter. Two sets of eyes turned to Egypt.

This town was fixated on Christmas lights. Egypt tucked her gloves in her pocket. Heat she could understand. Everyone needed a working heater in this weather, but lights? Besides, the blackout wasn't her fault. Balls of used gum rolled around her fingers. At most, she had caused a slight delay in their repair. Last night's blizzard was the real culprit.

"Cade's working on it."

"She speaks. Ooof." Frederick rubbed his ribs Babbette had just elbowed.

"Of course, she speaks, dear. She's probably just a little shy. Cade's not a monster, even if he's completely lacking in manners."

"Babbette Hutchins, meet Egypt Starr. Egypt, this is Babbette."

The woman's name pinged off random thoughts and stuck to a related bit of information.

"The baker's wife?"

"The baker. And this is my Frederick."

Frederick ripped his hairnet off and bowed.

"We figurine couples are going to have to form our own club."

Cade cleared his throat and shook his head. Confusion knotted Egypt's inside. He wanted no mention of the figurine. Did that mean he thought she wasn't his match?

"Egypt Starr. A magical name. She'll fit right in our little—"

"Bakery." Babbette elbowed her fiancé. "I recognize a fellow bread lover when I meet one. Which do you prefer? Sticky buns or Danish?"

"Actually, I—"

"A toasted bagel with cream cheese," Frederick volunteered.

"How did you know?"

"I may not be able to make coffee but I know a woman who needs to recoup her energy from a strenuous night." The spry man dodged another elbow attack and removed a package of cream cheese from the refrigerator.

"Frederick." Babbette tossed a cinnamon raisin bagel onto a plate.

"Yes, love?" He placed a kiss on her red cheek while easing the serrated knife from the cook's pudgy fist.

"He's right," Egypt injected. Was their behavior foreplay or the beginnings of a premeditated murder? "We stayed up late decorating Cade's tree."

"Of course, dear." Babbette winked at Cade.

"It's true." Grinding filled Egypt's ear. She relaxed her jaw. Maybe the woman wasn't being coy; maybe she had a twitch.

"Plain or cinnamon raisin?"

"Cinnamon raisin."

"Cade." A ruddy-cheeked man stomped inside the bakery. His red hair waved over his head like a rooster's comb. "We're starting a game and need another player. You up for it?"

Although the question was aimed at her companion, the man's eyes never left Egypt's face. Recognition tiptoed through her mind. She had seen his face before. The memory eluded her until she noticed his indigo eyes. He had eyes like Cade's.

"Not today, Sloan."

"I brought an extra pair of skates." A pair of old-fashioned ice skates rattled against his leg.

"Go ahead, Cade. Watching you will help pass the time until I leave."

"She's leaving?" Sloan's gaze slipped off of Egypt and out the window. "That might explain the lights."

"Cade's going to fix the lights."

"I'm leaving with her." Cade pinched two packs of Big Red off the counter and tucked them into her pocket.

"Do you think that's wise?" Babbette slid a paper plate over to Egypt then picked up the knife.

"Wise?" It was happening again. They were speaking English, yet she didn't understand the conversation.

"Hockey's a dangerous game. She could get hurt, especially considering your family's reputation."

Melted sugar glistened on the blade. The mound of sticky buns had been torn asunder.

"It's finished." Cade pointed to Egypt's torn sleeve.

"Reputation? What reputation?"

"I'll tell you when you're older, Sloan."

"Older? I'm older than you." Sloan stepped closer to Egypt, but Cade blocked his view. He stood on his toes and peered over his brother's shoulder. "How did her sleeve get torn, Cade? Did one of your Blue Coats attack her?"

"An icicle attacked my jacket."

"Congratulations on surviving one, dear." Babbette patted Egypt's hand.

"One what?" Sloan looked from Babbette to Cade.

Sloan appeared just as confused as she felt, she consoled herself. So whatever was going on wasn't a town secret. Which didn't explain exactly what it was.

"Frederick, get the lady another bagel. She's gonna need her strength."

"It was an accident."

"They always are. Would you like a drink, dear? You just name it, and it's yours."

"For pity's sake, Babbette, this isn't her last supper." Cade slapped a ten-dollar bill on the counter. "Besides, the icicle was the third not the first. Give me a cup of that cocoa while you're at it."

"We have only enough for one." Frederick wagged the empty carafe at them.

"We'll take it." Egypt flinched as her shout echoed around the room. So, she had spoken a bit loud—she had finally understood part of the conversation. Bits of cornmeal dribbled from her fingers as she grabbed the cup.

Cade plucked her plate off the counter and grinned at her.

"I'm willing to share."

"I'll hold you to that."

"What reputation is Babbette talking about, Cade?"

"Are you still here, Sloan?" Cade nudged his brother out of the way, pressed his shoulder against the door and ushered Egypt outside.

"Answer the damn question."

"Don't swear in front of Egypt," Cade growled. "Or there won't be enough of you to carry home in a bucket."

"Ooh, I'm scared."

"Save it for the ice."

"You should have taken Babbette up on her offer, Egypt. Cade's gonna need help getting home." Sloan jammed his Stetson on his head and stomped away.

Cold air raced across Egypt's skin. Her flesh shivered over her bones. Steam wafted up from the open cup and warmed her face.

"You gonna inhale it or drink it?"

"Drink." Rich chocolate caressed her tongue. Cinnamon kicked the taste buds that had ignored the creamy smoothness.

"You're not going to share, are you?"

"I said I would." She filled her cheeks. Taste buds tingled as the liquid rolled across the palate. She handed the drink to Cade then retrieved the rest of her breakfast.

"Don't worry, Princess. I'll save you some."

"What reputation was Babbette talking about?"

"We Dugans tend to take our hockey seriously and personally. Lately, one of us has ended up mildly battered."

"Mildly battered?"

"Cuts. Bruises. A black eye or two. Sven is pretty much the only one who'll play with us anymore." He handed her the cocoa, dumped her plate in the nearby bin and helped her into the sleigh. After wiping his hands on his faded jeans, Cade fished a pair of sunglasses out of his pocket and set them on his nose.

Egypt watched as the chocolate powder floated to the surface of her drink. There was more to his family's legacy than hockey. "If violence is your family's legacy, why did Sloan ask about it?"

"Sloan's not the brightest bulb on the string." Cade guided the reindeer up a hill. Bright-colored mittens waved at him as they passed a herd of children. Red sleds, blue sleds, plastic and wooden ones cut tracks into the hill. Shrieks and laughter darted among the trees while children lobbed snowballs between makeshift forts.

"So, your family's legacy has nothing to do with you running me down with the sleigh or the Christmas tree or even the icicle?"

"No. Why would you think that?"

"'That's three.' You told Babbette I'd survived three attempts."

"So you have. What do you think of our rink?"

Egypt stared at her two reflections in his sunglasses. He was definitely hiding something. She would let him think he'd won this round.

"I don't see any other players."

Aside from the golden sunbeams stretched across the icy surface, the pond was empty.

"Looks like we're the first to arrive." He laid the antique skates across her lap then pulled a pair of black ones from under the seat. "Are you sure you don't want to play?"

"No, thanks. From what you said I'd probably end up with several broken bones."

"Well, we can skate together until the others get here. Get your skates on, Princess." Snow crunched under his feet as he jumped out of the sleigh. "Don't tell me Her Royal Highness can't skate."

"I can skate." Her fingers were thick and clumsy as she attached the old-fashioned blades to her shoes.

"Prove it."

"I will." She slipped out of the sleigh and tromped across the snow after him. Prove it. She would prove she could skate. How hard could it be? Everyone said it was like walking, and she was doing just fine with that.

Shaved ice arced through the air as Cade skidded to a stop in front of her.

"We'll take it slow." He held out his hands.

"I can skate." Cold air stung her teeth. One blade tapped the ice. Her right leg moved forward leaving the rest of her body behind. Her left quickly joined it. Her shoes slipped. Pain burned across her ankles as they dipped toward the ice. Her arms cartwheeled in the air. She couldn't do this.

Arms slipped around her waist. Strong and safe.

"I thought you could skate."

Cade lifted her until only the blades touched the ice.

"It's been a while."

"How long has it been since you last wore skates?" He glided pushing her before him.

Her knees locked in place. Was this how a plow felt?

"Skates? We never had skates. We used to go in our shoes."

"That's called slipping, not skating. Do you trust me, Egypt?"

"Yes."

Cold air washed down her back. Panic choked her. Where was he going? He couldn't plan to leave her in the middle of the ice? Her legs trembled. If she fell she could always crawl to safety.

"Relax. I won't let you fall." He circled in front of her. He grasped her arms and skated backward while pulling her forward. "Now, pretend you're walking."

"Walking?" Her voice cracked. The tips of her gloves bent as her fingers dug into his sleeves. Her right leg eased forward; the left quickly chased after it.

"Steady. Good. Good. Bend your knees. Yes. You have it." He widened the distance between them.

Her torso leaned forward. He closed the distance, and she straightened.

"Don't let me go. Don't let me go."

"I won't until you tell me."

They circled the rink. Once. Twice. Three times. This wasn't so bad. Her confidence returned.

"Okay. Let me go but don't go far."

Her fingers convulsed in the air before she curled them into fists.

"Start turning, Egypt."

"Turning? No one said anything about turning." The edge of the ice loomed closer.

"Just put one skate in front of the other."

Egypt stared at her feet, willing them to follow his instructions. To her surprise, the left eased in front of the right but kept going. Her toes pointed in opposite directions and her legs tried to follow.

"Cade "

"I'm here."

Fingers tickled her waist, but it was too late. White rose up to meet her. She caught a glimpse of Cade's skate, a black rectangle ramming into her dirty sneaker. Her knees hit first. The impact rattled her teeth. Bone ground against bone as her palms smacked the ice. For an instant, her descent stopped. Fissures raced across the ice. The air crackled like a bowl of Rice Krispies on steroids.

"Cade " She was going to die. The whole trip had led up to it. First the sleigh, then the tree, followed by the icicle. The spirit of Christmas was going to murder her.

"I'm here, Egypt."

The ice parted like waves of grain before a wagon wheel. Some chunks clinked together while others leapt onto the remaining ice. Cold stung her fingers before her digits fell numb. Water defied gravity to race up her sleeves.

"Don't panic. We'll get out of this." Cade flung his body backward, wrenching her from the water.

Mud oozed down her gloves to plop back into the water. Why hadn't the crackling stopped? Egypt's heart pounded, climbing up her esophagus into her mouth. Giant cracks radiated from behind her.

"There has to be a faster way to kill someone."

"You're not going to die."

201

The ground slipped under her feet like sand during an earthquake. Beads of water shot into the air. Her jeans slurped up the frigid water. Tiny icebergs bobbed against her thighs.

"Son of a..." Grinding teeth filled her ear. "...bitch."

"Swearing, Princess?" Cade's arm slipped around her waist.

"It's justified. I just hope I don't lose a shoe." Mud sucked at her sneakers. The water parted as she forced first one foot forward than another. "This is how I run in a nightmare."

"Hang on, Princess."

Water bored holes in the snow as Cade lifted her. Egypt wrapped her arms around his neck as tremors seized her body. All she needed was to fall into the snow. Paris wouldn't mind if a human Popsicle showed up for her wedding. Copper exploded inside her mouth as her chattering teeth nicked her tongue.

"Hey, Cade. Where are you going?"

Egypt glanced over her shoulder. Four men stood along the banks. Each one wore identical grins of amusement. Great. What good was humiliating her if there wasn't an audience?

"Home."

"You broke the ice." Sloan slashed the air with his hockey stick.

The chest under her ear rumbled. "Not now."

His arms tightened bringing her closer to him.

"Look on the bright side, Cade." The brown-haired one grinned.

"Which is?" he asked as he stomped by his grinning siblings.

"You can tell your children you saved their mother from certain death."

"Yes." Sloan pressed his hand to his chest. "I'll swear you jumped into the icy water to save her."

"Right up to his knees."

"Eat—"

"Cade," Egypt said into his throat.

"Sugar plums." A vein ticked in his jaw as he set her in the sleigh.

"Sugar plums?" The brothers exchanged glances.

"Cade doesn't swear anymore. Egypt doesn't like it." Sloan elbowed the nearest brother.

"Sugar plums. Oh, our next hockey game should be real...enlightening."

Cade ignored his brothers as he took his seat beside her.

"Cade."

"Yes, Princess."

"If I wear my earmuffs to your next hockey game I won't be able to hear anything." Egypt draped the quilt over their legs and scooted closer to him. "Do you think I'll miss much?"

Cade wrapped his arm around her shoulder and snapped the reins over the reindeer's rumps.

"Not a thing."

Chapter XIX

"Sorry about my brothers." Windows rattled as Cade slammed the front door.

"I have siblings of my own." Her glove splattered against the wooden floor. She bent to pick it up. Her fingers might as well have been a claw in an arcade game for all the feeling they had. She cornered her glove with her shoe and forced her fingers to close around it.

"Don't worry about that." He grasped her free hand and tugged off her other glove. It joined its mate on the floor. "Let's just get you warm."

"I'm not the only one who got wet." Warm. If he kept massaging her fingers, she would get more than warm. Already her trembling had subsided to bone-shattering quakes. He exhaled on their clasped fingers. Her flesh began to tingle from the sultry breeze. "Aren't you afraid your fingers will just break off and roll across the floor?"

She eased her hands from his ministrations. Enough of his teasing. If he insisted on warming her, she wanted his hands on more than just her fingers.

"Pete would pick them up for me." Chattering teeth ruined his smile.

"And probably eat them." Droplets of water squeezed from the hem of her sweater. This was her chance. If he stayed

204

there would be no turning back. "We need to get out of these wet things."

He nodded and peeled off his leather jacket.

"This never should have happened. The icicle was supposed to be the last." Distraction slowed his words. He gripped his flannel shirt but made no move to remove it.

The button of her polo shirt dented her finger. Had the strip tease ended before it had begun? Not if she had anything to say about it.

"The last attempt on my life?"

"Yes." He slipped the top two buttons from their holes and yanked the shirt over his head.

"I see."

His flannel shirt joined her sweater on the floor. Anger rippled the muscles under the woven threads. Heat unfurled in her belly and thawed her fingers. She had found a cure for hypothermia. Cade's stripping would melt any frozen woman. She blinked as he tugged the thermal shirt from his waistband. Share his charms with others. Not likely. Her generosity ended with Cade.

Her thermal shirt landed on top of his. Keep him talking, Egypt and he'll be naked before he returns to you.

"So, you've been trying to kill me?"

Water squished out of her socks as she stepped out of her shoes.

"No. No, I don't want you dead. Far from it."

Her fingers closed around his bicep. Warm skin pressed against her palm. Let him think she needed someone to lean against as she peeled off her soggy socks. He would find out the truth soon enough. Her primitive self stirred, testing the boundaries of her flesh.

"It's the Curse." He hopped on one foot while he rolled his black socks down his legs. "When a Dugan man is interested in a woman...things happen."

"Things? Like death?" Her shaking hands reached for her waistband. *Almost there. Don't back out now, Egypt.*

"Not death, just accidents." He fumbled with his button fly. "My dad said his courtship involved flaming desserts, avalanches and a stomach pump. At least you got off easy. No trips to the hospital."

She kicked free of her pants and rested her hands on her hips. She would shuck the rest of her covering once she knew where she stood.

"You're interested in me?" Her gaze dropped to his recently exposed briefs. *Good Lord. Wasn't the cold supposed to shrink a man?*

"Can't you tell?"

"Oh, yeah."

He cocked his head to the left. Egypt cleared her throat and forced her gaze to meet his. Their state of undress hadn't sunk in yet.

"You like me so much you tried to kill me."

"Not intentionally. I mean, you could really only blame me for the sleigh. The tree and icicle were beyond my control."

"So, you're only responsible for one time?"

"Well, you *were* in my care, so I can claim all three tries." His pectorals bulged as he plowed his fingers through his hair. "I just don't understand. By rights, the icicle should have been the last."

He was the perfect mate, broad-shouldered and narrow hipped. Give him a loincloth, and he could have graced the wall of any cave.

"But we fell through the ice."

Primal instinct roared in her veins, shattering the veneer of civility. Her senses heightened, smashing rational thought. This was the world of a man and a woman. Elemental. Raw. Needing. His chest hair cushioned her fingers. Heat licked her hand. His left nipple puckered as she outlined its circumference.

"You should have been safe." He captured her hand but didn't break the contact. His pupils dilated. His spine straightened, the start of an all-out war as the primitive self battled the gentleman for control. "That pond had been frozen solid since, well, forever."

"It happened." Her hand slipped out of his hold. Her pulse echoed in his chest. One beat, two hearts. "I'm all right. Just a little cold."

"Are you cold, Egypt?" His hand moved towards her lacy bra. Muscles bulged along his shoulders as he forced his arms to his side.

"I was." Egypt shrugged her shoulder. The red bra strap slid down her arm. Her heart raced to match his, two runners sprinting toward their destiny. "Now, I'm strangely hot and wet."

"Hot and wet." Cade's gaze skipped over her breasts, down her belly and stopped at her red panties. His nostrils flared. His head reared back. The prey had finally caught the scent of the hunter. Fight or flee. She would have him. "I'll get you a towel."

He dashed past her, skirted the couch and darted into the bathroom.

Egypt released her frustration on a ragged breath. No wonder women hated peep shows. What was the fun of looking if you couldn't touch? Flesh slipped under her fingers as she kneaded her hips. There had to be a way to entice him into the primal forest where she dwelled. She just needed to think, to combine the best of the prehistoric with the modern.

A flutter of paper caught her eye. She jerked the pad out from under the cushion and flipped through the pages.

"Here. This towel should be big enough for you to cover up, er, dry off with." He held the navy bath sheet in front of him, a flimsy shield at best.

Egypt's heart expanded pushing the air from her lungs. A smiling woman reclined on a bed. A nude smiling woman with her face. When Opportunity closes one door he usually opens a window. This particular opening happened to be on the ground floor.

"Was this what you were up to last night?" Her hips swayed as she stalked toward him. He had baited his own trap. All she had to do was spring it.

"What is that?" He peeked at her over the top of the towel.

"Your sketch pad." *Slowly, Egypt. He has no place to run.*

"I—"

"You said I could look at the drawings."

"Not all of them." He inhaled sharply then straightened his shoulders.

Now he would fight, himself more than her. Nature would conquer nurture. She paused two steps away and watched as her mate filled the gentleman's skin. Humans were animals, after all.

"Then you should have done a better job of hiding it."

"I thought I had." He tossed the towel onto the chair and dugs his fists into his waist. Proud and arrogant. He posed for her inspection, waited for her to come to him.

"Under the cushion is not a very good hiding spot. You put it there last night before taking me to bed."

His aroused flesh strained against the towel hitched around his waist.

"I did not take you to bed, Princess."

"Maybe not physically." She turned the pad around so he could see the sketch. "But you did in your mind."

"My mind didn't do you justice." His gaze caressed her flesh as it fed the fire blazing within her.

"Is this how you see me?"

"I see much better now." His gaze raked her from head to toe. His chin rose as he crossed his arms.

The wait had ended. She closed the distance between them and filled her head with his scent.

"Cade, how long have you been undressing me in your mind?"

"Don't," he groaned. The civilized man's flag of surrender.

"Why? And don't tell me you're not interested. I can tell despite the towel."

"I'm interested." His hand curled around the knot holding the towel closed.

"Then why not?" Her fingernail scratched a trail down his forearm. She tapped on his hand. They were wearing too many clothes.

"Do you understand what you're asking?"

"Yes." She freed his hand and pressed her palm against his. The towel remained in place.

"There's no going back."

"I certainly hope not." She raised her face to his, like a flower seeking the sun. His gaze burned into hers, pleading with her to stop, begging her to continue.

"I won't be ignored or fobbed off onto one of your friends." His fingers slipped between hers. He lowered his head and teased her with a butterfly kiss to her bare shoulder.

"Make love to me, Cade."

"Yes, Princess."

Firm lips pressed against hers seconds before his tongue invaded her mouth and stroked her tongue.

Reality had improved upon her dreams. He tasted of chocolate, tart raspberries and desire. Pain radiated from her nipples as her breasts ached for his touch. Crisp chest hair tickled the tight peaks but it wasn't enough.

"Touch me." Her words echoed against his palate.

"I'll need my hands." He stepped back and tugged free of her trembling grasp.

"Sorry."

"Don't be. I'll touch you any place I can." He flicked the loose bra strap with his finger then traced the lacy edge to the front clasp. "You're beautiful." His thumb teased her nipple before he palmed her breast. "Your body's so responsive. It's like a piece of clay waiting for my touch."

His nose grazed her shoulder before his teeth closed around her earlobe.

Tingles sprinted down her arm. The sensation short-circuited her nervous system. Her lungs gulped in air. Her heart beat to an unknown tempo.

"Lately, I've had this need to be a work of art."

"Works of art don't catch cold." His hands cupped her shoulder blades before gliding down her back and slipping under her panties. "Your clothes are wet."

"Then why don't you take them off?"

"As you will."

He shoved her panties over her buttocks. The fabric tickled her legs as it fell to the floor. A pinch of his fingers later and her bra gaped open. His hands smoothed her body's contours, completing not creating.

Her senses extended beyond her physical being into him. She felt the pressure against his skin as he fit his body against her.

"Shall we go to bed?" He placed a kiss on her forehead. His lips trailed down her temple over her jaw then captured her lips.

"Oh, definitely."

She stepped backward pulling him with her. She knew the perfect spot for their first mating. She dropped to her knees on the bearskin rug in front of the fireplace. The patch of fur bent under her fingers.

"I meant the place with the mattress."

"Later."

"Later," he agreed.

Muscles bulged as he settled over the top of her. Her hand closed around his hard length. Life pulsed against her fingers. He stroked her belly, waking dormant nerves. His tongue rasped against her nipple. Warm puffs of air dried her damp flesh before his mouth found hers. His finger eased through her intimate curls and touched her center. Her body liquefied, preparing for their union.

"Now, Cade," she groaned into his mouth. Her legs wrapped around his waist as with one sure stroke he joined what nature had made separate. Together they journeyed to the beginning of time, and their souls were made one.

The bed dipped as Cade returned to her side. Now she looked like the woman he had sketched. Sated and satisfied. She could barely lift her head onto his shoulder. The heat of their union had melted her bones.

"I'd love to sculpt you." Lazy fingers traced the curve of her spine before collapsing on her hip.

"In the nude?" Fearing she might drip right through the box spring, Egypt tossed a leg over his. Nothing had prepared her for their union. She had been completely naked yet snugly warm; powerful, yet she couldn't raise a finger to swipe the hair out of her eyes. Love and sex were a potent combination.

"Oh, yeah."

"My mother wouldn't approve." Stubble scratched her forehead as she nestled closer. Too bad she couldn't bottle his scent. Guess she'd just have to hope he rubbed off on her.

"Speaking of your mother..." He placed a kiss in her hair and tucked the blanket around her shoulder.

"Cade, will you accompany me to my sister's wedding and reception?"

"I would be honored." He yawned.

"Cade?" His chest rose and fell in measured increments. The heartbeat under her ear slowed.

"Hmm."

"Go to sleep."

"Yes, Princess."

Her body floated into the land of dreams. The mist coalesced, forming shadows then solid objects. Her sister's face swam into view. She twirled across the floor. Her skirt mushroomed as she sank into the chair in front of the vanity.

Another woman stepped from the mist. She, too, wore a wedding dress. Her frothy veil framed her heart-shaped face in the oval mirror. Karen O'Connell, Paris's best friend. Unease slithered up Egypt's spine. Why was Karen wearing a wedding dress? She wasn't getting married. A large diamond sparkled on her ring finger. Or was she?

"I'm so happy for you." Paris sailed off the chair.

"Thanks, I never thought I'd be so lucky." Karen tucked a brown curl under her crown of white roses.

"Do you want to try on my veil?"

"Can I?"

Paris set the wisps of netting over Karen's wreath. "When's the wedding?"

"May. I want to be a spring bride. Mom hopes to reserve the country club."

"You'll make a lovely bride." The words stumbled from Egypt's lips like pieces of lead. Steel bands squeezed her chest, crushing her heart. There had to be some mistake. Cade belonged to her.

Cade stepped into view, his face hovered near Karen's. A smile teased his sensual lips.

"There you are. Do you have any idea what it took for me to find you?"

No!

Sweat stung Egypt's eyes. The room spun as she sat up in bed. Her heart hammered at the bones jailing it. Cade didn't belong

212

to her. He was Karen's. *Karen's.* She kicked the blankets off of her. Cold air banished the impending hysteria.

She could survive this. She had survived it before. She flew down the steps and skidded to a stop. She would never introduce Cade to Karen. Never. He was *hers.*

She had to leave.

Yes. Cade couldn't be allowed to attend Paris's wedding. Egypt jumped into her jeans, crammed her bare feet into her sneakers and stuffed her arms and head into her sweater. She would explain it to him when she returned.

"Egypt?" His lazy voice drifted down the stairs.

Cade. Her gaze flew to the banister. She had to leave. The room dissolved in a kaleidoscope of color. Now, before he found her. What was she forgetting? Nutz brushed against her leg. She scooped up the cat, yanked the hamster cage off the shelf and raced out the door.

Chapter XX

"You could at least smile." Paris removed the veil from her head and set it on the counter.

"How's that?" Egypt forced her lips away from her teeth. It was the best she could manage. After all, a heart was required to feel happiness, and she had left hers in Holly.

"I'm not a dentist checking to see if you're flossing, I'm your sister. Now, unzip this gown, we're running behind."

"Sorry." Like an automaton, Egypt went through the motions. He hadn't followed her, hadn't even tried. Another test, Egypt? Okay, she admitted it. She wanted him to chase after her, needed him to prove her dream wrong.

"Look, Egypt, if you're really this upset why didn't you say something. Darrell and I could have gotten married later in the year."

"It's not that." Darrell? Who cared about Darrell? It was Cade she needed. Cade she wanted. She hung Paris's dress on the hanger.

"Then, what is it?" Paris held the silk blouse against her chest as the door opened. Karen sashayed into the room. Her white dress sparkled in the fluorescent lights.

"It's just—"

"Did you soap the windows? Honestly, Egypt. Tell me the truth. I don't want to miss our flight to San Francisco."

"No." Why did Karen have to wear white to Paris's wedding? Egypt forced her eyes to meet her sister's. "It's Cade."

"Cade? The mechanic Mom wanted you to bring?"

"Yes." From the corner of her eye, Egypt watched Karen hone in on Paris's veil. It was happening. Her dream was coming true. Her heart battered her breast. Not all of it. Cade wasn't here. Power surged through her. She had done it. She had thwarted that nasty dream.

"What about him?"

"He's not here." He wasn't going to meet Karen. Cade was hers. But did he still want her? She had run away without an explanation.

"I noticed."

"I want him." There she said it.

"So, why didn't you invite him?" Karen asked, twirling the veil in her hands.

"I couldn't. I want Cade for myself."

"Stop twirling the thing and try it on. You know you want to." Her sister spun on her heel and faced Egypt. "You dreamt about him."

"Yes."

"Who was he with this time?"

"Karen."

"Karen?"

"Me?" Karen flicked the veil out of her face.

"Well, then—"

"There you are." The door crashed against the wall as Cade stormed into the room. "Do you have any idea what it took for me to find you?"

"No..."

Cade's reflection stood by Karen's. A diamond winked from her ring finger. This wasn't supposed to happen. Egypt's heart pounded in her ears. Cursed fate. She may not be able to change it, but that didn't mean she had to watch it unfold.

She hiked up her skirt and dashed out the side door. The grass muffled her footfalls. Faster, faster. She had to get away. Her heels tapped against the asphalt. Moonlight bounced off her Volkswagen's roof.

Footsteps pounded behind her seconds before hands closed around her waist.

"There's nowhere to run, Princess."

She pounded at the arms holding her, struggled against the surge of yearning.

"You don't belong to me."

"We agreed that I did."

"That was before." Willpower drained out of her. She couldn't fight him anymore. Her head lolled against his chest. How could something feel so right yet be so wrong?

"Before what?"

"Before I saw you with her."

"Her who?" He spun her around, forced her to face him.

"Karen O'Connell, that's who."

"What in the hot toddy is a Karen O'Connell?" Anger chased the confusion from his face.

"That would be my friend, the one you almost trampled chasing my sister." Paris moved by Egypt's side. Her blouse hung askew from being buttoned incorrectly. "Hot toddy?"

"And just what was I doing with Carrie?" He forced the words through his locked teeth.

"You were marrying *Karen*."

"Sh—sugar plums. Give me your shoes."

"What?" Hope filled her arms and legs. He hadn't noticed Karen. She had changed her dream.

"Your *shoes*." Cade hefted her onto his shoulder, carried her a few paces then plunked her down on the rounded top of her Volkswagen. "I am taking your shoes."

He slipped first the right one off then removed the left. He looked at the offensive items and tossed them to her sister.

"I didn't walk here, I drove." Her toes wiggled against her nylons.

"You can't drive without a few choice pieces of car engine." Wires and caps dangled from his fist. "Which I have thoughtfully relieved your car of. Not even Duct Tape Dugie can fix your car. You belong with me, Princess. Now and forever. The only person I am marrying is you."

"But I saw you with her. In the mirror. Just like in my dream."

"You're perspective is skewed, Princess. You were the only woman I saw in the mirror." He set his hands on either side of her hips and leaned forward.

"Me?"

"I thought we had settled this before I made love to you."

"But—"

"You agreed. I even have the ring."

"Ring?"

"Surely you've heard of the tradition? Man and woman exchange rings, priest says a few words then the couple can legally fornicate without fear said woman's father will inflict serious bodily injury upon said honorable man."

"I think he's proposing, Egypt," Paris whispered.

"You want to marry me, Cade?"

"Among other things, but it's the only deed I'm willing to do before a crowd this size." He nodded to the crowd circling them then pressed his fingers to his lips and shrilled a loud whistle. "Pete, get over here, you mangy mutt. You have the ring."

"Pete bought me a ring?" Was this really happening? Or would she wake up in her bed at her parent's house alone and aching.

"I *made* you a ring."

"Is this what you were doing last night?"

"I had to finish it." He removed a velvet box from Pete's jowls then lifted the lid and flashed her the contents. "Well?"

217

Two sapphires twinkled from a band of woven yellow and white gold.

"It's beautiful."

"Not the ring. I want your answer."

"If you don't want him..." Karen sidled closer to Cade.

"I want him."

"Good. Now, let's go home." He scooped her off the car and turned around. "I need to check on some lights."

"Wait." Margaret Starr planted herself in front of them. "Where are you taking my daughter? We have a wedding to plan, and she hasn't even set a date."

"Spring." Egypt rested her head on Cade's shoulders. He had taken her home the moment he had taken her in his arms.

"Spring's good." He stepped around her mother and carried her to the side of the reception hall. "She won't need shoes then."

"How did you get here, anyway?"

"The sleigh."

"You drove the sleigh here? No wonder it took you so long."

"Not exactly."

"What do you mean, not exactly."

"You'll see." He set her on the front seat, tucked a couple of quilts around her then climbed aboard.

"The sleigh looks different."

"I borrowed it from a friend. Comfy?"

She scooted closer and threw half her blankets over his legs. "I am now."

"Then hang on." With a flick of the reins, they dashed across the parking lot. Halfway to the exit, Egypt noticed the reindeer hooves no longer touched the ground.

"Cade, just who did you borrow the sleigh from?"

"Kris Kringle."

"Santa Claus?"

"He let me pick out my own Christmas gift this year."

Epilogue

"I'm glad that's settled." Pete tucked his rawhide bone between his paws and eyed the newcomers. That cat was up to something. His hackles had never failed him before.

"Me, too. Me, too." The wheel squeaked as Stitches increased his speed. "It's a wonder humans survive at all. Can't smell the pheromones. Nope. Nope. Nope, they can't."

"The little fur-covered treat has a point." Nutz stretched his hind leg straight out in front of him and licked the fur over his thigh.

"You're just upset because you didn't get to be there." Pete rested his chin on the bone. Maybe he should bury it. The feline would never look for it in the yard. Cats hated to get their fur dirty.

"I arranged the whole thing."

Nutz turned that unblinking stare his way. Pete wrapped his tongue around his bone and sank his teeth in the soft, already-chewed part. The only safe place for his bone was inside his belly.

"Typical feline. Always taking the credit for the good stuff."

"I'll let you sleep on the couch next to me."

Pete climbed onto the sofa, shoved his bone between the cushions and lay down on top. He chewed his nails for good measure then rested his head on his paws.

"That's because I caught you playing with my squeaky steak."

"That was an accident." Nutz blinked then stared at his twitching tail. "I was trying to move it."

"So you did. Five times." Why had Cade's mate tolerated such a creature? Everyone knew that humans belonged to dogs. It was the natural order of things.

"Egypt, come back to bed."

Pete's ears pricked at his pet's voice. Was it breakfast time already? He rolled onto his back. The bone scratched his shoulder in just the right spot.

"I thought I heard talking."

Egypt. Strange name, even for a human. Still, his pet had chosen well. She had small hands just right for scratching that spot above his tail. She tossed his ball even when he slobbered on it, let him sit next to her on the couch—and the things she did with his brush...

He would have kept her even if Cade hadn't. Too bad her taste in pets wasn't as gifted.

"Shhh. Don't let them hear you," Cade warned.

"Who?"

"The animals."

"The animals are talking?"

Fabric rustled. Need scented the air. His pet made him proud.

"It's Christmas Eve. They always talk on Christmas Eve."

"I thought that was just a fairy tale."

"Like flying reindeer?"

"I think it would be interesting to talk to them. Why don't you want them to hear me, Cade?"

"Because they don't shut up for the entire hour. It's like they save it up the whole year and bam—you're up at midnight listening to them explaining the different tastes of leather."

Pete scratched his nose. One time he had mentioned leather—and he had been a pup at the time. Humans had long memories. Naughty-and-nice-list long. Pete's lids drifted closed. He never did find that other Italian loafer. Italian food was the best.

"Have I thanked you for coming after me?"

"You have. But you can thank me again. Of course, without your shoes I won't have to travel so far for the next rescue."

"Will we spend Christmas with your family?"

"Only the morning. We'll visit yours in the evening."

"Can we take the reindeer?"

"That's a once-a-year thing. The sleigh only flies on Christmas Eve."

"Then how will we get to Dragoon's Springs?"

"We'll manage."

"Cade."

"Hmm."

"I love you."

"I love you, too, Egypt. I'm even glad I tried to kill you."

"Me, too."

Humans talked too much. It's a wonder they didn't forget what they were doing. Movement whispered in Pete's ears. Soft paws on a wood floor. That cat was moving.

"Where are *you* going?"

"I want to talk. I don't like that cat food she's been feeding me."

"Get back here. This year, they get to rest."

"And next year?" Nutz looked up the stairs then back at him.

"Next year, we wake them up at eleven with a rousing chorus of 'Jingle Bells.'"

END

About the Author

LINDA ANDREWS lives with her husband and three children in Phoenix, Arizona. When it was announced to her family that her paranormal romance was to be published, her sister pronounce: "What else would she write? She's never been normal."

All kidding aside, writing has become a surprising passion. So just how did a scientist start to write paranormal romances? What other option is there when you're married to romantic man and live in a haunted house?

About the Artist

CHARLES BERNARD is an illustrator and graphic designer who has worked for Columbia House and the Famous Artists Schools in Westport, Connecticut. He has created cover art for various publishers, including story illustrations for *Analog Science Fiction and Fact Magazine*.

More Books
by Linda Andrews

The Knights of the Living Five

A Knight's Wish
Dancing in the Kitchen
A Hint of Magic
Ghost of a Chance

Daughters of Destiny

Gillian
Fiona
Brianna (2012)

The Christmas Village
Some Enchanted Autumn (2012)

Enjoy a Sample

Daughters of Destiny

FIONA

LINDA ANDREWS

CHAPTER 1

London Docks, England
May 1892

Someone was behind her. Awareness prickled the back of her neck. Fiona Grey peered through the darkness and the thick pea-soup fog, searching the alley for a place to hide.

There. Perhaps the doorway...

Before she could move, a hand covered her mouth. The unmistakable odor of male assaulted her nose as a forearm pressed against her chest and another hand closed around her upper arm. Fiona's heart picked up tempo as the man's hard body pressed against the length of hers. She stiffened in his arms. In all her twenty-one years, she'd never been treated this way.

She twisted in his hold. How dare he!

"Shh..." Ale-scented breath hissed past her ear seconds before his hold tightened.

A moment later, her boot heels bumped over the cobble-stones. Merciful heavens, where was he taking her?

Instead of anger and fear from his grip, a pleasant tingle raced through her. Most peculiar. Sure, she craved a bit of excitement, but she preferred to experience a kidnapping within the covers of a book, not in person.

The restless spirit of her dead fiancé, Milton Davis, hovered near the center of the alley. His opaque form appeared in shades of gray against the yellowish fog and glow of gaslight.

— *I say, he's being a bit rough, isn't he?*

Rough? The stranger's grasp exuded determination, not cruelty or punishment. Of course, given her wealth, he wouldn't want harm to befall her and risk his ransom. No, he presented only a minor annoyance. As for the other presence in the alley...

Fiona glared at her not-so-dearly departed fiancé. Did he truly think such an observation would help her? Of course she didn't precisely need his assistance. She had looked after herself for two years.

Wiggling a bit in her captor's hold, she brushed her weapons with her fingertips. The stranger held her only because she allowed it.

Milton adjusted the cuffs of his gray burial suit.

— *Don't look at me like I'm infested with beetles, Fi. I did not encourage this midnight jaunt. I thought London to be a civilized place, not some godforsaken den of iniquity.*

Fiona cast her gaze upwards. Milton hadn't encouraged her escape from the *Revere*, but he had urged her to walk slowly so she might see who followed her. Had he known she would be grabbed? No, she refused to believe he would endanger her life just to prove the dockyards were no place for a lady.

She wiggled. And just what manner of man was this stranger? Granted, this was her first kidnapping, but he seemed to be going about it in a rather peculiar manner. Instead of carrying her off to a waiting carriage, he appeared to be manhandling her into the very doorway she'd planned to hide in. She inhaled sharply. The scents of sea and soap filled her lungs. Alarm rippled through her—something did not ring true.

"I mean you no harm, madam." The man's breath was hot against her ear and tart with the smell of alcohol. "I must have your compliance and silence if we are to escape the docks."

Compliance and silence. This man was no common sailor. Indeed, his speech was refined, his vocabulary educated. A captain, then? Fiona struggled to fit the facts to her conclusion. In her experience running her family's shipping company, captains swaggered not skulked, and few wished to escape their beloved ships.

— *Ha, I believe you owe me an apology, Fi.* Milton smoothed the lapels of his burial suit. *I surmised a sailor to be the perfect guide out of this place. He wishes to escape just as much as you.*

"Mmoo uph pht." Her jaw moved against the man's palm, felt the rasp of skin against her lips. The calluses were wrong, and the hand was soft—too soft for a salt, young or old. She waited for fear to ice her skin. Instead, a sense of protection warmed her.

"Do you understand?" the stranger whispered.

"Umph." Fiona jerked her head once then stilled.

"Your complete silence, please." He gave her arm a little shake. "I can assure you those who lurk in the mist would not grant you safe passage."

Her shoulders straightened. Safe passage. So, he was no kidnapper. She fought the tendril of disappointment. Ah, well, she'd had enough adventure for one night.

Clearing her throat, she sighed then jerked her head to indicate her compliance.

"I will release you now."

His hand lifted off her mouth, but he kept it near her head. She remained still. Would he bolt down the alley if she turned to look at him? She counted to twenty. Thirty. At forty, he hadn't moved.

Milton fingered the dark spot where the cleft in his chin had been.

— *Are you well, Fi? You seem rather quiet.*

Quiet? She was silent, as requested, and stared at the wooden door in front of her face.

Fiona cleared her throat and tapped her rescuer's shoe with the toe of her boot. He remained a statue by her side. She turned slightly. He was taller than Milton had been, with a straight profile and strong chin.

"Pardon my ignorance," she whispered when he still hadn't moved, "but isn't haste a virtue at present?"

"Indeed, madam, indeed." He slid his hand down her arm and laced his fingers with her gloved ones.

Shock coursed through her. She fixated on their clasped hands. How could the press of a stranger's palm against hers seem more intimate than Milton's kisses?

"Where is your child?"

In the murky lamplight, she watched his dark brows meet in a V above his aquiline nose.

Child? Fiona glanced around her. *Milton*. He had heard her talking to Milton and thought her companion to be a child. Fortunately, Milton didn't seem to make the connection.

She stepped away from the stranger then turned to face him. Her gaze flicked over his shadowy features. She doubted he would accept her denial, so she must find another means to distract him. Fortunately, most men possessed vanity and pride.

"Is a child pivotal to your rather, um, theatrical assistance?"

He stiffened. "Theatrical assistance?"

"Lurking in the shadows, sneaking across the clearing and tossing stones in every direction." She tugged her hand from his grasp. Three fingers waved at him, one for each of his actions.

"See here, Madam, I am a..." He swallowed hard. "...an Englishman. My actions were dictated by reason not...not by a pampered Parisienne." He flicked the velvet collar of her cape.

What kind of sailor knew about fashions, Parisian or otherwise? This man was not as he seemed. Had he heard of her or her family? *Faith, Fiona, this is another country.* The Greys' membership in the First Four Hundred probably meant nothing to the English.

"Monsieur Worth designed my wardrobe, not—"

"Yet another point of honor succumbs to the folly of fashion," he growled.

"Honor!" She tried to make the connection between her cape and her honor.

He placed a finger to her lips, stilling her shout but not quelling the outrage shaking her frame.

"You agreed to keep your silence."

Her teeth clicked near his finger. She tossed her head and stepped back.

"*You* offered to guide me through this maze." She drilled his chest with her index finger.

"I cannot allow you to leave your child behind."

Child. Affronted pride would not dissuade the man from his topic. Interesting. If only she had more time to consider the puzzle he presented.

"You cannot—" She swallowed her rising voice. A close version of the truth would assuage his concerns and, more important, get her off these docks. She hoped.

"Precisely. Furthermore, I insist you collect the infant immediately." He glanced over his shoulder. "Time is of the essence."

Cursing drifted down the alley.

— *Make up something, Fi.* Milton flitted toward the voices. *I'd recognize Bosson's voice anywhere.*

Bosson. Fiona's heart kicked up-tempo. She didn't want to meet Bosson in a drawing room, let alone in a dark alley.

"Madam, please." Her rescuer plowed his fingers through his hair. His seaman's cap rolled down his back and plopped onto the ground.

"I have no child, and my traveling companion is dead." She tried to ease around the stranger's bulk, but he blocked her way.

— But not forgotten. Milton winked at her. *Now, urge the fellow in that direction.* He pointed the way she had been traveling before the man had grabbed her.

"Then with whom were you conversing?" Confusion thickened the man's voice.

"My companion." Fiona shifted to the other side. The man filled the doorway. How was she to urge someone that large to move in *any* direction?

— Perhaps you should not mention me, Fi. Milton drifted close and stuck his face near the stranger's. *His kind aren't exactly known for their intelligence.*

Fiona shook her head. Outside of her family, she had yet to meet a man who was.

The stranger cocked his head to the side.

"You just said—"

A loud banging from the direction of the railyard interrupted him.

"Sir, may I remind you that I am a *lady* standing on a decrepit dock in the wee hours of the morning? I have no baggage, unless you count the menace lurking in the shadows."

She glanced at Milton. He crossed his arms.

— That's a fine way to treat your protector.

Fiona resisted the urge to roll her eyes. She carried her protectors on her hip.

"Perhaps we might quibble another time?"

"Just so." The stranger offered her his hand. Warmth surrounded hers as she accepted. He tugged her out of the doorway and down the alley, taking the right lane when the path forked. "This way."

"Are you quite certain?" Fiona glanced at the buildings towering above her. "I believe I followed this path before." And ended up back where she had begun.

"I can assure you, I have my bearings."

For a while, silence reigned as they rushed down the narrow lanes. Dawn pushed back the darkness and the fog thinned, allowing her a better look at the buildings. Fiona eyed the mortar and pestle visible through the cracked paint on the building's swinging wooden sign.

"Didn't we pass the apothecary's shop before? I only ask because it appears quite familiar. And look at those golden balls." She pointed to the next placard. "I'm certain that is the same pawnshop."

His fingers tightened around hers. "Madam, I am fulfilling my part of the bargain. Do you not think you could reciprocate?"

"If you need to concentrate–"

— *Must you provoke the man, Fi?* Milton huffed. *Do you wish to arrive at your uncle's house tonight?*

How had she forgotten how sore men became when questioned?

"Very well." She pressed her lips tightly together. She would be compliant and silent.

Gradually, the crowded lanes and alleys of Wapping gave way to more modern buildings and somewhat cleaner streets. Conversation drifted out of the fog. Grunting filtered from a nearby alley. The acrid air burned her lungs. Her guide coughed.

"Commercial Road is ahead. I've a cab waiting."

Fiona nodded once, opened her mouth then shut it with a click. A group of men emerged from the mist—dockers with meaty fists swinging at their sides.

Her rescuer looped an arm around her shoulders.

Fiona resisted the urge to stiffen at his intimate liberties. The territorial move protected her from the workers' leers. Determined to help in this ruse, she leaned against his side, rested her hand on his chest. Funny, she hadn't realized how cold she was until she felt his body heat. His heart thudded against her palm. It beat almost as fast as hers. Guess he wasn't accustomed to the excitement, either.

The crooked street emptied onto a wide lane. A hansom cab wavered like a phantom in a yellow arc of light. Disappointment pulled on her, and she pushed out of his hold.

"Your coach, I believe." Relief weakened her knees. They had made it.

"'Ere now, ye didn't think the likes of you could escape us?"

Fiona pivoted. Behind her, two men stepped from the thinning fog onto the cobbled street. The smaller one tossed a knife from hand to hand. Bosson, the *Revere*'s first mate, pointed a rusted revolver at her rescuer's heart.